# Lights Above Cass

# Lights Above Cass

Marilyn Brokaw Hall

ISBN:     Hardcover    978-1-6485-8406-0
             Softcover    978-1-6455-0861-8
             eBook       978-1-6485-8407-7

Matchstick Literary
1-888-306-8885
orders@matchliterary.com

# Readers' Favorite Book Review(s)

Lights Above Cass by Marilyn Brokaw Hall is a science fiction novel that will be loved by fans of thrillers, drama and, of course, science fiction. Lights Above Cass by Marilyn Brokaw Hall was an emotional novel but very entertaining at the same time. Reviewed by Rabia Tanveer for Readers' Favorite

Lights Above Cass by Marilyn Brokaw Hall is a blend of thriller, military action, and mystery, a story that opens with an intriguing premise Mystery, suspense and uninterrupted action are among the elements that set this novel apart. Marilyn Brokaw Hall has done an impeccable job with the plot. The twists are plentiful, and I enjoyed the way she creates premonitions in the story. The reader has the disturbing feeling that something awful is going to happen, but it is hard to say what it is. The author's ability to capture strong imagery and to use clear descriptions adds to the enjoyable reading experience. The characters are elaborately developed and with interesting backgrounds. Each is created with flaws that make the reader look forward to how they will behave in moments of conflict. Lights Above Cass is fast-paced and filled with memorable characters. Reviewed by Ruffina Oserio for Readers' Favorite

Author Marilyn Brokaw Hall has crafted a multi-genre and multi-layered work that enriches readers in many ways during the reading experience. Part military fiction and part sci-fi mystery in its initial conception, the plot twists and incorporates more and more content as it builds, until we find ourselves questioning society and the way we treat others. It was truly refreshing to see diverse and well-represented women in a science fiction work, particularly in an alien abduction sub-genre. A truly excellent plot line and conceptual creation and, overall. Reviewed by K.C. Finn for Readers' Favorite

Lights Above Cass immediately reminded me of Close Encounters of the Third Kind, a 1977 sci-fi film that I watched several times in the past. Of course, Lights Above Cass is a 'close encounter of the Fourth Kind' in which humans are abducted by a UFO or its occupants. The stories of people who were left behind after their love ones' abduction are melancholic and touching. The intriguing and mysterious series of alien encounters and abductions leads to an ominous truth for humanity, one that serves as an important reminder of how fragile our world is especially in the hands of ignorant people. Overall, a fascinating tale. Reviewed by Lit Amri for Readers' Favorite

Lights Above Cass by Marilyn Brokaw Hall is an intriguing novel based on unresolved historical events. Being raised by a science fiction fan who was fascinated by the Roswell incident and UFO abductions, my interest was piqued in the first paragraph. The account reads like a combination of the television series Project Blue Book and the acclaimed movie Close Encounters of the Third Kind. However, as impressive as those screen productions are, this story goes a step further, bringing the inexplicable and mystifying occurrences to a dramatic and chilling conclusion. I found it refreshing that rather than twisting the facts to meet protocol, the primary characters acknowledge and assimilate the fantastic and irregular information they are given. This is a superb novel that I recommend to UFO enthusiasts who enjoy science fiction books exploring the enigma of Roswell and alien encounters. Reviewed By Susan Sewell for Readers' Favorite.

*No more secrets… no more lies,*
*Eyes once clenched tight now wide open.*
*Not too late... don't hesitate…*
*It's up to you… it's up to me,*
*What each of us chooses to see.*

# Acknowledgements

To my husband, Orman, my rock on this planet, I love you. To my loving children Tracy, Charlie, Trent, and Alicia and grandchildren Bailey and Ada, I love you so very much. To my Mom and siblings, Mike, Ray, Eric, Gloria, and Janice, you are always with me in my thoughts. Thank you, Patti Jackson, Debra Turner, Jenna Howells, and Debbie Triplett, for your hours of reading and listening. Thank you, Mary Inbody for your insight as well as your guidance and encouragement.

# Acknowledgements

# CONTENTS

# Chapter 1

## Control Tower, March 18, 2020

The unidentified craft sped at twenty-thousand kilometers per hour directly toward the base. It became quite clear to the controller in charge the blip on the monitor was not one of their military drones or spy planes. This base was in a highly restricted no fly zone for any other aircraft except for those that belonged to the base. When visitors came to the base, they were flown in on unmarked planes with the windows blackened out so they could not see from the air where they were going. It was easy for the controller, Corporal Brett Anderson, who had been trained in identification, to determine that it was neither a commercial flight on the wrong path nor was it any enemy airplane. Whatever this was, the unidentified object was moving at a fantastic speed; and would outmatch any of the airplanes housed on this top-secret base. *Could this be a real UFO I'm seeing on the screen? Looking at it from this perspective, it seems to be defying any other conventional explanation I can think of, but if I am wrong and report this to my commander it could be quite embarrassing, he thought.* Corporal Brett Anderson watched as it made unbelievably sharp dives. *With maneuverability like this that craft must be using an electromagnetic field. I have to report this to the commander.*

Corporal Anderson oversaw military aircraft as Chief Controller, specializing specifically in the identification of spy aircraft. He and his team of controllers were responsible for all flight safety, the movement of all incoming and departing aircraft. As the Chief Controller he was well-versed on their specialized aircraft. He had graduated first in his class and was able to identify aircraft types, monitor their speeds in flight, their position in the air, and was knowledgeable about the location of their navigational aids if needed for the crafts assigned airspace.

What he identified on his screen tonight didn't resemble anything he had been specifically trained to recognize, nor that he had ever seen before. However, he was aware indirectly that he worked at a facility which purportedly knew more about extraterrestrial spacecraft than anywhere else in the world. He was proud of that fact and had sworn secrecy regarding this highly classified information, though he had personally never seen any proof of alien spacecraft existence. This specific information was well above his pay grade and was considered as on a *need to know* basis. Any reports that he saw which he thought might reference possible sightings were highly redacted. The only thing he was certain of was that the base he was assigned to lay hidden forty-five stories below the surface of the mountain top for which the base had been constructed. The control tower where he worked was in a remote valley adjacent to the underground base. He was not permitted to discuss that information off base either. As far as his family knew, he was stationed in Antarctica for the next four years and any information he obtained while working here would need to be taken to the grave.

Unsettled with what he was witnessing on the satellite feed and the radar screen from the air traffic control tower, Corporal Anderson couldn't stay seated. He found himself pacing back and forth as far as his headset would allow without it pulling loose from his head. Staring directly at the radar trace activity his heartbeat sped up, forcefully pounding against his chest.

"Dixon, are you seeing what I see here on the screen?"

"What is that, Corporal? Do you think it's a UFO?"

"That's what I think it is, and I am going to have to call and wake the Captain."

Corporal Anderson spoke firmly into the phone connected to the headset, "Yes, Captain Bryant, I am aware of the time, sir." He didn't dare glance at the clock on the wall for fear he would miss capturing something vital on his screen.

Private Mark Dixon watched Corporal Anderson raise his eyebrows in frustration over the conversation with his superior. Private Dixon was just glad he wasn't the one making the call to the commander. He had been on the other end of several conversations with Captain Bryant that hadn't gone very well and did not envy Corporal Anderson at this moment.

"I wouldn't have wakened you, sir, but I've never seen anything like this before, sir. I really think you should come up here right away and see this activity for yourself. I hope you don't think I'm being insubordinate by saying that, but you should come now, the sooner the better." Corporal Brett Anderson was pretty sure his captain had already hung up the phone. Hearing only silence he himself disconnected the call and returned to the duties in front of him demanding his attention. He was certain he was following the correct handbook protocol by alerting his commander. If he was wrong, Corporal Anderson knew there would be hell to pay for dragging Captain Bryant out of bed in the middle of the night. With what he was observing, he was willing to take that risk for the sake of the highly classified base and all who were stationed here.

Captain Jamal Bryant, Director of the Aerospace Defense Command Intercept, shoved open the solid steel door with a forceful push. Private Dixon turned hearing the door slam against the wall chipping the paint and sending a white chalky powder to the floor before it bounced closed. He would need to put in a requisition for a new door stop once this panic was over.

Rushing toward the radar screen, Captain Bryant was out of breath from running up three flights of stairs without waiting for the elevator due to the sense of urgency in the controller's voice. He tried not to show he was short-winded as he spoke, but had to stop and take a couple deep breaths anyway.

"Good job, men," was all he had time to say in recognition. When Captain Bryant saw the radar screen, he knew exactly what he was looking at since he himself had witnessed an alien craft firsthand in the air, but he decided to withhold that information for now. Captain Bryant remembered how the spaceship flew close to the treetops at a low speed hovering near a mountainside for several seconds before it accelerated, climbing to altitudes which he couldn't follow. Captain Bryant also remembered when he had been in pursuit of the thing, he had reported it to ground control right before he lost instrumentation and communication with the tower. Later he wondered if the alien craft was somehow responsible for the planes' malfunction. Captain Bryant had been able to capture data of the UFO on his flight recorder that day; however, when he landed the jet, its fight recorder was promptly removed. That was the day he had first believed in creatures from outer space and sought to work in the area of finding more of them. Now it seemed one was coming to play in his backyard.

Captain Bryant began shouting orders to both soldiers in the control room. This craft was not going to get away if it landed, not with him seated in the all-glass command tower. "Sound the alarms, Private Dixon," ordered Captain Bryant.

Corporal Anderson took this as an indication his commander agreed that the object being tracked on screen was a possible hostile craft by the way it was comporting. Not that he had seen one for himself, but he had heard lots of stories of pilots who reported unidentified craft and had them on their flight recorders. These blips spreading across the screen were certainly alien looking to him. He also recalled hearing rumors that spacecraft had the ability to affect the scientific instruments of bases in other countries. Corporal Anderson hoped this would not be the case tonight. He checked his instruments, confirming there was not any malfunctioning of the radar equipment as the crafts crossed over into the restricted air zone. Corporal Anderson and Private Dixon relayed the orders to the ground crew, the soldiers on the ground, and the pilots in the air as soon as Captain Bryant issued their orders.

Alarms blared around the perimeter of the military base. Red lights flashed inside the interior hallways of the facility; the highly classified installation located deep in the Appalachian Mountains. The entire base was surrounded by a specialized non-lethal electric security fencing equipped with intruder detection cameras along with state-of-the-art guard towers that were stationed along the perimeter lines. Yellow warning signs were posted along the outside of the security fence usually stopped any ground intruders who attempted to sneak onto the base. Mostly lost hikers were found and redirected, or an occasional reporter who tried to take photographs needed to be escorted back down the mountain The perimeter also had ground sensors and listening devices that would detect even the smallest of intrusions such as black bear. If that did not stop them, the Special Forces team would shoot to kill, if necessary. This was the first-time unidentified lights in the sky became a threat to the base. Over the past fifty years unidentified flying objects were occasionally reported in other parts of the state and across the country, especially in the western states like Washington, Montana, Arizona, and New Mexico but this was the first time an unidentified spacecraft visited the base which housed the bodies of the Roswell crash.

Tonight, high alert alarms were sounding both inside the heads of the soldiers and all along the outpost's perimeter. Soldiers readied for an air attack by utilizing NORAD radar, a network of satellite, ground-based and aerial radar to detect, intercept and engage any air threats. The new radar system was only used on this specific base due to its specialized capabilities with amplitude radar, three-dimensional view and state-of-the-art design The radar was showing this ships size as being twice the size of a football field.

Captain Bryant grabbed the back of a black leather rolling seat at an empty desk, pulling up close to Corporal Anderson. "Just exactly what do you believe we have here, gentlemen, and when did this activity first begin?"

Corporal Anderson's face flushed with worry that he had not called his commander soon enough. "The satellite sensors started going crazy at approximately 0200 hours, sir. At first, I thought it was just one craft, but eventually the radar screen picked up more. The shape of the original craft and flight pattern didn't match up with any type of aircraft I've been trained to identify, sir. I know this sounds completely crazy, but Private Dixon and I tracked that thing going way faster than the North American X-15 with its Mach speed abilities. There were several smaller blips on there too but they just up and disappeared completely off the screen within — I'd say maybe less than ten seconds of the radar identifying them. If I had looked down, I would have completely missed them. Do you think Russia or the Israeli's have developed some new type of spy plane? My mind keeps going to UFO but it's hard to wrap my head around the idea of them being real."

Captain Bryant not wanting to validate his true opinion of the spacecraft just yet stated, "It's possible. Putin puts a lot of money in technology. I guess Pete Knight holding the worlds speed record for flight sure would have enjoyed seeing this crafts speed. It's hard to say who this belongs to until we get a closer look at one of these babies. It would be unusual for any of their aviators to bring a plane of that nature in this close for fear we might force it down and steal their valuable technology. It could also be that whoever is flying doesn't realize our detection capabilities or that we're here watching. There's always a possibility they want to defect from their country and if that's the case I would be more than happy to assist them in taking this magnificent technology off their hands. After watching this unusual flight behavior on screen, I doubt this is the case though with what we are looking at on here. No, this most definitely reminds me of something I witnessed about fifteen years ago, but we shall see, men, when and if it gets closer. I have a feeling in my gut that life here on the base is about to change."

Noticing Private Dixon crossing his peripheral vision, the captain rolled his chair toward him. "Private, is that coffee hot?" Without waiting for an answer, he reached for the Styrofoam cup taking it from the soldier. He took a gulp before rolling back and setting it down on the counter. With a nod of satisfaction, he stated, "Just what I needed — a jolt of java. Thank you." Pointing to the radar screen, he continued, "Corporal Anderson, it looks like its friends are back from wherever they went."

The blips on the screen continued to flash erratically. On a normal shift in the tower the blips just pulsed along in a slow monotonous pulsating, like a normal sinus rhythm from a heart monitor. What Captain Bryant observed pulsating were as many as six unidentified objects crowding the sky on-screen, quickly approaching them. The aircraft's flight path at this point was aimed directly toward the glass control tower. If whoever operating it did not change course immediately, the tower would be destroyed. He was trying to decide if they themselves needed to evacuate the tower but knew he would be court-martialed if they did since all the orders would need to come from the tower.

Captain Jamal Bryant's finger pointed toward one of the pulsating lights on screen counting down in a calm, deep, Southern voice over the intercom, "Unidentified aircraft twenty miles and closing, fifteen miles, ten miles. Prepare weapons. Do not engage the craft unless I give the final command. I repeat do not engage. We need to determine their intentions and remain standing down until engaged."

Corporal Anderson and Private Dixon sat glued to their seats with headsets on issuing orders for the safe clearance for the take off for each helicopter leaving the ground. The air force crew prepared the Jet Intercept planes with enough munition to shoot the crafts down, if necessary.

Five miles from base, the spaceship stopped its advance. From their perch in the tower, the three soldiers no longer required satellite or a radar system to monitor the craft they were tracking. They estimated the length of the mother ship to be twice the size of a football field. The lights were blindingly brilliant as they shone in all directions, forcing the light out into the darkness that surrounded it and masking the full moon behind it, making the night sky appear even more ominous. The craft hovered, waiting for what, Captain Jamal Bryant did not know.

Blackhawk helicopters armed to the teeth were in the air awaiting further orders from Captain Bryant, either to attack with deadly fire and fury or stand down. The chopping sound emanating from the Apache propellers padded the sound of the blaring alarm. Special Forces on the base were prepared for the worst. Their mission was to defend this base and its secrets regardless of cost.

Once the helicopters reached where they last detected the unidentified craft, the copter pilots set down in a clearing approximately a half mile from the site. Unable to see where it landed their only explanation was that it must be hiding in plane sight. Air Force military boots hit the ground running; trained military canines led the way through the pitch dense forest. Unsure of what they would find when they got to the craft landing site, Sergeant Trevon Loch's special team of men and women were trained to fight and were ready to give their all for their country.

As the soldiers closed in on their prey, the dogs cowered. Their ears no longer perked up and their tails hung down flat against their hind legs, very unusual behavior for these brave beasts. They were trained by soldiers to obey orders as any other soldier normally would. The dogs were to attack first unless otherwise ordered to stand down.

Tonight, a sense of eeriness settled upon the squadron of soldiers. They were not used to being in this posture here in the mountains on US soil against this type of alien threat. Neither were the German Shepherd's they had brought along. If the craft landed near this area, there were no lights to identify its specific coordinates. The soldiers wore camouflage uniforms with their faces painted to help them blend in with the forest vegetation providing extra cover under the full moon. Except an occasional owl, coyote, soldier snapping dead twigs under their boots, or intermittent panting of the dogs, all remained quiet in this part of the forest. They knew they were close from the coordinates received from tactical command.

Sergeant Trevon Loch motioned his platoon with special hand signals to stop, get down and listen. Time passed quietly and at a snail's pace. His troops were disciplined; they could wait out any enemy no matter how long it took. Tiny hairs on the back of his neck stood up giving him a chill. Sergeant Loch knew exactly what that meant from being in Kuwait. Over there he had a sixth sense about hidden bombs. They would stay put until he understood the danger clearer and was able to devise a safe plan of attack.

Without warning, light emanated from under the ship creating sparks from the cloaked craft. The heat it generated intensified, creating sizzling mounds of dried grass and leaves. Within seconds it left behind only minute orange glowing bits of disintegrated, cooling ash. A deafening whirring noise created a sense of chaos among the dogs and the soldiers. The obsidian sphere rose two hundred feet in the air within seconds, rotating in a circle. Trapezium-shaped lights blinked randomly near the expansive windows of the craft. The occupants inside appeared more frightening than the soldiers expected, in the time they were able to see the aliens inside the spacecraft and wrap their heads around what they were witnessing. The craft vanished within seconds.

Sergeant Loch identifying a form left behind ordered, "Hold your fire." Attempting to refocus his eyes from the blinding light, Sergeant Trevon Loch noticed a single silhouette standing in the center of the field directly under the light of the full moon.

The human form was easy to recognize since it was aided further by the fading glow of embers lighting the field. It was a young woman. She appeared to be in her mid-twenties. Her shoulder-length blonde hair appeared as if it were floating in the air due to the updraft created by the craft. She was wearing a mid-century cotton house dress. Sergeant Loch immediately noticed when he approached her that she was missing her shoes. There was no way that she had walked here barefoot this late at night on her own. He knew instantly that she must have been aboard the craft. The young woman stood quietly gazed off into the darkness of the forest, unaware of her current surroundings or the soldiers quietly approaching. Her pale skin and stone-like stature resembled a concrete statue one would normally see when visiting a park. As Sergeant Loch came closer, he noticed two other females lying on the ground, hidden by her shadow. They were not moving; he wondered if they were possibly in some type of trance or paralytic state.

# Chapter 2

## CIA Meeting, March 18, 2020

Captain Jamal Bryant stood before the squadron of soldiers led by Sergeant Trevon Loch, Corporal Brett Anderson, Private Mark Dixon, and CIA Special Agent in Charge Jesse Finch. "Ladies and gentlemen at approximately 0200 hours this morning, on March 18, 2020, I was notified by our chief controller of possible unidentified objects entering the air space surrounding this top-secret facility. After identifying it was neither a military drone nor spy plane, Sergeant Trevon Loch's special forces squad was assigned to take lead in engaging or capturing the craft."

Captain Bryant's assistant rushed into the room and quickly began distributing packets of information on the alien aircraft. She took a seat near the captain who leaned down as she whispered something in his ear. He nodded in acknowledgment before she got up and left the room.

Captain Bryant began again, "As I was saying, once on the ground it was determined that the craft had the ability not only to fly at speeds of approximately twenty thousand kilometers per hour, but also hide in plain sight right under our noses on our own playground. In some ways, I believe these aliens are toying with us. I don't like it one bit. It would be an embarrassment if this information would happen to leak to the media. The only way this top-secret information can be controlled is through the men and women in this very room today." He turned on the screen behind him showing the radar tracings that had been recorded live just a few hours before, displaying the aircraft blips. The next Power Point revealed the radar system capturing the UFO speed, as well as 3- D, close-range images of the ship. "I don't have to tell you how important this information is. We have forty-five stories of secrets inside this facility, and only a third are directly related to what you witnessed last night. Our science and technology divisions are expansive as some of you well know. Others that are here today — well let me just say you are now on the *need to know* list and reporting to Antarctica or aboard the next space station shuttle to the moon for an extended visit could be in *your* real future if leaks occur. Please take a few minutes to review the information in front of you. It is classified, and you are more than welcome to read the entire packet here. There is a confidentiality statement at the end which each of you will sign before leaving. Nothing leaves this room, ladies and gentlemen, in writing or by word of mouth."

Several soldiers who were aware of the secrets quickly signed their statements, closed their folders, and stood following the captain to get coffee and a doughnut before he began speaking again.

"Corporal Brett Anderson and Private Mark Dixon, you are now reassigned to report directly and only to Sergeant Trevon Loch. He will fill you in on any special assignments in the future; and welcome to the special team. Agent Finch as always, I expect you will fill your agents in on the women that were retrieved last night. Once you have more information, I will need a report back from you by... let's say 1600 hours today. It appears I have a meeting with General Kearns later tonight. Special Agent in Charge Finch, I believe the general expects you to be in that meeting as well. He will be flying in from the Pentagon, and as you and I know, he will be expecting more than we will have had time to prepare." Agent Finch nodded his understanding of the expectation for himself and for his agents.

Corporal Anderson quickly flipped through the information in the file before him. He was very interested in reading anything he could about the facility he worked in and its history with UFO's. Most of the information in the beginning of the packet gave the history of how the Armed Services Committee was involved when Doctor J. Allen Hynek had been Director of the Center for UFO Studies. He remembered hearing Doctor Hynek had a central repository for all UFO materials in Evanston, Illinois and wished he could have seen some of the things they had collected during that time. Now it appeared the most classified materials were stored here. According to the briefing, Doctor Hynek ran a program called '*Project Blue Book*' from 1966 to1969. He and his team of agents were responsible for the investigation of UFO sightings across the country. The agents interviewed the abductees attempting to debunk the report. Either way, they had to make a final decision on whether the sighting or abduction was true or false. Corporal Anderson now realized why CIA Agent Jesse Finch had been pulled into this meeting. It would be his men, with the Central Intelligence Agency, that interviewed the women from the spacecraft. He turned the page, reading that the Aerospace Defense Command decided the whole thing was a waste of time when Doctor Hynek ran the operation and reported that alien life was a farce; he knew the Christian population would not accept that there was life on other planets, being that, it might cause its followers to doubt Creation as it was reported in the Bible. So the director demanded that the Pentagon immediately terminate *Project Blue Book*. Apparently, this decision was also satisfactory to the CIA, since it gave them a way to hide the real facts. The agency had determined without a doubt that unidentified flying objects could be a national security risk and took the program into its own hands, taking it deeper under cover. Here hidden in the mountains, the program was far away from government critics, who were voted into office every two, four or six years; some of those would have chosen to decline to open their eyes to the idea that maybe our biggest enemy and our largest threat to the entire world as a whole might just be from another galaxy and not from Russia, North Korea, China or even the Middle East. Due to alien technology, it seemed they were much closer to us, and we to them. That thought had been too terrifying for the previous director to handle.

Special Agent in Charge, Jesse Finch, concluded the meeting by saying to the group, "In your packet you will see that there are four types of close encounters with unidentified flying objects listed. The first encounter type is that you see a UFO; the second is you find evidence of a UFO; the third type is you make contact with the UFO inhabitants; and the fourth kind is you are abducted by the aliens. So, using that scale, early this morning our soldiers in the radio control tower, Corporal Brett Anderson and Private Mark Dixon, witnessed firsthand what these alien ships are capable of, regarding speed and maneuverability. Sergeant Trevon Loch and his Special Forces witnessed evidence of the ship and its ability to hide in plain sight. The women they left behind were abductees aboard the ship and fall in the last category; encounter of the fourth kind. This was not the first abduction we've come across. My team had plenty of proof of alien existence prior to now. We just couldn't discuss this information with anyone outside of our own team of agents, until today inside this room. According to the studies they did at the time they determined that ordinary citizens wouldn't be able to handle the thought of alien creature abductions. We have no way of protecting common citizens from being taken, nor can we get them back. The abductees just show up when the aliens are finished studying them. We have found in some instances, they don't always put them back where they found them. Sometimes, they are clear across country or in another town. When we were able to recover the spacecraft and the dead aliens from that Roswell site back in 1947, and the one in Aztec, New Mexico in 1948, we understood at that point that we needed to put our evidence in a safe, secret, hidden facility underground, where no human or alien could ever gain access. As you leave this room today I hope you understand how important this project is for mankind."

# Chapter 3

## Cass, W.V. Missing Females, March 18, 2020

Thirty minutes later, Special Agent in Charge Jesse Finch stood before his most trusted men in their underground meeting room on the twelfth floor. He began issuing new assignments. Since the occurrence on the base the prior night, their plans had drastically changed.

Agent Finch was generally referenced by others in the CIA as the 'James Bond' of the bureau. He was not nicknamed *007* for his black wavy hair or his piercing dark eyes. It was because he could read most people like an open book. Of course, that only worked one way. He himself was unreadable, according to those who knew him. His mysterious behavior sometimes left his coworkers frustrated. But, in the end they always got their man or woman, and usually some secret commendation from the General. His team trusted his instincts with their lives and careers.

Jesse began working for the Central Intelligence Agency ten years prior, in the missing persons division. He never dreamed his career would lead him here. In fact, during that period he never knew here even existed; until he received a promotion along with special instructions to arrive at the air force base in Martinsburg, West Virginia. From there, he was driven to an undisclosed underground facility in the Allegheny Mountains, near Green Bank, home of the Green Bank Observatory, where he met with General Frank Kearns to receive this new assignment.

Jesse soon discovered he would oversee investigations of unexplained missing persons. His new windowless office was in a concealed facility, where watching and listening by scientists at the National Radio Astronomy Observatory was top secret. Any unusual activity was reported directly to him as part of his teams' ongoing investigations.

Special Agent in Charge Jesse Finch secretly interviewed and personally hired his own team from the best men in the CIA employment data base. Special Agent Vic Foster originated from Albuquerque, New Mexico. He came well recommended with a degree in homeland security and a very appealing secret military background. Special Agent Riley Harris transferred to the team from Scottsdale, Arizona. Special Agent Colin Bilodeau originally from Ruston, Louisiana joined six months ago bringing his valuable National Aeronautics Space Administration skills to the investigative team. Jesse also had his own scientists, physicists, physicians, engineers and forensics teams housed inside the mountain.

As Director of Missing Persons, Jesse and his team investigated persons that were taken or as some called them: abductees — as in being abducted by aliens or disappearing into the strange lights in the sky. It was their job to investigate these reported missing persons and try to determine why they were chosen. If taken and returned, they interviewed them thoroughly using hypnosis by scientists, to see if they were able to remember any of their time away. The forensic team gathered samples of their blood, hair, and skin to determine if there were any changes or uncommon chemicals in their bodies. His engineers were able to create models of what the abductees saw inside the ships and sketch models of the different types of aliens they had encountered, to determine their possible position and profession aboard the ship. Jesse and his team were focused on determining why these people were taken, if they were indeed taken. He also supervised the scientific division of forensic studies and alien genetics.

He was dedicated to his work, and the of hours he put in didn't matter in this important study. To him there was no middle ground. Some people who reported they had been taken, he discovered, had lied to get publicity and their names in the *National Enquirer* and he did not want his team to get involved due to the agency's secrecy, but other stories seemed to ring true. Those were the ones his team tracked. Over the years he and his elite team crisscrossed the United States, from one abduction report to another, investigating UFO sightings in places like Roswell, New Mexico; Rachael, Nevada; Phoenix, Arizona; and Dulce, New Mexico. Last night Jesse found himself receiving the most interesting case yet dealing with UFO's, and it was right under his nose, right here in West, Virginia. Today they would begin putting the pieces of the puzzle together.

"Good morning, Special Agents Bilodeau, Foster, and Harris. Today is an exciting day for all of us in this room. We won't be flying to Nevada as originally planned for a look at those cave drawings." Jesse could see relief on their faces since they had all traveled more than they wanted over the past few weeks. "Instead, it looks like we have our work cut out for us right here, after speaking with Doctor Charity Armstrong. There will be a lot of ground to cover and little time, as usual, to get the investigation completed. I've attached on this board in front of us, a photo of a particularly interesting little town. Like other places we have investigated, it has proven to be a very interesting hot spot for UFO activity. I really don't want to say more about the women because I want you to come to your own conclusions as you do your investigation." Passing out packets, he continued to talk. "The name of the town is Cass, West Virginia. It used to be a booming lumber town years ago. Cass was named after Joseph Cass, of the West Virginia Pulp and Paper Company. What made this town so prosperous was the C&O Railroad, which linked the timber from the surrounding mountains to it, creating labor for several thousand men. There were twelve logging camps in the area bringing in men and families to work the logging camps and mills. This, gentleman, is where our investigation will begin." He waited for the agents to pull the information from their individual packets before continuing.

"So, how far back are we talking about, with the possibility of ufology in this town?" asked Colin.

"Good question about UFO activity in the area, I find it very interesting that since 1941 numerous young women just up and vanished from this particular community. Some woman may have just run away while others died or disappeared under strange circumstances. Still, no bodies have been found for approximately a dozen Caucasian females all in their twenties from this area. Now, I have reason to believe there is something more disturbing and more along the unexplained happenings type going on here, something never considered by extraterrestrial naïve law enforcement in the past. Doctor Charity Armstrong's team has identified the women left here during the night using DNA evidence in the missing person's data bank. I have reopened some of the female missing person cold cases for the Cass area. As time goes by, there may be more. I am assigning you to reinvestigate their backgrounds. Leave no stone unturned, gentlemen. Start with their birth and give me a detailed report of what you can find up to the day they went missing. Or if you find they are truly dead, you have my permission to attempt to determine who did it and why. But only if you can get that accomplished quickly, which may not be an easy task. Once completed, turn it over to the local police and let them have a run at it for prosecution. If you do find a body, this is when our forensic director, Doctor Sara Meskins, will step in and complete any exams on the deceased. We need to find as many of these women as we can, alive or dead. Include information on what they did for a living, who were their families, who did they love, and what happened with those families and loved ones after they disappeared? One last thing — if they did have someone like a significant other or spouse, I need to know if that person is still alive. I'm sure you will find some that are not still living, since we are looking at a time frame of approximately seventy-eight years. Do not give any information. Only obtain information. If you start feeling the urge to spill your guts… call me, and we will determine who is on the *need to know* list together. I know this is rather unusual, but due to this new discovery our protocol on how we work these isolated cases from Cass are very different and probably will be the most exciting assignments we have done so far in this department. This part is very important for our report. Once this information is obtained, I will be able to give you more details on this top-secret assignment." Jesse pulled black thumbtacks from a clear plastic case and pinned photos of multiple missing women on the cork board by the photo of the town.

Vic put his assignments back in the packet and started to get up to leave, thinking he might have to work with forensics again, and that meant he and Sara Meskins would need to be on speaking terms again soon.

Turning to the agents, Jesse was still deep in thought about the women that arrived from aboard the ship, "Oh, I almost forgot. There's a deadline attached this time. I need all this information within the next five days. Gather as much intelligence as you can. Report back to me as soon as possible. Download your reports, so when we meet again at the end of the week everything will fall in place. Call me day or night if you run up against questions, or if I can be of assistance in the operations room. I can access anything you need that you don't have at your fingertips. We are up against a fast approaching deadline. I am hoping we have five full days to pull this data together. It's just an estimate on the timeline. I will be meeting with General Kearns tonight, to discuss the occurrence on the base; which I am sure you have heard rumors about. I don't want to discuss it completely at this juncture, for reasons I am not ready to disclose. I will say that by keeping you out of the loop I am doing you a big favor. I don't want what I need to tell you about the women here to affect the information you gather. I want you to be thinking about the ones you are interviewing outside this facility, not anyone here. I also don't want the people you interview to know we have their loved one, if in fact we do. They might feel your emotions, or see it on your face. Don't promise them anything. If they themselves have been aboard an alien ship, we most assuredly will be bringing them back here for examination and hypnosis. Once I have all your data, there may be other reasons to bring other people you interview here as well. That will also be determined later. The General will be expecting answers and you can bet he will be breathing down our necks until we have what he thinks is enough data. Do you understand?" Biting his lower lip, he thought of the women located on floor fourteen, in area seven. Jesse hoped they found the answers he needed soon.

"When can we see them, sir?" asked Special Agent Vic Foster, eager to see for himself someone who truly had been aboard an alien craft.

"Not until you're done, Vic. They are with our doctors and scientists being examined from head to toe. They haven't spoken yet. I'm not sure if they can or if they are in shock. Time will tell. There's lots to do, so let's get to it, men. Any other questions, or have I made myself clear in what I need from you?" Jesse had given them more information than he wanted to, but knew his agents would linger until he acknowledged the women's return to Earth aboard the spacecraft.

Jesse heard a resounding yes from the agents, along with a low moan and some whispers as he left the room. The agents had a long week ahead, which meant no time at home after just flying in from Washington state the day before. He expected he had sparked their interest just enough to stimulate them to get their assignments completed as quickly as possible.

Jesse went to his office to make a quick call to his wife, Bette. He had moved Bette and their kids from their home in Harrisburg, Pennsylvania to Lewisburg, West Virginia so they would be closer to his work, but now he wondered if it was a mistake since he traveled the countryside and was gone more than he was at home. He wasn't sure it was fair of him to move his wife so far away from her family. Only time would tell.

"Bette, it's me. I'm sorry I'm not going to be able to come home this weekend for the birthday party. I know he only turns ten once." Jesse picked up his son's photo. Alta looked just like him when he was that age. "Look under the bed, I put a gift for him under there just in case something came up and I couldn't make it home. It's a chemistry set. All boys his age enjoy learning about chemicals and experiments. He'll love it, believe me. Tell him I said just to be careful and read the instructions. I think there's one where he can make his own invisible ink. Tell him to send me a letter so I can try to decipher it, okay? Just don't let him blow up the house; he needs to play with it out in the garage. He probably won't even know I'm not there."

"Jesse, of course he will notice and more importantly, I will know. It really bothers me; I don't like you being gone all the time like this. You never talk about your work to me. I have no idea what you really do. You don't tell me anything. Secrets, secrets, and more secrets — that's all I hear you say anymore. You could have another family somewhere else, for all I know. You don't, do you…?"

"Of course not, Bette, that's silly even saying such a thing. Everything I do, I do for you and for our family. You must believe I love you. I really need to go for now… I'm sorry. If you need to speak with me, you know you can always dial the switch board, and they will find me immediately, if it is an emergency." Jesse didn't have time to deal with Bette's constant nagging him about his job. She never nagged him about his paycheck. *If she only knew what I really did. Surely, she would understand, or would she?* He wondered. He was sworn to secrecy so he would never tell her what he really did. He had taken an oath to his government and a different one to her, and he would honor them both the best he could. When he had time, he would come up with a plausible alternative to his real secret job that he might tell her so she would finally get off his back. Lies, lies, and more lies… that's what his home life with Bette had finally come to.

# Chapter 4

## Rose's Story, 1939

Rose Gilbert was just finishing her shift at Maxton's Diner when a few of the loggers from the Whitaker station arrived, wanting their dinner. There was no way Millie was going to be able to handle tonight's crowd; or so Millie Maxton needed to be persuaded into thinking by Rose, so that Millie would let her stay and work. Besides having a bunch of hungry loggers from the logging camp to handle, just like clockwork that good-looking chisel faced Jackson boy had walked through the diner door. Rose had had her eyes set on him for some time now and she was determined tonight was the night. Rose was hoping, if Noble noticed her around enough, he might just ask her out.

Rose slipped into the back where Millie was cooking and whispered in her ear her intentions for the Jackson boy, waiting to see if her boss would approve. Millie wasn't the actual owner, but she was married to Ralph Maxton, her real boss. Ralph was ten years Millie's senior, but she still called most of the shots when Millie wanted something, she usually got it.

Ralph had been a widow with two small boys when Millie came along and rescued him from grief, after his wife had passed away. She stole his heart. Ralph took satisfaction in his rough exterior of generally sounding bossy, but without Millie, Ralph well knew he would have finished his life on the creek bank with a jug of moonshine and a bullet from his Colt revolver. He now kept that gun behind the counter next to the register for protection, not for harm. Ralph was a mess before Millie. She saved him, the boys, and the diner, making life for them all bearable again. He knew he could never repay her for all the love she gave him and the boys. Ralph Maxton appeared in the doorway carrying a medium-sized burlap sack over his shoulder filled with potatoes and a smaller one stuffed with large sweet onions. "What's all the chit chatting about, ladies? Rose, if your shift is done you better git home girl. My wife has lots of work left to do," adding extra gruffness to his voice to make his point.

"Ralph, I just asked Rose to stay a little while tonight, that's all. She agreed to help me work the evening shift. I just told her I needed her since I was feelin' a little extra tired today — so don't you dare say no. See how swollen my feet are tonight?" She raised her ankle in the air. "I sure could use some help. It looks like it could get a might busy, and with me a carryin' this baby of yours... I could certainly use the help just for tonight that's all." Millie stamped her swollen foot to finalize her statement.

Ralph tossed the sack on the floor leaving a dusty mark of dried clay, dirt, and burlap particles on the floor, "Good. She can start by peelin' and choppin' potatoes and put on that big kettle of water for the boil."

"No, then there will be too many cooks in the kitchen. If I'm back here, I can prop my feet up some. Rose there's no need for you to work the kitchen with young single men out front." Millie stared at Ralph, "Besides, you know potato peelin' is Denver's job. He needs to learn the business, too. He's fifteen and as lazy as sin just layin' on his bed readin' those Marvel comic books of his, over and over. He's never gonna learn how to fly anyways, and you know it."

Ralph snorted — *Women... she was right again.* He walked away to check on the pork roast, and drag that good for nothin' boy from his bed. Millie was getting her way tonight.

To Rose, Millie said, "Here honey. Take these apple pies out front and set them on that carousel behind the counter. Put on a clean apron, and straighten up your hair, too; no sense in starting the shift in a soiled manner with possible suitors sittin' about, just waitin' on a pretty girl like you to take their order," Millie winked at Rose.

Rose hugged Millie, whispering in her ear, "You can have half my tips tonight. Thank you," she hurried from the steamy kitchen.

Rose could tell Noble Jackson was interested in her, too. Every time she had the opportunity to glance his way, Noble tried to pretend he was following some conversation at the table trying to laugh at the appropriate times while drinking beer with the guys after their meal. She noticed after all the other guys left, Noble lagged behind. Rose was hoping it had to do with her. She cut a large piece of apple pie placing it on a tray with two cups of coffee, thinking Noble might need the caffeine to keep him awake on the drive home to Cass. Rose carried the tray out to the table where Noble was seated.

"What's this for?" Noble asked, starting to get up to leave after realizing he had suddenly lost his nerve to ask Rose for a date.

"It's for you and me. I haven't had a break all night, and since you are the only customer left, I was hoping you might share a piece of hot apple pie with me. I made it this morning all by myself. I suppose it will be time for me to close up and walk home after we eat."

Noble lowered himself back into the chair, "You can't walk home in the dark, Rose, that's dangerous. Besides, it's raining someone could hit you on the side of that slippery road. Where do you live? I can drive you home in my truck when you're ready to go."

Rose smiled, putting the pie between them. She cut into the crust and apples with the fork and held it up for him to take a bite. "Do you know where the Baptist church is over off Main Street?"

"Umm… this is very good. You made this, huh? It tastes like my mom's. She used to put extra cinnamon in her apple pie too. Sure, I know where that church is. I think I was there a time or two when I was younger. My mom liked to sing mostly in the opera house, but she was pretty good at singing hymns, too. I play my dad's guitar when I'm not working. What about you, do you sing?"

Rose finished her bite of pie and shoved another forkful of deliciousness in his direction. He took the fork this time and the pie and pulled the plate closer to him. Two could play at this feeding game, he decided.

"I play the piano at the Baptist church on Sunday mornings. My sister Ruthie thinks she can sing…," Rose stifled a giggle. "My dad is the preacher there. You should drop by on Sunday morning and bring your guitar. You could play a couple of hymns for my father. What kind of music do you play anyway? He would only like to hear religious hymns."

"A church girl… huh, I never figured you for the type, Rose. You're always laughing with the guys in here." Thinking he might have offended her, Noble tried to revise what he had previously said, "Oh, wait a minute. That didn't quite come out the way I meant it to, so don't take that the wrong way. I'm just a little surprised you have a minister for a father, that's all." Feeling embarrassed, they both sat quietly at the table, worried that their conversation wasn't going as either of them had planned.

"I'm not interested in playing guitar for your father, Rose; only for you, if you are interested that is, so let me get that point straight before you decide to get mad. Mostly I play music I hear from the logger camps. There is a lot of history in the music they play. I've written a few songs of my own, too. It helps me keep some memories alive that I don't want to lose. I think you might enjoy hearing those songs too, if you gave them a chance. Someday I might write one about you." He took a bite of the apple pie instead of offering it to Rose, thinking he had better just shut up.

"Don't worry, I'm not upset. I understand what you mean. No man wants to try to come between a minister and his daughter." Realizing she was pushing him away instead of what she really intended, she said. "That's why I brought it up tonight. You need to know what you're getting into, Noble Jackson, especially before you kiss me. So, I'm putting my cards as they are… right out here on this tabletop for you to see. Look at me, Noble — I'm just a girl like any other girl, regardless of who my daddy *is* or *is not* in this one-horse town. So, don't judge me by my preacher dad."

"Rose, you're not just *some* girl to me. You have to know that by how many times a week I eat in this diner and the way I look at you when I'm here," Noble reached across the table and took her hand. "Okay, eat up this last bite of pie, and I'll give you a ride home. We'll see about me bringing my guitar over on Sunday afternoon, if the weather is good, so we can go for a ride in my truck," flushing over admission of his thoughts to her, he looked down. Rose was different than any girl he knew. She was sincere, honest and beautiful. Noble knew he had to be careful because Rose Gilbert, whether she knew it or not, already had him wrapped around her finger. When Noble tried to get up, his legs felt weak just from the thought of being alone with her in his truck.

Rose heard a bang behind the counter. Looking over, she saw Ralph giving her the stink eye, "I think Mr. Maxton is ready to lock the door. He might start getting mean if we don't leave. You about ready to give me that ride?"

***

Noble pulled his truck under an old sugar maple tree growing close to the street. The large soaked leaves limited the amount of drizzling rain on the windshield. The leaves provided them with plenty of cover while they sat in the truck cab and finished their talk.

"Noble Jackson, you better not stand me up on Sunday, you hear? Don't go ruinin' my plans."

"Plans. What plans are those?" Noble put his most serious face on display.

"You'll know my plans — when I think you're good and ready and not a minute sooner," Rose pointed her finger at him in a teasing manner. She reached across the truck seat, kissing him on the lips. Rose grabbed the door handle on his side of the truck with a yank. She jumped across his lap, sliding out of the truck into the pouring rain. She turned to face Noble, laughing at her bravery around him.

Noble watched Rose laugh and was mesmerized by her presence as the rain drenched her hair and dress, causing it to cling to her wet skin. He touched his lips where she had last been and closed his eyes, smelling her scent on his clothes, and knew at that moment he would never let her go. He shifted the truck into reverse, coasting backward just as she closed the front door of the house.

Rose ran into the house, skipping up the front steps. She heard her father in the kitchen, so she yelled toward his direction, "I worked a second shift at Maxton's to help Millie, and got all wet on the way home. I'm going to dry off and go straight to bed. I'm exhausted, Daddy. Do you need me for anything, or can I go straight on up to my room?"

"No, I don't need anything, sweetheart; you go get dry, so you don't catch sick from that cold rain. Don't forget, you are supposed to help clean the church tomorrow with your sister, Ruthie. It needs to look good for Sunday morning service when Reverend Linnell does his site visit. He's also bringing his two sons with him, so I've invited them all over here after church service for lunch. That needs planned out, too, but talk to Ruthie. I know she was working on a menu today."

Shivering from her rain-drenched clothing, Rose needed to change. She couldn't wait any longer, "Yes, Father." Rose bolted up the stairs to her bedroom. After undressing and putting on her nightclothes, she sat watching herself in the vanity mirror as she tried to get her dark blonde hair plaited into braids. Once pinned up, she could just let it dry overnight and deal with the kinks and curls tomorrow. *Ruthie can have either, or both of those Linnell boys; I just hope Noble shows up. Otherwise, I might get trapped by two fathers wanting to join families with their common thread of religion, and that's not how I dream my life will be. I want love and adventure to take me places to see and do things that nobody has even dreamed of yet, so — Mr. Noble Jackson, you better be here Sunday afternoon to rescue me.* Rose pulled her diary from under her bed and began listing all the fine qualities Noble possessed. She placed it back inside her sewing kit where she was certain it would not be found by Ruthie, and returning the sewing kit back to its spot under the bed.

\*\*\*

When Noble slept that night, he dreamed of nothing but Rose...

\*\*\*

As it turned out, Ruthie didn't care if Rose had someone else in mind to marry; she liked both Linnell boys, and would be happy with a marriage proposal from either one. "You know it doesn't matter to me, but our daddy is the one that will make the final decision on whether you can marry anyone else. I'll help you out this once, Rose, and tell him I am worried that neither boy will ask me for their hand in marriage. So, to make the odds better for me I have asked you to not be interested in either, giving me the chance I need to get into that family, but I warn you, Rose, you better not change your mind and later try to take one of those boys from me, or I will tell Daddy so many lies about you and that Noble Jackson that he will never want you around as his daughter ever again."

*Ruthie is such a brat*, Rose thought; feeling a little sorry for the Linnell boys, especially the one that chose her sister. "Fine with me. I only want Noble, and no one else. You can have your fancy high society status in the Linnell family, and all their money to go with it. I just want to be free to love the man I have chosen for myself."

*** 

Four months later Ruthie married, changing her last name to Linnell, and Rose was free to marry Noble, her true love. Rose moved to Cass with Noble. They set up homestead in a simple, but sweet little log cabin near the logging camp where he worked, with the money he had gotten from the sale of his parent's house in Marlton. She quit working at Maxton's diner and started taking in laundry for some of the single men living in the camp to help ends meet.

# Chapter 5

## Crescent Moon, March 22,1941

After two miscarriages, Rose couldn't decide if she was ready to keep trying or just give up. Depression had her in its claws and was digging in deeper. She knew Noble wanted children, but for some reason she just couldn't give him what he or her father expected. At this point, they didn't even care if it was a girl or a boy.

The last time Rose had visited the doctor was on Friday morning, March 22,1941. Confirming she was pregnant again, he could see her uneasiness grow into an uncomfortable silence. As she finished dressing, he made notes in her chart.

"I know you're worried about miscarriage, again. It's written all over your young face. You need to listen to me this time when I say. 'Go home, get off your feet, and let Noble take care of you while you are in this condition, if you want this little one to survive.' There's a new medication if you want to try it that might help. Diethylstilbestrol, but my female patients have such a hard time saying that big long name, so I'm just calling it DES for short. She watched as he shuffled behind his desk. Placing his half-smoked cigarette in the brass ashtray, he handed Rose a prescription. "Take this over to the drug store. You might want to pick up a pack of these while you're there," he said, holding up a pack of cigarettes labeled Lucky Strike across the front in red and gold. "The smoke can be very calming, and it can't possibly harm you since you exhale it right back out." He picked the cigarette up, inhaling deep and slowly, he exhaled the gray smoke in her direction. "See what I mean? It's very relaxing?"

Rose coughed and nodded to her doctor, closing the office door behind her as she left. She decided not to stop anywhere on the way home: she didn't really have the money, and she wasn't ready to tell Noble she was pregnant again. Getting his hopes up too soon would be a definite mistake. Maybe she would talk to her dad on Sunday and see what he said. *Daddy might give me the money for the medicine if he wants a grandson from me that bad.*

Rose took her time walking home from town. It had rained for several days in a row, and the road from town was muddy with deep ruts developing in the unpaved road from the March spring thaw. When cars approached, she quickly moved to keep from being sprayed by the muddy water from head to toe. Even doing that, Rose still managed to get little dried mounds of caked dirt on the back of her calves by the time she reached home.

\*\*\*

Later in the afternoon, Rose finished taking down the last load of wash from the line. The clothes were cold and stiff from the harsh wind. Rose placed the laundry outside the front door on the porch to be picked up. She decided to take another hot bath to get warm before eating dinner, not expecting Noble home until late. He had already told her he planned to have a beer or two with his friends and play his guitar. Noble said he had a new song he wanted them to hear and that he would play it for her when he got home. Feeling tired after her dinner meal, Rose fell asleep on the couch waiting for Noble.

\*\*\*

March 23, 1941

It was getting on past midnight when Noble's hound, Ring, sounded his alarm. With each throated howl, he bellowed like a train whistle while standing on top of his wooden box, staring up at the night sky. The thin crescent moon above him was in its waning phase.

Rose hurried through the dark kitchen to look out the window, wondering what Ring could be so riled up about when she tripped over her forgotten shoes. An abundance of bright blue light flooded the backyard and spread into the kitchen, distorting her vision causing her to lose her balance. She knocked over a chair along with some of Noble's mother's crystal dishes stacked on the side cupboard. Rose landed hard on the floor as the broken glass shattered around her. She screamed from the searing pain in her wrist. Pulling hard to remove the shard of bloody glass, her severed artery sprayed the kitchen wall. "Too much blood lost," — Rose mumbled before she passed out.

The lights vanished from the sky. Ring, their obedient dog, hopped down from his perch and went back inside to curl up in his wooden box. All was right in his world, as the hound heard his master's truck slow to an abrupt stop in front of the house.

Noticing the lights were off inside, Noble thought as he drifted off, *Rose must already be asleep. I'm just going to close my eyes for a minute or two before I go inside.*

# Chapter 6

## Echoes of Pain, Spring 1961

Noble's hands were pulled taunt behind his back as he was hand cuffed by the officer. He heard their words echo in his ears, "Guilty, beyond a reasonable doubt."

Noble sprang to a sitting position on the thin mattress on the floor of his prison cell. He was the third man in for the night and last one in slept on the floor. Those were the rules the convicts made. It was one of a few things they themselves could control. With three men to a cell and one bunkbed there were always fights, but not about who slept on the floor.

Noble's cotton, black-and-white prison shirt stuck to his warm moist skin. The higher up the cells on the block, the hotter it got, even in late March. It wasn't the first time in the past twenty years he had awakened to hearing his sentence read aloud by Judge Plotnick and probably wouldn't be the last, not yet anyway. Noble lay in silence wondering how much longer he would be with his current cellmates. When he had first come to the prison, he was in solitary confinement for a year and never saw the sun. Noble was then placed in a cell with one convict who bragged constantly about the robberies he committed and encouraged Noble to brag about why he was there. Noble found Jerry's company annoying and many times over that year they came to blows. Soon, he was the one removed, and Jerry would disappear into the prison population. Sometimes Noble wondered if Jerry might have been a snitch placed there undercover to extract information from him about his wife. Maybe the superintendent finally figured either there was nothing to tell or Noble was keeping his own counsel, not trusting anyone while he was still trying to get released.

Noble appealed to the Judge in Pocahontas County, but it seemed to him that everyone in the county was related to Rose and her family either through her mom, her minister dad, or her sister Ruthie, who was now a Linnell, so the decision from his appeals always came back the same guilty, beyond a reasonable doubt, no leniency — and the sentence with it carried the death penalty. Noble was to be hung by the neck until dead, whenever the prison superintendent determined he had been punished enough while alive. It didn't seem to matter much anymore one way or the other. He was tired of just existing; no one could call this living.

Noble had no one left in his life who cared whether he was alive. He had had no visitors from the time he was brought to the prison. His dad had died when Noble was ten while reporting on a flood for the local paper, he tried to rescue another man and child from the rushing water; and all three were swept away. His Italian born mother, sang opera at the Pocahontas Opera House, but when he turned sixteen, she had a heart attack backstage. It had been years since Noble had thought of either of them. He was glad in a way that they died not knowing what fate had in store for their only son.

Noble's dream, this time, was not just of the sheriff; it was mostly of Rose. Where could she have gone? He could still see her face and feel the warmth of her smile when he thought of her. She never faded from his mind like some men said their women did. Those perfect pouting lips, blonde hair, and bedroom eyes were etched permanently in his mind. She had vanished in his dream just as she had in life. Afterwards, he was left alone in his dream to hear Sheriff Linnell's voice boom against the quiet inside his head, "What did you do with her body, Noble? We know you killed her."

Noble wanted to forget the sheriff, push him far away and bring back Rose. Oh, how he missed the musky smell of her skin as he slept next to Rose in their bed. Her perfect body intertwined with his as they made love. Noble only had those few sweet memories of Rose to keep him sane, and little time to think with all the noise and claustrophobia from three men in this dingy cell.

Today marked twenty years. It was 1962. Perhaps that's what had brought the nightmare this time. Noble lay down. Closing his eyes, he tried to force sleep, it wouldn't come. The other two convicts sharing his cell would be angry if they were wakened before their shift in the prison coal mine.

At least Noble didn't yell out in his nightmare like some convicts did, causing the guards to investigate. That always brought trouble one way or another. Some of the convicts locked up here were walking sticks of dynamite, just ready for a spark. Over the years, he had seen plenty of things he desperately wanted to put out of his mind — convicts beating, raping, or killing each other in the sugar shack, and a few guards joining the ruckus. It wasn't something you talked about either. There was a convict code. Keep your mouth shut and stay alive. Noble didn't know how much longer that would be since his last appeal was in January 1962. It had been rejected, so there would be no more appeals for him in hopes of getting out.

Noble heard the clang of keys and footsteps from the guards. Their heavy boots matched each other's steps as each boot met with the concrete floor. The guards enjoyed making an entrance. Their forceful behavior seemed to intimidate the inmates, helping to keep them in line. *What are they doing on the South cell block in the middle of the night? Who are they coming to get? What torture had the guards come up with during the night and at what inmate's expense?* Noble himself had been beaten, dragged to the basement, tied to a chair, burned with cigarettes, questioned for hours, and locked in a dark janitor closet so small that when he sat down, he still had to bend his knees, not able to stretch them out. Noble never told a soul when he was returned to the cell block. He never would. He knew the punishment would be worse.

The guard's boots stopped in front of the cell where he lay on the floor. He kept his eyes closed, faking sleep and not wanting to encourage them if they were just walking around. Noble hoped and prayed they would just go back to their office, drink coffee, and play cards until their shift was over.

The large metal key eased in the lock of Noble's cell door. It opened with a whining screech. He could tell by the guards' snickers and hushed voices they were up to something — very bad. One kick in his gut sent him seeking cover under the small metal bunk out of their reach. Without delay he scooted further out of sight since it didn't appear, they were there for him tonight, not yet anyway.

The mattress above him lightened instantly as the guards gagged Pete, yanking him from a deep sleep. "Someone's been naughty," the guard stated in a scoffing voice. Pete's hands were then cuffed behind his back before they dragged him from the cell. His bare toes scraped against the rough concrete floor, tearing skin and ripping toenails. Pete resisted, refusing to walk and trying to make it difficult for the guards to take him. Wherever they were going, he would force them to drag his full weight this time. Everything else was out of his control. Face taped he could not beg or yell out for help. No one would come. Only the convicts could be witness to what was in store. Unfortunately, he wasn't being taken very far tonight. Noble heard a low guttural sound from one of the guards as he hoisted Pete up and over the side of the walkway railing.

Smack! The weight of Pete's body echoed five floors down, meeting its end on the cold grimy concrete floor below. Noble heard a smirk of laughter outside the cell. Bill slapped Jeff on the back, "See there, I told you it would bounce from this far up. Come on; let's get that mess cleaned up before the new shift arrives. Make it at least look like a suicide so we can go get some coffee. Let day shift find it when they make their rounds so they will have to clean it up off the floor."

Jeff sneered, "Yeah, making day shift clean it up is like killing two birds with one throw. You said that thing would bounce, but you never said there would be no head left. Jeez, I bet his body feels just like jelly with all those crushed bones. What a mess!"

Noble scooted from under the bunk as soon as the guards disappeared. He vomited in the sink, and then quickly took the dead convicts place on the bunk. The mattress was still warm from its previous occupant.

Pete's body odor enveloped the cotton batting. He knew if he stayed on his own mattress the morning guards would be sure to question him closely since Pete would have had to pass him on the way out of the cell. Noble closed his eyes thinking, *that could have just as easily been me.* His heart pounded against his chest as if it were trying to escape; Noble was sure the other inmate who was lying above him could hear the sound. If he did, he didn't let on that he was awake. He was playing it smart. He didn't believe in getting involved in other convicts' problems. He was just biding his time until he got free. Some of the convicts on the floors below got up from their bunks pressing their faces against the steel bars to look out, to hear what happened. Someone announced it was just another suicide, so they went back to bed, not wanting to be seen up. The convicts in the cells on either side of Noble's never opened their eyes or even budged. They knew the guards would see them and know who might be witnesses to the recent event.

Pete was murdered for nothing. He was just a skinny, scruffy, red-headed kid who stole one too many cars, turned twenty-one and got himself caught. Not anymore, no second chance. He wouldn't ever be leaving this place. Pete just became a number on a twelve-by-four-inch concrete block in the prison cemetery. A few questions would be asked tomorrow about what happened; there would be no replies from him or the other convict. The guards already had their story: they were not sure how he got out, but he must have committed suicide. Stupid convict just couldn't take confinement anymore, would be their reply. Noble expected he would meet up with Pete again, back there under the clay dirt sometime soon with the grim reaper hot on his heels, too.

There was no bringing the memory of Rose back now, not after that gut-wrenching noise of finality. Her sweetness didn't belong here tonight, among the echoes of pain for the guilty and unjust.

# Chapter 7

## No More Appeals, 1962

One-week later two guards came for Noble, but not in the middle of the night. He was waiting in the breakfast line when he saw one of the guards point him out. As soon as his meal of white beans and biscuits was finished, Noble was accompanied out of the cafeteria in shackles by the guards. Neither of these guards worked on the South cell block where Noble was currently housed, so he knew they must be taking him somewhere new.

Noble was escorted to the superintendent's office, he stood in front of superintendent Stover's ornate mahogany desk while the armed guards stood on either side of him. The room was decorated with three flags — the Federal Bureau of Prisons flag, the West Virginia state flag, and the United States of America flag, each stood tall on a brass stand. There were multiple large framed commendations, from past governors on the health and welfare of the inmates in the prison. However, there was nothing left out in sight that could have been used as a weapon if a convict's motive was to attempt to break free and escape. Noble took it all in, as he suspected every convict did who stood before this man. It was the closest thing to freedom he had experienced in the past twenty years.

Superintendent Stover was a tall, thin man, dressed in a gray wool uniform. He cleared his throat as he quietly read, nonchalantly, through

Noble's file. He glanced at Noble's arrest mug shot showing black hair, brown eyes, chiseled face, and apparently, no beard when he was arrested. The report went on to read that Noble had quit school at age sixteen, parents deceased, and worked as a logger, until he was arrested at the age of twenty. The convict Noble Jackson had no prior arrests or offenses for burglary, assault, robbery, or anything else.

Noble's file summary was short and to the point; murder was his one and only crime. Superintendent Stover was fully aware that sporadically some men just snapped. Murder carried the death penalty in his state, which he thought was strange since some killers never received the maximum sentence, even when they had committed numerous other crimes. Most received imprisonment without the possibility of parole, but the judge from Pocahontas County had thrown the book at this one, as some would say.

Superintendent Stover started with a somber look, "Well, Convict number 99034, it appears you have lost your last appeal for the murder of one, Mrs. Rose Clair Jackson. I'm assuming from her name this was your wife — correct? Why didn't you just leave her? It would have saved you a mess of trouble if you had. It looks like this woman's body has been missing since March 23, 1941. Surely if she wasn't dead this Christian woman, would have shown up to visit her family home by now don't you think?" He cocked his head to the side, studying Noble while not really expecting an answer. "No, I guess not; especially if she has been dead all this time. Well, this isn't a social visit for you and the guards. I am hereby notifying you that as of today you will be transferred to death row until your final sentence is scheduled and carried out."

He smiled, exposing nicotine-stained, uneven teeth, as he gave his final remarks, "Well, as luck would have it, you will not be hanged by the neck until dead, as this order says, if you are worried about that. No, our new governor has seen fit to change policies in this state, and we here at the West Virginia Penitentiary will be receiving our brand-new electric chair early next week. It's supposed to be a more humane alternative to hanging. Of course, it will take time to assemble, and we will need to have the state electrician examine it for safety after it's built, so it works correctly. We can't have our prisoners injured while they are being executed, can we? No, that wouldn't look very good on my part." Looking sternly into Noble's eyes with his own steel gray ones and his lips pressed firmly together, Superintendent Stover wondered, *Why is it that some men never flinch, always insisting they are innocent until the day they are executed?* The Superintendent picked up the file on Noble once again, tossing it into the metal tray as a symbol of Noble's life being finished. "I think our work is done here, gentlemen." The Superintendent turned his back, busying himself with other trivial matters, signaling to the guards the meeting was over.

Later that day, Noble sat in his new cell on death row alone. There would be no more inmate conversations for him. The heavy metal door on his cage had one opening halfway up that the prison guards used to pass a tray for food and water at mealtimes; otherwise it was kept closed. There was no outside light from the sun, only the glaring lights from high above lit his cell. Time slowly passed; days ran into several weeks. Noble lost track of time; bored with his current existence, he lay on the small cot and slept. Being an inmate on death row, nothing really mattered anymore, and nothing was required of him, except he had to live until he was executed by the state, in the new electric chair. From where Noble now lay, he could see the names of all of the death row inmates who had spent time in this particular cell. Each inmate name crudely etched into the steel on the backside of the cell door. Noble decided he was not ready to add his name to the list.

*** 

Noble thought back to when he had first met Rose and to the last time, he saw his wife, as clear as she had always been. He needed this time alone with her memory. He worked as a logger from the time he was sixteen, right after his mom died. He had been as alone then as he was now. Rose worked the day shift at Maxton's diner over in Deer Creek. Noble remembered sitting in the crowded diner at a table with other loggers, enjoying a beer after his meal. It wasn't the first time he had intentionally eaten at Maxton's hole-in-the-wall. In fact, that week he had come to the diner every night just to get a glimpse of Rose before she left. He liked observing Rose engage her customers, but that night she didn't leave; she stayed a second shift. Now, he knew she had stayed for him. He loved hearing her laugh and watching her smile as she worked. Rose was friendly, outgoing, and drop-dead gorgeous. He couldn't take his eyes off her, and once she saw he was watching her, she flirted back while glancing in his direction every chance she got.

It was storming when the restaurant closed, and they finally talked. Noble offered her a ride home in his pickup. He wanted to introduce himself and ask her for a date, but lost his nerve. He was thankful she was so much braver than he when it came to introductions. From working at the restaurant and going to church Rose was used to engaging with strangers and making them feel like they already knew her. Four months later they married. Noble moved them to Cass, close to his job at Whitaker Station and they set up housekeeping. Noble wanted to start a family. But as Lady Luck would have it, Rose miscarried each of their two babies before she could make it into her second trimester. Having a child just didn't seem to be part the big picture plan for them. It was major disappointment both for him and for her father. Her sister, Ruthie, turned out to be their father's favorite of the two, proving childbearing was as easy as snapping a pot of sugar peas for her. Noble tried to comfort Rose and knew she was getting depressed with every day that passed, but he didn't know what to do to help her. What did she do to herself or where could she have gone?

So much had happened to him since he last saw her. Noble remembered kissing Rose at the front door of the cabin when he left for work that March morning. She handed him his gray metal lunch pail and thermos of hot coffee, just like she did every morning.

"I love you, Noble Jackson. I'll see you tonight," Rose stood smiling. He remembered she was wearing a thin blue cotton dress. The color brought out the violet blue hidden deep in her unusual eyes. Her messy hair hung loose, covering her slender shoulders, but she didn't care. She knew Noble liked it that way. It was his reminder of what they had done the night before. Rose waved in his direction as he backed up his truck. Noble always made a point to look in his rearview mirror for one last glimpse of her before he pulled away. Rose also never left the doorway until his truck disappeared from her sight. After he was gone, she would start her day of cleaning, cooking, and washing.

It was a typical morning, nothing stood out of the ordinary. There was no fight between them, as some would later say in the court room. There never was a word of anger passed between them. Of course, Noble was disappointed that they didn't have a child, but he wanted Rose regardless. She meant the world to him. Surely, she had not gone into the woods after he left and done something to herself. Rose had seemed a little depressed, but nothing that he would have been concerned of her harming herself. That's what Noble told the deputy later, but they didn't believe a word he said. The doctor took the witness stand, saying Rose had been in his office that very day, and he had confirmed to her before she left that she was pregnant again. Noble couldn't understand why she had not told him before he left for work. Anyway, the law had already made up its mind he had killed Rose, as well as their unborn child, concealing her body somewhere on their property. They were determined from the time they pulled Noble from his truck that he was guilty, after finding all that blood, and he would pay for his crime.

The sheriff formed a search party that sunny brisk March morning, it included people from her father's church along with a couple of blood hounds, but nothing was ever found. That still didn't satisfy the law, that Rose Jackson just up and disappeared on her own. Rose's dad was too well-known in the community, and someone had to pay the price. With Ruthie whispering untruths in Sheriff Linnell's ear, that person was to be Rose's husband, Noble Jackson. Who else could it have been?

Witnesses from Maxton's diner, including owners Millie and Ralph Maxton, talked about how sweet Rose was to them. Numerous customer statements described her character as angelic. By the time the audacious prosecuting attorney, A. R. Phelps, finished his closing argument, there was not a dry eye in the court room, and not one of the jurors on the panel believed Rose would have just up and left Cass of her own accord.

Noble didn't blame them; he thought Rose was an angel, too. The jury even referenced that specific term when they announced the verdict. "Surely, her body would show up at some point, so the town can give this sweet angel a proper burial," the judge repeated before the court was adjourned.

Noble couldn't think. Nothing made sense. It just didn't seem real. He tried to recall the events of that fateful day they came for him, March 23, 1941. Of that previous night, all Noble remembered was stopping after work to drink beer with a couple of guys from work and playing his new song on his guitar. A man was there collecting songs for a radio show from American Epic and he wanted to listen to Noble's latest song, *My Darlin' Rose.* After hearing it, he asked Noble to come to Charleston to record several of his songs. Noble stayed longer that night than he had intended, thinking of the extra money he could make selling or playing his songs on this radio show. It was dark when he drove up to the house, and he was very drunk from too much celebrating. Noble couldn't even get out of his pickup he was so intoxicated. He passed out across the cracked brown leather seat and never made it into the house to tell Rose the news. It seemed they both had things they needed to tell each other, but never had the chance.

The next morning, Noble awoke hearing the truck door creak open, thinking he was going to catch it from Rose, or maybe she would just climb in on top of him as she often did; Noble hoped it would be the latter. Instead, he was being roughly pulled from the truck cab. He was confused in this groggy state, but noticed a female standing on his front porch. Her hands concealed her face as she spewed guttural cries of anguish. The wailing flowed through the cracks between her fingers to echo off the hills.

Noble did his best to move toward this sound, thinking it was Rose and wanting to comfort her, instantly realizing his mistake. Instead of Rose, it was her sister. "Ruthie, what are you doing here, girl? What's wrong? Why are you crying like that? Where's Rose?" Noble tried to go toward her. He desperately wanted to get into his house, but the strong forearm of the lawman held him firm against the warm metal of the truck as he kicked Noble's feet apart to keep him off balance. Noble's cheek was flat against the hood's black steel in seconds.

"That's what we all want to know, Noble!" Ruthie screamed out her demand to him as she leaned forward hands on her hips, face wet, flushed, and contorted. "What did you do last night, huh? Did you two finally have a big fight?" She frantically moved across the yard, losing a shoe in the process. Reaching him, she shoved at his shoulder knowing he couldn't get loose to fight back. "Did you kill her, Noble, because she couldn't have your child? Answer me. Where is my sister? What did you do with her body, Noble? When they find what you did to Rose you will pay, I will certainly make sure of that."

"I didn't do nothing, Ruth. What are you yelling at me about? I got drunk celebrating a little too much and slept it off in the truck, that's all I know. Rose! Come out here, Rose. Quit joking around, you hear. It isn't funny, not one bit, so come on out."

"There's blood all over the kitchen wall, Noble, and the house is a mess, so there's no reason to stand here and lie to us. She ain't never coming out of that house and you know it." Heart-broken, skinny Ruthie lost her balance. She lay in the dirt, giving into inconsolable grief that her only sister was gone. Rose was dead, and she felt guilty for the things she had recently said to her dad about Rose. She might as well have killed Rose with her own hands, but Noble Jackson never needed to know that conversation.

Noble had no other explanations to offer her or the deputy. When the sheriff arrived on the scene, he hoped he could convince him to let him look for Rose. He tried to go into the house to see for himself, but no matter how hard he struggled, between the deputy and Sheriff Linnell, he couldn't break free. They shoved Noble into the back of that black-and-white cruiser where he was finally trapped. Feeling overwhelmed and defeated, he beat on the window glass with his forehead. There was nothing else left that he could do. Noble thought, *Rose has to be there she just has to. Where else could she have gone? Rose and I never fought. Ruthie has to know that, surely, she knows how much Rose means to him. She just isn't thinking straight.* He loved his wife with every breath he took. Noble could not forget how painful and frustrating that day had been for him.

Noble couldn't understand why they wouldn't release him so he could help search for her. If she was dead, he wouldn't give up until he found the degenerate who had hurt her, and he would make them suffer, before he ended their useless life. If that occurred, they would have him, by rights, in charging him with murder. But he never received that chance to prove his innocence. Noble was never able to see the inside of their home. He only heard the evidence that was reported to the jury during his trial.

Noble could still hear the deputy's statement that put him behind these prison bars. The Deputy swore on the witness stand, "Upon entering the home, I found blood sprayed all over the kitchen floor and the wall. There was broken glass everywhere. The blood found at the scene was the same type of Mrs. Rose Jackson's. He pointed to Exhibit A. It appeared to me that someone, probably her husband, Noble, who must have been drunk, attempted halfheartedly to clean up the blood, but in his drunken state the kitchen was just a disgusting mess. The house was locked from the inside, so who else would have had a key? When we exited the house the sheriff and I found the defendant, Noble Jackson, passed out drunk in his truck. Your Honor, there was a butcher knife with the defendant's fingerprints laying right on the counter. It had blood spatter on the handle, which also matched the blood stains in Exhibit A. One of the kitchen chairs was knocked over, and a stack of glass dishes was shattered. These two things on their own suggested to us there was a struggle of some sorts in the kitchen your honor."

Noble remembered yelling at the deputy on the witness stand interrupting his own attorney's objections, "Of course that butcher knife had my fingerprints on it; I washed it that morning before I left for work after Rose made my lunch. My fingerprints are all over that house because I lived there, too. I did not kill my wife! I loved my wife and will love her until the day I die!" His comments didn't help his defense attorney. They just showed the jury how angry Noble could get under stress.

# Chapter 8

# Death Row with Sparky

Marvin Gosset, one of the guards assigned to monitor the convicts on death row, stood outside Noble's steel door. He opened the metal slot just enough for Noble to hear outside the cell. Taking a drag off his cigarette, he blew it through the opening to attract Noble's attention before he spoke, "I hear ole Sparky's just about ready for his first victim. You're gonna be moved over to the dance hall soon, so you can make that long walk down the last mile. Don't worry I'll be down front waitin' for you." He cackled. "I hear it will be a sight to behold. First, they'll put a black hood over your head so you can't see. Heck, maybe I'll put a little bit of something on it ahead of time for you to smell how about that?" He waited for a reply then continued. "After that, they'll strap you to the chair. They're gonna stick some electrodes on your head and your body. After Superintendent Stover reads his final statement of your guilt, the state electrician is gonna send two-thousand volts of electricity down those thin copper wires and shoot electricity clean through your body. Heck, it'll probably blow the bottoms of your feet clean off. You ever see someone git hit by lightnin', boy? I hear there's and entrance and an exit wound. You're gonna smell just like a roasted pig on a spit in the summertime. I sure hope I get to sit in the front row. Why you'll be famous. It's just like the first hangin' here. I wasn't around for that one, but I'll be able to brag about the first convict I saw that took ole

Sparky for a fast ride to hell! Ha, ha, ha." He chuckled, smacking his hand on his thigh. Marvin was sure that would provoke Noble, and he sure enjoyed stirring things up when he was bored.

Noble leaped off the bed and ran to the door, bare feet scuffing against the rough concrete floor, but Marvin eased the slot closed, not allowing Noble the pleasure of sharing any type of human emotion. Noble smacked the steel door with his fists until they were bloody. Cursing until he was emotionally exhausted, he slipped to the cold floor. His time was almost finished. Death was coming for him soon, and now he knew its name was ole Sparky.

Late afternoon brought with it a visitor to the barren death row cell block. Marvin, the only guard assigned for the shift, was ebullient to have someone he knew to play a game of cards with, Jerry, whom he recognized as an undercover FBI agent, was terrible at playing poker so Marvin figured he could win a few bucks off him before his shift was over. "Jerry, what brings you all the way down here?"

"Bored out of my skull trying to get information out of a guy up on North block. I had to get out of there for a few days; after all these years this job is finally wearing on me. So, I was just roaming around and found myself down here. You all alone today?"

"Sure am, some new guy is supposed to start next week. There's only one inmate down here right now, anyways. So, there's not much to do but play solitaire and drink coffee."

"How about a cup of that coffee and a game of cards?" Asked Jerry.

Marvin laughed, "You got it. I'm always ready to take your money, Jerry." He poured two cups of coffee and sat down at his desk, motioning to Jerry to pull up a chair on the other side. Grabbing a deck of cards from the desk drawer, he shuffled the deck twice then cut it down the middle. He didn't want Jerry to think he was cheating or anything, so he placed the deck in the middle of the desk. "You wanna deal first game?"

Jerry grinned, "I have to warn you, Marvin, I've been practicing. I might even take some of your money home with me this time." He picked up the cards.

"Yeah, well we shall see about that, buddy," he motioned for Jerry to deal the cards then began searching in his pockets for loose change and pulled out his wallet.

Jerry dealt five cards to each of them before he placed the rest of the deck back in the middle. "How many cards do you want?" He waited for Marvin to look over his hand.

Thinking about his strategy Marvin said, "Give me two cards." He took a drink of coffee while he waited.

Jerry dealt Marvin two more cards from the deck. He looked at his own hand.

Satisfied with what he had drawn Marvin laid his cards face down on the desk. "I'll bet you two dollars," he said, placing his money in the middle of the desk.

"I'll take one," said Jerry pulling one card from the deck and discarding another one from his hand. Jerry took two dollars from his wallet saying, "I'll see your two dollars, and raise you a quarter."

Marvin asked, "Okay, whatcha got?" Ready to win he spread his cards out revealing his pair of aces while figuring Jerry had nothing better.

Jerry smiled displaying his straight flush for Marvin to view, "All hearts— five-six-seven-eight-nine-ten." He grabbed the money crushing the bills with his fist to make a point then placing the crumpled bills by his cup.

Marvin picked up the cards shuffling them extra this time. He dealt five cards to each of them again, "Ante-up." Marvin tossed two dollars toward the center of the desk.

Jerry followed suit saying, "I'll see you another dollar."

Marvin tossed a dollar bill toward the center of the desk.

Jerry wasn't feeling good about his hand this time around. He took four cards from the deck. He had nothing in his hand and was hoping for some better cards the second time around. *You never know what you are going to get. Replacing this many cards could be a significant risk but I have to take the chance*, he thought.

Marvin held two pairs this time sevens and nines, "Let's see you beat that." Bragging, he waited for Jerry to show his hand, hoping he had won this round.

Jerry frowned, "The kitty is yours, man. All I got is two kings, so you win this one."

Marvin gladly grabbed the cash from the middle stacking the dollar bills in a neat pile by his wallet.

Jerry shuffled the cards slowly. He didn't have this part down, not like Marvin who could shuffle cards with his eyes closed. So, he had to concentrate on shuffling, being careful not to let the cards slip and fall to the floor. He dealt them each five cards once more. Looking at his cards, he asked Marvin how many cards he wanted from the deck.

Marvin shook his head, "None for me this time. I'm fine. In fact, let's make it more interesting and raise the ante. How about ten dollars, or is that too high for you?"

Jerry appeared frustrated, but pulled out a ten-dollar bill from his wallet and tossed it toward the middle. He frantically looked at his cards again moving them around in his hand.

Marvin spread his cards on the table in anticipation of his win, "Three of a kind, now let's see you beat that hand." He smacked the desk, spilling his coffee then wiping at it with his sleeve, preferring to get his clothes wet rather than the money or the cards.

*Marvin spoke too soon,* thought Jerry. He laid down a full house—three-tens and two kings. "I guess that pile of cash belongs to me."

"Jeez, I thought for sure I had that game in my pocket. How about another round so I can get my ten back at least?"

Jerry put the money in his wallet. "Let's take a break. I need to stretch my legs." He stood up stretched and walked around, looking at the information taped along the wall. "I heard you guys got an electric chair down here." He looked wild-eyed at Marvin. "So, no more hangings down here. Is this information correct?"

"Yep, you got that right. Jerry did you ever see a hangin' here at the prison?" Marvin waited on Jerry's response; he had seen one and thought it was quite entertaining.

"No, I don't think I ever have. I'm usually locked up with one of the convicts, trying to extract some sort of information or other. So, I don't get to do much around here where I can be seen and identified by other convicts."

"Well you sure missed it … there won't be no more hangin's inside here. Heck the last one they did was John Spikes or Spokes something like that. Yeah, I think that was his last name. Anyways, he was a big fella, way too big for hangin'. He was so big, instead of snappin' his neck and leavin' him hangin' for a few minutes, that rope just ripped his head clean off his shoulders. You should have been here. What a sight I'm tellin' ya. Blood squirted in every direction. The women in the room watchin' screamed bloody murder. One even fainted, I think it was the wife, maybe. I had to leave the room because I was laughin' my you-know-what off over that, and seein' his head roll under the superintendent's chair while he was sitting there trying his best to look professional —well it was just too much for me. It was like he was saying, 'What are you talkin' about? I don't have no head under my chair.' Ha, ha, ha. You wanna take a gander at that electric chair? They finally got it all put together yesterday. I expect by Monday that guy in there will be meetin' ole Sparky," Marvin snorted as he motioned with his head toward Noble's cell. "I named it myself. I sure hope it catches on so I can take credit for the name, too."

Jerry turned in his seat, seeing the solid iron door behind him that held Sparky's first, future victim.

"Hey, while nothin's goin' on right now, come on with me and I'll introduce you to Sparky if you want to take a firsthand look at the ole gal. It's a fine piece of killin' equipment." Marvin was ready to brag about Sparky to someone, and it wasn't like he could take the chair home for his family to see, so this was the next best thing as far as he was concerned.

"Where's it at? I'll meet you there, I need to go take a leak first."

Marvin pointed to the end of the hall, "Just on the other side of that door, man. I'll go turn on the lights so you can get a good, close up look at her."

As soon as Marvin closed the door behind him, Jerry emptied a vial of powder into Marvin's coffee cup, stirring it until it was completely dissolved. Jerry hurried down the hall to meet up with Marvin.

"Wow, that's crazy! Is it safe to sit in just for a minute to try it out?" asked Jerry, running his hand over the smooth wood of the poplar arm.

"Sure, as long as the electric from this box is not on. See this handle here? You need to pull it straight down to get a good current going. At full power those copper wires carry a charge of two-thousand volts. Plenty enough to kill a man dead in just a few seconds."

Jerry sat down in the wooden chair, "Man, this is exhilarating. Can you imagine the voltage that will come through this thing?" Jerry shook his body as if he was getting a jolt of electricity.

"You got that right! You want me to see if there are any spots left so you can come down and see it happen for real next week? There's a signup sheet in the superintendent's office."

"Sure, who wouldn't want to see something like that. Thanks, buddy. Hey, I'm ready to win a little more of your money now, if you still want to play another game or two. That's about all the time I have left before my shift starts," he said looking down at his watch.

Back at the table, Jerry got the coffee pot and refreshed both of their cups. He pulled out a little bottle of whiskey and shook it, gesturing to Marvin if he might want some in his coffee to liven the flavor up.

"Sure, pour some in there —what's it gonna hurt? Heck, my shift will be over in a couple hours anyway." He held out his cup. Jerry poured a little in then added a touch more.

Marvin drank his coffee in a couple gulps. He wasn't going to let good whisky sit and get cold. He pulled out his log for the day and started making some notes since he had to have that complete before the end of the shift and didn't want to think about it later in case, he got tipsy. He wouldn't get paid if he didn't have any entries. Plus, it would look like he didn't feed his prisoner any food, which sometimes he didn't. He ate Noble's food himself, but truthfully did anyone really care? So what if his death row convict lost a pound or two? Sure, he knew the superintendent frowned on that type of punishment, but who was going to tell if the food was gone and it was entered that Noble ate it?

In the meantime, Jerry meandered over to Noble's cell and popped open the slot. "Yoo-hoo, anybody home down here on death row?" He laughed, enjoying his time with Marvin, but was bored when Noble didn't come to the door, so he came back to the desk.

Marvin was beginning to think Jerry had drunk more whiskey than he gave away. Marvin took the bottle and poured himself a half cup and drank it down straight. "Whew, that stuff is good goin' down, my friend!"

Jerry sat down at the desk and began shuffling the cards back and forth. "Hey, I got a crazy idea. Let's hook one of us up to ole Sparky and tap the switch just enough to get a tingle, to see how it feels."

"What! You can sit on that chair with the juice on, but no way am I gonna do that." Marvin liked this guy, but there were limits to how crazy he was willing to get. Sure he had played around with the hanging noose when it was available, but this was in a new category of crazy.

"Now wait a minute, you haven't heard the whole game yet. I've got three hundred dollars here burning a hole in my wallet. So, here's the game, we both draw one card from the deck and whoever wins high card wins one hundred dollars. But, in turn the loser must volunteer to get a tingle from ole Sparky. Are you game, or am I going to have to come back some other time and get one of the other guys to play this game with me? You know they will." Jerry pulled the hundred-dollar bills from his wallet and shook them in front of Marvin's face, goading him to play the game.

Marvin howled at the thought of sitting in the chair. He wondered if Jerry would be crazy enough to bring Noble out and put him in the chair. Marvin had been thinking about that all week, just doing little things to Noble, to show him who was boss. "Jerry, you're crazy, man. How do you feel about torture in general?"

Marvin pointed toward Noble's door, licking his dry cracked lips.

Jerry thought about it for a few seconds, "Maybe if we don't get caught, but let's do this first just in case something goes wrong when we get him out. We need to know exactly how to hook a man up first because you know he won't come with us in here willingly. We don't want to get charged with a murder rap, right?"

Marvin shuffled the cards, cut the deck in half three times, and placed the stack on the desk. He was starting to feel a little sluggish.

Jerry said, "You first since it was my idea," as he laid the one-hundred-dollar bill on the desk to entice Marvin.

Marvin took a deep breath, rubbed his hands together, and blew on them before taking the top card off the stack and laying it face up. "King of spades; let me see you beat that, bad boy." Marvin was feeling confident that the money was going to be his in just a minute. *Poor Jerry is going to get stung both ways, but hey maybe Jerry likes a little pain.* Marvin had heard some guys liked that kind of thing, but he had never met anyone that admitted it, until possibly today.

Jerry reached to the center of the desk, took the next card, and turned it over revealing the ace of hearts. "Whew, that was a close one." Jerry looked pleased that he was keeping his money.

"Oh jeez, I thought for sure I'd win your money," Marvin whined.

"Let's do that mile walk, as they say, down to see ole Sparky." Jerry laughed, putting his arm on Marvin's shoulder. "Don't worry; we'll play this game a few times, so you get more than one chance to win my three-hundred bucks."

Once in the room, Jerry insisted that Marvin remove his shirt and pants, so they could make sure the electrodes were placed exactly as the diagram on the wall showed, for safety purposes. Marvin even helped hook himself up, wanting to get this over with as quickly as possible. Jerry adjusted the leather arm and leg straps, pulling them tight, not letting Marvin see he was secretly wearing gloves, so the only fingerprints on the machine were Marvin's.

"Hey, I'm going to run and get that deck of cards and our money off the desk, so we don't have to go traipsing down the hall in our underwear later and get caught, or someone shows up out of the blue and steals that whole kitty right from under us."

"Good idea," Marvin said, looking down at the straps. "I'll just wait here on you, Jerry. Hey, while you're at it bring that bottle of whiskey too. Now don't walk off and forget about me." Still looking at his arms and legs strapped tight against the wooden chair, he cackled drunkenly at the sight of being found in this predicament.

"Are you kidding? I've got to see this thing through to get my hundred dollars' worth. This is the best game I've ever played while working here." He tap-danced out of the room, causing Marvin to laugh even harder.

*Man, I sure wish we had a camera. Me strapped to this chair would be an out-of-sight photograph. Maybe next time,* Marvin thought, while he sat in the chair waiting patiently on Jerry's return.

# Chapter 9

## Chalk One Up for Ole Sparky

While Marvin rested his heavy eyes to wait, Jerry ran down the short hall. He slipped around the desk and grabbed the large steel key to the cell door of the cell where Noble was being held. He unlocked Noble's door, pushing hard to make it open wide.

Noble was standing in the center of the cell in a boxer stance. He was not sure what was going on out in the hall, but if Marvin and whoever was with him came for him, he was determined to put up a fight. Noble thought he recognized the voice mocking him through the hinged slot, but their voice didn't add up to being outside of a cell. Nor had he seen that person in some time.

"How did you get in here, Jerry? Wait, never mind. I knew you weren't a convict the whole time we shared that cell. So, now you're down here after me again." Noble paced around the room with fists clenched. "Come on — if you want a fight, I'll give you one, but make it fair. Haven't you given me enough grief without doing to me whatever you and your buddy Marvin out there have planned? I've suffered plenty for a crime I didn't commit. You want to know what I'm in here for? They said I killed my wife. Well it's a lie, I never touched Rose. I loved her with all my heart." Noble didn't really want to fight. Mentally exhausted and weak from hunger, he sat down on the bed. Having nothing more to say, he just didn't care anymore.

"Noble, I'm not here to hurt you. I'm here to save *you*. So, you need to come with me right now if you want to live. He looked down at Noble's bloody knuckles. "Well, I didn't plan for that. We'll have to improvise. Come on; let's go before we both get caught."

They hurried from the cell. "First, I want to show you something," Jerry opened the door to reveal Marvin connected to the electric chair. Noble couldn't believe his eyes; Marvin was just sitting there in his boxer shorts sleeping with a smile on his face, looking like the happy drunk he was. *What was going on in this place today?*

Only partially dozing in the chair, Marvin opened his eyes to see his prisoner, Noble Jackson, out of his cell. Marvin started to tell Jerry they didn't need Noble yet, then realized he had been tricked, and maybe drugged by the way he was feeling, he was now seeing tiny blue birds floating around Jerry's head.

Jerry walked over to Marvin, slapping him hard enough across the face to leave a red handprint in its place. "Just to set things straight, my name is not Jerry, it's Randy Sea. And you have to be the most stupid and evil human being I have ever known."

Noble didn't know what to do when he saw Marvin being abused. *Should I try to help the guard get free? If I do, Marvin would just torture me again, maybe even shoot me.* He wasn't sure if he could trust this Randy Sea, whom he had spent a year off and on with him in the same cell all the time calling himself Jerry. They certainly never got along during that time.

Randy walked behind Marvin and ever so slightly pulled down on the handle that released the electricity. "Did that feel good, man?" He watched Marvin squirm, strapped to the chair. Marvin's trembling, contorted face turned sideways as he searched for Randy behind him, "Let me out of this chair I'm beggin' you. It's not right. Noble Jackson is the convict, not me, he should be the one sittin' here... not me."

Randy laughed, "I think not Marvin. Noble isn't guilty of anything, except being found guilty by a bunch of uninformed, easily swayed jurors that felt sorry for the local minister whose daughter was missing. Now *you*, on the other hand, were not even tried for the crime of rape of my cousin, Penny Jean. Do you remember what you did to her, huh?

You got her pregnant and destroyed her life. She tried to get rid of it, but I heard she died or maybe you killed her. All I know is she disappeared after what you did to her. Penny Jean leaving just like that with no word, is not something she would have done to her family. You are the slime of the earth, and you deserve to die a little bit at a time, and this... is the right place and the right weapon to make that happen," Randy Sea pulled the lever a little more this time.

Marvin screamed in pain as urine ran down his leg, pooling next to the chair on the concrete floor. The liquid flowed over the copper coils, catching Marvin's underwear on fire and causing the rest of him to burst into flames.

This caught Randy by complete surprise. He and Noble ran from the smoky room, abandoning Marvin to his deserved fate, still strapped to the chair. The electric jolt and smoke in the room sent an alarm to the central office. Alarms were sounding all over the prison as the entire facility's electrical system went down. The doors to all the cell blocks opened automatically, creating complete pandemonium inside the prison. Fights broke out between the guards and the prisoners on the blocks and in the yard. Convicts attempted to escape from the ominous, Gothic buildings of the stone penitentiary. Guards working in the turrets began firing off shots with their powerful rifles, killing several convicts and wounding others in attempt to slow the prisoners' escape and prevent them from breaking through the wire fence near the front gate.

While all this commotion was going on, outside and in the cell blocks, Noble quickly dressed in Marvin's prison guard uniform. He put the gloves Randy had worn on his hands, and ran for the car that Randy Sea pointed out. In case, they got stopped, his hands would be covered. Once in the car, Randy handed him a jacket with GUARD stamped across the back. They disappeared out the back gate, grateful that the guard stationed there was still asleep from the coffee Randy Sea had secretly left for him earlier.

*\*\**

Several hours later, Randy pulled onto a dirt road that led to a discreet hidden cabin. "I need you to wait here for two weeks. No one will look for you in this area, it is owned by the FBI so just stay indoors. Everything you need is inside. My half-sister, Virginia Sea, is moving to Arizona, and you will be going there with her under an assumed name. You can begin a new life for yourself out there. Don't try to come back here, Noble, not for any reason. I don't know what happened to your wife. She must be dead. You should change your hair cut and grow a mustache, but not a beard; Virginia is a hairstylist, she can help with that. She can help you find a job with these new identity papers, too. I don't know if we will ever see each other again, so good luck. I just want you to know, I'm doing this because I believe you are innocent, and I was not about to let you be murdered in that electric chair for no good reason. I would have come for you earlier, but I was stuck in a cell next to a serial killer all week. He will be moving down to death row next week, now that I found out where his last victim is buried. Marvin Gosset, on the other hand, deserved everything he received, maybe more. Before you go, I have one more thing to give you. You can look through it once you are inside." Randy handed Noble a package.

Noble got out of the car. He watched Randy Sea drive away. He walked over to the porch swing and sat down. He opened the packet, and there inside were his songs that he had been working on when he was first taken to prison. The one on top was titled *My Darlin' Rose*, and the last page was a letter to Rose telling her he forgave her if she was still alive and had left him for someone else. He still didn't want to believe she was just dead. Now, he knew where his songs had gone, Randy Sea had protected them for him all this time.

# Chapter 10

## What Happens in Florida Stays in Florida, 1960

The ink-filled needle penetrated deep under her skin. Jacqueline closed her eyes, squinting at first, to try to block out the pain, but it didn't help. Adrenaline rushed over her. Finally gathering enough courage, she opened her eyes, she watched as the needle darted in and out, working its pattern in scarlet red. The heart was complete, along with two tiny green leaves; only the artist could see the tiniest of lettering inside each leaf. The light buzzing sound ceased, and the second tattoo with its hidden secret was complete. Smiling at the completed tattoo Jacqueline was pleased at the design that Max had chosen. Max was always one step ahead and Jacqueline knew the moment she saw the pattern it was perfect for them.

The tattoos they got earlier in the week to honor each other were now healed. Max pulled Jacqueline close and kissed her tattoo. It was the last day of spring vacation at Miami Beach, and they wanted to spend it soaking up enough memories together to last a lifetime. Neither could forget for one second that everything in life was precious and comes with a cost. Reminiscing about the first day they met, as the two walked along the beach together squishing wet sand between their toes watching the ocean's tide rush past, washing them clean.

Jacqueline was a fifth-grade science teacher. She began her teaching career at Cass Elementary School in the fall of 1960. That was the year both of their lives changed forever.

"So, tell me again when you first fell in love with me."

"Max, I've told you this story so many times over the past year and a half that you should have it seared into your mind by now." Jacqueline smiled, thinking back at their first chance meeting and how it affected them both. "It was the first day of school in the principal's office. I was so nervous about starting my teaching career. The principal said he was going to assign me a mentor for my first year, so I wouldn't feel alone, and since you had a background in science, he thought we would start off by having some common ground to talk about. Little did he know at the time, he was not only assigning me the best teacher as a mentor, but when he introduced us that morning, I would fall instantly in love with you. There I was, sitting in his office so nervous but giddy, too. I couldn't wait to begin my first day of teaching the children in *my own* classroom. A few minutes later *you* walked in wearing that navy jacket, with those piercing baby blues looking right straight at me. Honestly, I never heard another word he said to either one of us. I just stood up, put my trust in you, and followed, not looking back. Outside of work, you have offered me pure, unbridled seduction with no guilt, no punishment, only pleasure, and my life balances shifted. Nothing is more important to me than you, Max." Looking down at their feet Jacqueline said, "See, look at our footprints here in the sand. I am still following you, and I will be beside you until the day I leave this earth. I want us to always be together. I never want to lose you. Anyway, our whole love story is written in my diary for you to read. I want to write a book about us someday, about our struggles and the secret life we've shared. I just hope we have enough time to experience everything we want to see and do together. How can something this perfect last? The thought of it just frightens me sometimes."

"I know, Jackie. I'm terrified every day that someone back home will find out about us, and the thought of accusations chills me to the bone. There is so much madness in the world, no acceptance for us, not yet... *you* are my only sanity. I'm still overwhelmed by the thought that you were so willing to lose everything for me, just when your adult life was beginning."

"If someone ever finds out, promise me you won't leave me. We will always be stronger together. You know that, right? Feel our *strength*." Jacqueline pulled Max's hand to her lips. Closing her eyes, she squeezed her hand tight. "Promise me, whatever happens to us, you will never let me go. Please don't ever forget me and what we have."

"I promise, with all my heart." They held their matching heart tattoo's side by side. "This is my vow to you."

"And mine to you," Jacqueline said before they finished their last walk along the deserted beach, then later catching their flight for home.

\*\*\*

Jacqueline and Max, by necessity, parted ways in a less friendly fashion at the airport. Instead of lovers, they were back to appearing to be just friends, acquaintances, teachers at the same school who had perhaps found themselves, by happenstance, on the same flight home from vacation.

Later that night, before Jacqueline went to sleep, she added a new entry to the beginning of her book. *Dear diary, I thought when I bought you when I started school, I would be putting notes in here about my thoughts as a teacher, maybe bits of gossip or even family events. Never thinking at the time, I would ever write anything special about what was happening to me, never thinking I would ever find that special person to make my life complete, but that is not the case. Instead, I have documented my story of true love with my Max within these pages.*

# Chapter 11

## Jacqueline Kaleta Investigation,
## March 18, 2020

Special Agent Colin Bilodeau pulled up in front of the three-story brown brick senior housing development. The sign on the outer door welcomed visitors to Armstrong Village. No buzzer was needed to get through to the entrance; from there he looked for the manager's office, hoping he could find who he was looking for without driving around all day. He had already been to the family homestead. No one living there had even heard of Greta Daniels. The family living there now had bought the house two years prior in auction. So far, his only tip was from the courthouse clerk. "Go try the senior housing development, over off of Delmont Avenue. If she ain't there, talk to the undertaker. That's I know to tell you," he said before he shuffled some papers and walked away.

Looking up from the gray metal desk, Miss Dazy Jones locked eyes with the six-foot-two, dark-tanned, blue-eyed, friendly looking Agent Colin Bilodeau. *What a welcoming sight for sore eyes you are after dealing with plumbing issues all morning,* she thought. She decided she would be happy to hear any problem this man wanted to talk about. "What can I help you with, honey?" That's how she greeted everyone, regardless of their age, but this guy well — she really meant what she said.

"Good afternoon, Ms. Jones. I wondered if you could point me in the right direction to find Miss Greta Daniels, if she lives here that is."

"Oh, Miss Daniels sure is here, all right. She hasn't been called home yet, thank goodness. She's still just as feisty as ever, if you ask me. Are you a family member by any chance? I don't remember seeing you visit before." Part of Ms. Jones job was to discourage solicitors trying to get to the residents, so they wouldn't be fleeced by scammers trying to steal their money. She smiled, waiting for his reply. If he was a scammer, she would show him the door in a second whether he was tall, dark, and handsome, or not. Those were the rules.

"No, I'm not family. I'm here on business." Agent Colin Bilodeau flashed his badge in her direction, not really wanting to leave his card with her since she seemed like a busy-body to him, but a friendly busy-body. His badge seemed to do the trick; she jumped from her seat in surprise, causing her rolling chair to bump against the wall behind her. *That's a new one; never a dull moment around here,* she thought.

"I believe Miss Daniels is playing bingo in the dining hall with a few of the other residents. Would you like me to take you to her, or do you want to meet with her somewhere in private?"

"In private, please. Which apartment belongs to Miss Daniels? I will meet with her there."

"Let me just go get her, and we can all go together to her apartment. That way she won't be too alarmed." Smiling, she scurried down the hall in her red pencil skirt, clicking her black heels on the shiny white tile before the agent could say another word.

Agent Colin Bilodeau followed Dazy down the hall, leaving some distance between them, to allow her time to escort the elderly woman out into the main hall. When Miss Daniels appeared, he quickly took charge of the situation, no longer needing the nosy Ms. Jones.

"Good afternoon, Miss Greta Daniels, I am Agent Colin Bilodeau. I wonder if we could have a few words alone in your apartment regarding a personal matter."

"Certainly."

Turning to the apartment manager, he said, "Thank you, Ms. Jones for your assistance. I believe I can handle the situation from here, unless of course Miss Daniels decides to run." His joke caused all three of them to laugh at the thought of Miss Daniels running anywhere at her age. Agent Colin Bilodeau found his southern charm useful in meetings like this. Being friendly went a long way sometimes in extracting just the right information. Besides that, lying to the Central Intelligence Agency was a criminal offense, punishable by law.

Once inside the small apartment, Agent Colin Bilodeau sat opposite Miss Daniels in the living room. He began sizing her up, thinking she looked to be in her mid-seventies, around the same age as his dear sweet grandma. She walked stooped over from arthritis, too, he suspected. Miss Daniels used a hand-painted decorative wooden cane which he thought gave her some class. He wondered if she had painted the design herself since he also noticed several other hand painted items in the room, as well as some beautiful art pieces on the wall. She seemed to have her wits about her, for which he was glad.

He graciously took a long sip of sweet iced tea from his glass that she insisted he accept. "I don't get many visitors anymore. In fact, I can't remember anyone stopping by for quite some time. Just about everyone I know, or knew, is dead. That happens when you start to get up in years, so remember that while you are still young, Agent Bilodeau. I don't even have a cat." She placed her cane next to her leg, carefully leaning it against the edge of the green sofa and waited on his response.

Colin didn't want to start off their conversation on the wrong foot, but he needed lots of answers. "Miss Daniels, I am here today to talk to you about someone I understand you knew back in the 1960s. Do you remember Jacqueline Kaleta, by any chance? Most of the teachers she worked with at the time are either deceased or have dementia and can't remember anymore." He waited patiently on her response, hoping her memory was still clear, she was his last resort. Every other lead had not panned out in getting any information on Miss Kaleta.

Greta picked and pulled at a long green thread on the couch arm, twirling it in a circle with her index finger one way, then changing direction in a mesmerizing repetition. "Well, of course I knew Miss Kaleta. She was a teacher at Cass Elementary. She taught the fifth grade, and I taught the third grade. She's been dead for many, many years; I'm not surprised when you say you can't find much about her, she was a very taciturn person. Let me rephrase that comment. It wasn't that she was standoffish or unsociable; she was just quiet around some people. Why would you be interested in hearing about her now, from me?" she asked wondering if they had finally found her body, but not letting on that she would be interested if they had. She suspected anyone from Cass during that time period would be interested in hearing gossip of what had ever happened to one of their best grade school science teachers since Jacqueline Kaleta had suddenly just disappeared without a trace, leaving everything she owned behind.

"How well did you know Jacqueline Kaleta? I am interested in finding out about her life, what she was like, what she did in general, how she was raised. I know that's asking a lot from you, just being a coworker and not family, but I haven't had much luck in finding folks like yourself to ask. Just any little bits of information you can give me to put together a picture in my mind of who Jacqueline Kaleta, the woman, was would be very beneficial to me. I know her parents are deceased. I haven't been able to find any other family; whatever you can tell me I assure you would be much appreciated."

Greta nodded, "I understand and will try to tell you what I can remember. It was a long time ago. Miss Kaleta was twenty-three when I knew her. We taught school together, but I already told you that, so I'm sorry for repeating myself. I remember her saying once that her parents were first generation Polish, if that helps in anyway. I think she might have moved to Cass from over in... I'm sorry I can't remember where she was from before she moved to Cass. Anyway, it was possibly to a spring open house, the first year she started there. Maybe you already have where she was originally from in your records, Agent Bilodeau? Her dad had a leather tanning business over in Elkins for years. That's it. That's where she was from. I knew I'd remember it in a minute or so."

"Did you or any of the other teachers get together outside of school? You know, the unmarried ones, I mean."

"Are you talking about the old spinsters?" Greta laughed at the thought.

"Oh, I hope I didn't offend you by my question, I was just trying to find out who she spent time with when she wasn't at school, maybe a boyfriend?"

"I understand what you mean, Agent Bilodeau. I was just trying to make a point. In today's world, young women have the luxury of not being expected to get married until they are good and ready, if they get married at all, but during that time period people talked if a woman wasn't married by the time, she was twenty. The community would consider her a spinster at the age of twenty-five. Can you believe that? Women today have so many advantages over women raised when I was young. It seems so many of them don't take to heart what we suffered through and earned for them, or maybe they take it for granted. That's what I was trying to say. If today's women are enjoying the right to do something, you can darn well bet women before them went through you-know-what to get that *right* for them. But that is not why you are here. You want to know about Miss Kaleta, not what an old thornback teacher has to say about life and the lessons we've learned along the way; another time perhaps."

Agent Colin Bilodeau smiled, "Thornback, that's such an archaic term to call women who are single, don't you think, especially when men are just viewed as bachelors if they are unmarried by a certain age. The word bachelor has kind of a romantic ring to it, compared to thornback or spinster, don't you think. I grew up in Louisiana with my grandma and grandpa raising me the better part of my life. They had a lot of interesting stories to tell me about the South and its treatment of women and of slaves in general. I was taught at a young age to respect women. So, what you are telling me is that you are one of the mystical dragons that stood mighty and refused to be tamed. You should be proud of who you are, Miss Daniels. That's how I was raised — to be proud of where I came from and who I am."

"Thank you, Agent Bilodeau. I see, you were raised by good family. Jackie, as I called her when we weren't at work, also played the piano at the First Baptist Church in Cass on Sunday evenings. I believe she was mostly a loner before we became friends since we neither were married. I think she was quite the book worm. She carried a notebook that she constantly wrote down questions in, so she could go back to the library and research in the schools' set of Funk and Wagnalls encyclopedias. Can you imagine what she could have accomplished today with a computer at her fingertips? She was a very talented teacher. Her students were lucky to have been taught by such an intelligent individual. Sometimes she would go hiking with me. As I remember, everything fascinated her in the forest when we took our walks in the woods. She helped me catalogue the flora and fauna that we found in the forest just off Dickens Run Road and up the mountain range out there. Together we wrote articles and submitted them to various science magazines and digests."

"That's impressive work."

"We were considering writing a book of science for grade school children together, but she died and that was that. I never went back to the woods after that day. I remember once she told me she had a feeling there wouldn't be enough time to do all the things she wanted to do to really experience the world and not just live in it." As she trailed off in thought, Colin heard her say, "She had the most beautiful blue eyes."

Colin pulled the file from his briefcase, laying it open on the coffee table. "It says here in this report that you were with her the day she died. Is that correct?"

Greta put her hands together and crossed her thin ankles, waiting for his next question, not bothering to answer what he had just asked.

He was watching her body language, and it spoke volumes, "It also says here you were in the woods when a black bear somehow came upon you and Miss Kaleta. By some miracle, you were able to escape, but it continued to chase Miss Kaleta, and she fell or jumped off the edge of a cliff into the river." He was determined this time to wait on her response.

"That's what I told Sheriff Thacker when I got back into town."

"And they never found her body in the river? It just seems strange to me, that if you both were out there frequently that she would have known when she was getting too close to the river's edge." He took another drink of the sweet tea that was growing on him, reminding him of his days at home back on the bayou.

"No, they never did. No one ever talked about that point that I can recall." She put her head down. Greta was hoping Agent Bilodeau would have some information for her at this point. She was tired of all his questions.

Agent Colin Bilodeau cleared his throat, "Well, Miss Greta Daniels that is a very sad story, losing a friend and coworker so tragically. I mean a story which I don't believe a word of. So, now that you have lied to me why, you don't finally come clean. You do know it is a crime to lie to the government, right? Tell the truth for once, and set yourself free from this misery you've forced yourself to carry all these years."

Realizing he had caught her in a lie, Miss Daniels stood up quickly, almost causing herself to lose her balance. Her heart raced, and she grabbed for her cane. Greta ambled over to her paisley cloth-covered embroidery kit. She was done with that string always causing her such irritation. She pulled out her tatting scissors and gouged at the string on the couch, leaving a deep dark hole in its place, like a surgeon would to remove a human heart.

Greta dawdled to the kitchen window, looking blankly out toward the pines thinking, *All these years I have lived with so many lies. My family and friends they believed me. But I know the truth and the truth has eaten a big dark hole in my own heart. So many secrets — and no one to tell. No one that would love me if I told the real truth.*

"They're all gone you know. There's no one of importance in my life left to tell the truth to. No one really cares at this point in my life."

Agent Bilodeau followed her to the window. He reached for Greta's hand, "Who was Jackie really, and what exactly did this extraordinary woman mean to you?"

Greta burst into tears. "She was my lover. Is that what you were searching for? Jackie was my best friend in the world. I will love her until the day I die. God — I miss her so much. There, I said it out loud. Are you happy? It was the sixties, a time when the cost for truth was very high. We were grade school teachers. There were so many expectations for women back then. Being a lesbian, well I'm sorry, it just did not fall neatly into any category of being acceptable in society. She played piano at the church. They would have slammed the door in her face. If anyone at the school found out the truth about us, all that we worked for and all that we hoped our lives together might be would have been stripped away. In an instant, we would have been ruined. We weren't child molesters; we were two consenting adult females who were in love with each other. I didn't want that for her, and she didn't want that for me, but our love for each other was strong, so we walked a silent path, a tight rope together without a safety net. One gigantic secret our families and friends never found out."

Agent Bilodeau patted her bony shoulder, "No one else ever needs to know that part of your lives. The love you shared with her sounds very special. Thank you for telling me the truth about your relationship with Miss Kaleta. Now come and sit down and tell me what really happened to Jacqueline Kaleta on March 23, 1961." Agent Colin Bilodeau walked back to the chair and sat down, giving Greta time to pull herself together before she gave her response.

Greta stretched out on the sofa, not having the strength to sit upright any longer, she closed her eyes. She rubbed her forehead with her wrinkled fingers as she spoke. "If I had told the truth in the original report, no one would have believed me. You know that, too, absolutely no one. The deputies would have either dug around until they found out that we were lovers, then they would have accused me of killing her, or they would have decided I was crazy and put me in a sanitarium to try to cure me. You know what those places were like back then — houses of horror for rapes, abuse, where lobotomies, they were the special of the day. You must understand the story I told was to protect me. She would have wanted it that way. Jackie was already gone. There was nothing left I could do for her, except keep her reputation safe."

"So, what really happened that last day?"

Greta pulled up her sleeve, "See this heart tattoo? Once on vacation in Florida we got matching ones. That's how we were tied together — with our love through this heart. Our initials are inscribed in the green leaves. She always called me Max for short, my middle name is Maxine. Just in case she slipped up, someone would think she was dating a man named Max."

"We were in the forest just off Dickens Run Road that morning. It was early, so there was still dew on the ground. I remember it being very tranquil, even more so than usual. You could say even a little creepy, now that I think back on it. I told Jackie it felt like someone was watching us through the trees. She told me I was just being paranoid, and she pulled me to her and kissed me, whispering in my ear what she wanted from me to try to get me to stop being so paranoid. I was afraid we were going to finally get caught and our lives ruined. It kept running through my head what our plan was if that happened, which was to take the money we both had saved and disappear. As we walked along, we started noticing this weird clear webbed slime hanging in strands from the trees. It was like graybeard that hangs from the trees down South, I'm sure you are familiar with that, but smooth watery strands of slime. That's the only way I can explain it." She raised her hands palms up and frowned.

"I understand what you are talking about with the slime. It's like angel hair. Please go on."

"You do? I never knew what it was called?" Greta took a deep breath, thinking about the strands before she started her story again. "About a quarter mile from there, we heard this weird roaring trumpet blare noise up in the clouds, so intense in my head that I felt dizzy, nauseated. It really affected my inner ear. I couldn't walk on any further. I needed to sit down and get my bearings, but Jackie, my curious girlfriend had to see what it was and refused to wait. I think she thought it was close to her house, and she was worried it had something to do with the house, so she ran ahead, concerned about the noise. That's when I saw that beam of bright blue light come down from the sky. By the time I caught up to where I thought she was she was gone. Whatever it was — I know this sounds silly, but honestly, I think maybe a spaceship took her. I kept screaming 'Jackie' over and over, but she never answered. By that time, I had come full circle and came out of the forest behind her house. I knew she was gone, so I slipped in the house, removed any evidence of our relationship, some photos, and a diary. I hurried home to call the sheriff. I told him she had been chased by a bear and fell in the river. He believed me and began a search, but of course, they never found her in the water, nor did they even find a bear. The only deadly thing they did find in their search was a den of rattlesnakes. That's the last I heard anything about the case. The sheriff told me I was not privy to any updates on her case, he could only give information to her family and I would have to talk to them about Jackie. Jackie was mine and I wanted to scream it from the rooftops, but I had to keep my mouth shut and keep working." Greta sat up as straight as she was able to on the sofa. She looked at Agent Bilodeau then said, "So what now? Are you going to put me in jail for lying all those years ago?" Greta held out her wrists.

Colin didn't say a word. He just sat in silence, watching Greta and wondered what his boss, Special Agent in Charge Jesse Finch would say when he handed in his report in on Miss Jacqueline Kaleta and her significant other Miss Greta Daniels, aka Max.

Greta, unsure what Agent Bilodeau was thinking, stated emphatically, "Don't tell me you found her after all these years?"

Agent Colin Bilodeau didn't respond. He just looked at her, seeing the pain in her eyes as she searched his face for answers— that he did not have and could not give to her.

Miss Greta Daniel's started to cry then shouted, "Oh, dear God! Is my Jackie still alive? Is that why you're here? If she is, I need to see her, to be with her. Surely, you understand our bond." She yanked up her sleeve again, revealing the wrinkled, sagging heart; her vow of love until the day she died, or how was it that Jackie had said it? *Until I leave this earth.* Oh, how ironic her promise had been.

# Chapter 12

# Eve Wells, A Time of Innocence

Eve Wells never knew a stranger from the time she could walk. If someone looked at her and smiled, she believed they were her friend. Eve was born deaf-mute on May 15th, 1946. Her dad sent away for a book on sign language as soon as they realized she couldn't speak.

Eve's mom took ill and was taken away to the tuberculosis sanitarium in 1950, to spend her last days in an iron lung. Before she left, the Baptist minister and his wife promised her that her daughter Eve would always be welcome inside the doors of the church. They also encouraged their parishioners to learn sign language, so wherever Eve went in town she could communicate and feel at home.

Eve could be as quiet as a mouse, and sometimes hid from her dad. On one spring day, she sneaked into the bedroom of her Uncle Stanley's house, curious as to all the comings and goings. She hid in the bedroom closet the day her cousin was born, watching the whole delivery with fascination and horror. When everyone was gone, she sneaked out from her hiding spot and took him from his baby crib. Sitting in the rocking chair, she fell asleep holding Stan. From that day on, Eve visited the child every day until the family finally made her stop.

Jim signed to his daughter, hoping to make her understand, "Eve you can't go over there anymore, at least not for a while. You have worn out your welcome and you have to stay home."

"Why, Dad? Stan loves me." Eve gestured.

"Yes, I know he loves you, but he needs to learn to talk like other kids do, and he will with you not around so much. Eve, Stan is not like you, he has a voice like me. I don't mean to say he is just a boy. He can speak and he can hear." Stan touched his mouth and next his ears.

"Okay, I go see Stan tomorrow, just not today," Eve gestured with a grin, her eyes twinkled with delight, hoping she would get her way.

"No, one time a week," Jim held up his index finger. He showed her on a calendar where he had marked when Eve could visit Stan.

Eve grunted, made a sad face, tossing the calendar on the floor before she left the room. She could see her time with her little cousin, Stan, was over until he was older, but at least they would still be friends.

***

1963

Eleven years passed. Eve, now seventeen, worked in the back of her Uncle Stanley's bar. She had seen a young man at the hardware store several times. She noticed he smiled at her as he worked. Eve wanted to communicate with him, but unlike most of the folks in town he was a newcomer and didn't know how to sign. She waited outside the back of the store for him to take his break, and when he did, Eve slipped up behind him, covering his eyes with her hands.

The young man grabbed her, not realizing at first that it was Eve. He was confused why she would do what she did. *Is she flirting with me?* He wondered.

Eve laughed, kissing him quickly on the cheek before she ran to the back door of the bar.

He stood there watching her until she disappeared through the door. That's when he noticed the book that she had left behind on sign language. It was lying on top of a wooden keg of penny nails by the door. Now he understood her quick visit. Eve wanted them to be able to talk. He slipped the book into his pocket and went on about his work.

Several weeks later, Eve was walking home after dark, from church, when she saw an interesting light in the sky. As it got lower, the light disappeared into the trees. She decided to investigate where the light was emanating from. Once she found its location, she decided she would bring her dad back to see the pretty light too.

Two aliens captured Eve and pulled her inside their ship. She fought them as hard as she could. Their oversized and unusual looking eyes terrified her, not to mention their nonexistent ears or small mouths with no lips. The aliens would not allow her to use hands, thinking she would continue to hit them, and not realizing she needed her hands to communicate. One of the aliens tried to offer her some liquid to drink to help calm her down, but she knocked the beaker from its grasp, breaking the glass. The alien became angry and shoved her down to the floor, holding her in place with its heavy foot. When Eve opened her mouth to scream, the other alien poured some of the liquid into her mouth which prompted her to gag and choke, but she swallowed some of the liquid anyway, causing her to relax and fall asleep. The two aliens stood in the doorway of the lab. One motioned to the alien doctor who was standing over her. It spoke in a robotic beeping type voice, "What do you think about this one, should we take her like we did the others or leave her? She doesn't seem to be able to communicate, but she might be useful in our other studies."

"No, we will leave this one with a special gift and come back later to retrieve it. I'm done here. Take her away."

Later when Eve awoke, she realized the aliens had carried her off the ship. They left her sitting upright in the grass. The ship disappeared in a flash of light.

Eve jumped up and began running through the woods. She screamed, but only guttural noises echoed through the trees from her mouth. Not paying attention to where she was going, Eve fell down a small ravine, the rocks and tree stumps tore at her dress and her exposed skin. When she tried to stand her legs stung. She was covered in a mixture of blood, dirt and leaves. Eve didn't hear her dad's voice calling her name, but she did recognize his form standing on the ridge above where she had fallen. She grabbed ahold of a root and began pulling herself up. When Jim heard the noise below him, he shined his flashlight in her direction to see what the noise was. That's when he saw his daughter, Eve; she was covered in blood and dirt, her clothes were half torn off, her long brown hair was matted with dried brush and stickers. Jim couldn't think as anger consumed him. Who would even think to hurt his daughter? Jim didn't know, but when he found that person, there would be hell to pay for what he already assumed they had done to his daughter.

Of course, Eve was so terrified she couldn't even put into signs or gestures what had really happened to her, or what she had even seen that night on the spaceship. She just clung to her dad and wailed in her guttural voice as he carried her back to his truck.

# Chapter 13

## Eve Wells Investigation, March 18, 2020

Special Agent Vic Foster walked into Imel's Saloon, a dingy county bar. It was only eleven a. m. Not too many folks hung out in bars this early in the day, but this is where he was told he would be able to find Stanley Imel. He took a seat in the corner so he could see who came and went. The seating wasn't unusual for him, anywhere he went he always made sure he could observe what was going on. He had done this since his military days. He noticed two men, both in their mid-fifties playing poker.

A dirty-blonde-haired woman scurried over to their table with cold mugs of beer from the tap. She splashed some of the foam from one glass when she set it down. "Heck, Sandy, watch it will ya? We're playing a serious game here."

"Oh yeah, all I see here are two old lazy farts that ought to be working, but are too lazy to hold down a job." She picked up her cash from the winnings on the table and walked away.

"Someone needs to teach that woman some manners."

"Don't worry about it, Jake. She's just in a bad mood. That kid a hers is back to using meth again, so cut her some slack."

"Really, I didn't know about the meth. Okay, Phil I know she needs this job, so she should at least be civil don't you think. After all, we are paying customers."

"Yeah, I guess you're right, but sandy's right too. We are lazy." Phil laughed then punched Jake in the shoulder.

Sandy could hear them talking about her from behind the bar. "Humph," she shook her head as she pulled a damp cloth from under the bar, wiping it down with all the strength she could muster in her arm.

A stocky-built older man wearing a brown flannel shirt stormed through the back door carrying a crate filled with beer glasses. He plopped the crate on the bar, coughed a couple times, and stormed out the back to get another load of supplies. It seemed to Vic that no matter where the man went in the bar, noise followed him one way or another. Finally, the guy finished his immediate chores, groaned, and roughly sat down on a wooden stool at the end of the bar.

Sandy, the bar maid, busied herself by emptying the crates and putting stuff away. Vic looked down at his watch to check the time, wondering if he was going to have to wait all day to talk to the guy he was there to speak with.

He walked over to where Sandy stood behind the bar, picking at loose strands of her ponytail in the mirror. Vic noticed she had a nice figure. She probably had been a catch back in her day, but the worry lines on her face gave her true age away now. Setting his glass on the counter, Vic said, "Excuse me. I was told I might be able to find Stanley Imel here. Do either of you know what time he usually stops in here?"

"Stops in, well you're standing right beside him," Sandy laughed, revealing a broken front tooth.

"I'm Stanley Imel, but people around these parts just call me Stan for short. My dad was the last Stanley Imel, as far as I'm concerned. He died last year, so I'm the only one left." As the bartender and owner, Stan tended to talk too much when it really wasn't necessary. "What can I do you for, mister?" Figuring him for a salesman, Stan waited for the stranger's pitch.

"I'm Agent Vic Foster; I'm from the Department of Defense, and would like to talk to you about someone I am looking for." He flashed his government badge causing Sandy to burst into tears.

"Oh my God, what has that son of mine gotten himself into now that a freaking government investigator is here?" she burst out.

Jake punched Phil in the arm before whispering, "Why did you have to bring up that her boy was on Meth? That government guy might have heard you."

"How was I supposed to know who he was? Let's just leave, slip out the back door right now." Phil started scooting his chair back.

"Just stay where you are. Keep playing cards. We haven't done nothing wrong," said Jake under his breath.

Vic raised his palm in Sandy's direction, still looking at Stan, "No, miss, this conversation has nothing to do with your son. I'm with the government; however, I'm not with the Drug Enforcement Agency. I'm just here to ask Stan some questions about a personal matter not to investigate any drug activity in the area."

Both men playing cards whipped around in their seats at the noise of Sandy crying and hearing the word DEA brought into the conversation at the bar. Phil fell backward in his chair, creating a loud commotion.

"Everything okay, Stan?" questioned Phil, not knowing what else to say, but feeling obligated to say something since they had made such a ruckus, causing everyone in the bar to glance over in their direction.

"It's fine, boys. Sandy's just a little unnerved today, that's all. You know how she gets sometimes about her boy. Don't get your boxers in a bunch. Go on back to your game and enjoy yourselves. Can I bring you another beer?" Without waiting on their reply Stan pulled two beers from the tap and took them to the table. "On the house."

"Thanks, Stan. We were just a little concerned something was wrong with Sandy that's all," Phil added.

"I know and I appreciate your concern. It's all under control, don't you worry about that," Stan assured them. He turned his attention to his bar maid, "Sandy, go get yourself straightened up. Try to pull yourself together. I need you today so don't let me down," Stan warned.

"Okay," Sandy whispered as she scurried to the restroom in the back to fix her makeup. Sandy was sure Stan would fire her after that display and her recent track record of not coming to work on time. She wouldn't be late or miss work if that son of hers would get his act together and stop using meth with that stupid little tart down the street. That boys' beautiful teeth were going to rot clean out his head, and for some reason he just didn't even care.

"Sorry about all the drama around here. It's not usually this crazy until after dark. Now, what can I help you with agent?"

"Is there some place we can talk privately? I have several questions of a personal nature."

"Heck, you can ask me anything right here at the bar. I might not answer it, or I might not know the answer, but you can ask either way." He poured two draught beers from the tap, setting one in front of Vic.

"Fire away," Stan took a long drink from his before he set the mug on the bar.

Vic decided he liked this guy, thinking, *Stan Imel has spunk, he seems a little crazy, but he gets it done just the same.*

"I'm looking for information on a young woman named Eve Wells." He pulled out her photo and placed it on the bar in front of Stan. "Do you remember her?"

Stan picked up the photo of Eve, "Why sure, Eve Wells was my cousin. She's been dead for years. Why do you want to know? Nobody has asked about her for a very long time."

"She's still listed as missing in the old missing persons database, kept by the United States government. What makes you think she's dead?" asked Vic.

Stan placed her photo back on the bar, "Oh, I know she's definitely dead. I'm pretty sure I seen her put in the ground, or at least her grave dug, but no one saw me." Stan stopped for a minute to take a gulp from his mug. "When Maybe messed up sometimes women died."

Vic looked confused, "Maybe, what does maybe mean?"

Stan coughed several times to clear his throat then took another gulp of beer. "Sorry, all that cigarette smoking over the years has got my lungs all messed up." He looked around at his establishment. Behind the bar, on the wall, was a long line of family photos. Right smack in the middle of them all was a picture of him with his grandparents, Walter and Maybe Imel. "Well, I guess it won't do no harm in talking about Maybe since she can't be arrested for anything now that she's dead."

Vic noticed Stan was the anxious type, always having to have something in his hands. Stan began picking up beer mugs, examining them under the light for cracks, wiping them off and stacking them in neat rows. Vic thought, *Stan must be contemplating whether he really should talk to me or not.*

Stan looked up from the beer mug he was holding and directly at Vic, "Maybe was my granny. Her real name was May Elizabeth Imel, but I nicknamed her Maybe for the things she done. She helped young women when their time of the month didn't come when they expected it should have. Do you know what I mean by that?" He waited on an answer from Vic.

"Are you telling me your grandmother, Mrs. Imel, performed illegal abortions on pregnant women?"

"Yes, that's exactly what I'm saying, and some of them died." Stan went behind the bar, opened the register and placed the cash from the bank deposit bag in the corresponding slots for ones, fives, tens, and twenties.

"How do you know she did this? Did you witness her doing this firsthand, or just hear about it from someone else?"

Stan closed the register with a resounding ding. He pulled his Mountaineer ball cap off then smoothed his hair before he replaced the cap. "I was around twelve when I figured out for myself that she removed babies. One hot afternoon, I found one out back in a shoe box. There was blood on the outside of the box, so I was curious. I wanted to see what Grandpa had put in there, but it wasn't Grandpa's doings. There was a tiny baby's body inside the box. It was just placed in there all bloody. She must have been in a hurry. I remember seeing she had wrapped it in a pink striped dish towel. Maybe saw me out the bedroom window. That's when she came running after me. She swatted me with a willow stick right across the back, all the time she yelled at me. She told me to go home if I couldn't mind my own business. I never visited Maybe one time after that day. Didn't even go to her funeral."

"I don't blame you. It sounds like she had a pretty bad temper. She was probably trying to protect you from seeing what you did."

Stan shook his head, "Yes, she certainly did. You are probably right. She didn't mean for me to open that box. I still went to visit Gramps, but I never stepped foot in the house to see her. I thought she was a mean old witch of a woman, even before I knew what else she did." Stan pulled out his pack of Camel's, tamping the top of the pack on the counter to settle the tobacco inside. Every time he thought about his grandma, he wanted to smoke. Remembering his own rule of not smoking in the bar, he put them back in his pocket for later.

"So, what happened to your cousin, Eve?" Vic's interest was piqued.

"Well, I heard she was coming home one night from church, but didn't show up back at the house when she should have, so her dad went out looking for her. She liked going to church. The folks there always treated her nice. Now I don't know if you know this or not, but Eve was deaf, and she couldn't talk either. Well she could, but not the normal way. She used hand signals, shrugs and gestures, she also grunted out bits of words that she tried to mimic with her mouth sometimes."

"It must have been hard for her to communicate."

"Heck, Eve could talk to just about anyone in town. The locals had been around her long enough to pick up some of her sign language. My mom said she thought I was doing sign language the day I was born by the way I picked it up and talked to Eve. To me, it was as easy as riding a bicycle." Stan stood up, walked to the end of the hall trying to control his emotions before he came back.

Vic wondered if he was going to get the information he needed from Stan, he could see that Stan was disturbed by their conversation.

"Sorry about walking away. I have put Eve out of my mind for so long it's hard to talk about her." He didn't wait for Vic to respond. He just wanted to get it over with. "Well anyway, some guy hit her over the head, took her in the woods, and raped her. Sweet girl. As if she didn't have enough to deal with already, besides having that done to her. It just wasn't right! When Eve woke up, she staggered toward home. Her dad found her. Poor Eve, she was a hysterical mess. He didn't tell anyone other than the immediate family. I heard him telling my dad. All her life, Eve's dad, my Uncle Jim, just wanted to keep her safe, but he failed, and it was hard for him to take. A couple months later, her belly started pooching out. Well, no way Uncle Jim was going to let her have some rapist's baby. He didn't want her to think about that rape, day after day, taking care of that baby. Every time he saw her, he got so angry, not at her, but at whoever done it. He sent her over to see his wife's mom, May, to see what she could do about the situation. The family never saw Eve again after that. No one even mentioned her name."

"Really? Well I'm sure you wouldn't have, after you already got in trouble once. Getting hit with a willow switch would have been enough for me not to bring up the subject."

"You got that right. I heard the sheriff ask about her. Probably the minister wondered why she had stopped coming to church. That's when Uncle Jim told them she was missing, that the family had been searching the woods for her. The sheriff formed a search party, but after five days just gave up."

Vic took notes of their conversation on his iPad. "The missing person report is dated March 23, 1961. Do you know where Eve is now? Do you think she died from a botched abortion?"

Stan shook his head, saying in a low voice so the men in the bar couldn't hear their conversation, "Well, I believe she might be buried behind the barn at the old farmhouse. They couldn't really have a funeral or bury her in the cemetery after what happened without Maybe's getting charged with her murder and going to prison. I saw Grandpa and Uncle Jim digging a hole one night out back behind the barn, but they didn't see me." Stan sat quiet for a few seconds before continuing, "Heck, I wouldn't be surprised if there weren't other women buried there, too. My grandma had a lot of young women that came to visit her. They would just show up to spend the night. Maybe had a little room built on the back of the house where they could just come and go?"

Vic had heard enough. He stood up this time, "Stan, I'm going to need you to take me there. I need to see this family farm. I have a strong feeling you are right about what happened to your cousin, Eve."

"Okay, just let me tell Sandy to watch the bar." He put the bar towel he had been twisting in knots behind the bar before he yelled for Sandy.

As they drove south toward the Imel farm, Special Agent Vic Foster got more background on the Imel's. "Is your grandpa Walter still alive?"

"No, he got kicked in the head by a mule in the barn and that was that. He never woke up."

"What about your Uncle Jim? Is he still around?"

"Well yeah, he's getting up in years now. He fell a while back, so his son put him in the nursing home in town, just off Main Street. I suspect he'll be there till he dies."

"Thanks. I think I'll stop by there and talk to him later today, if I have time. I need to get a little more information about Eve from him once we look at the farm."

# Chapter 14

## Maybe's and Walter's Farm

"Jesse, this is Vic. I'm out at the Imel farm with Stan Imel; he is Eve Wells' cousin. He's the grandson of Walter and May Elizabeth Imel, they owned a farm here in Cass back in the 1960's. They're Eve Wells' grandparents as well. Eve's mother was their daughter and she was married to Jim Wells. He is the only one in the group still alive, and he is in a nursing home. The farm looks pretty run down. Stan says no one's lived in it for at least the past fifteen years, perhaps more. Stan's dad was Stanley Imel Senior. I am here with Stan, just to keep things straight. I don't think this investigation is going to turn out to be what you are looking for, as far as our missing women from Cass. My guess is, it will probably end up a murder case, rather than a ufology case. But at least we'll know one way or another, what happened to Eve Wells. Apparently, Stan's grandma, May, was performing backroom abortions here, on the farm."

"Seriously? So, is May still alive or what? If she is alive, she could still be charged if you find a body."

"No, both she and her husband are deceased."

"Did you obtain the abortion information from the grandson?" asked Jesse.

"Stan says he saw his grandpa and Eve's dad digging a grave back behind the barn, somewhere around the time Eve disappeared. My gut tells me she's buried under the dirt behind that barn. So, what do you want me to do, turf it to the local sheriff so, I can come back to the office and work on another case, or stay a little longer to see what more I can find?"

Jesse didn't answer for several seconds, stopping to read a message from Bette on his cell phone. "No, stay there and look around. I'll notify the local sheriff to get a warrant for us to search the property. We need to do a dig behind the barn in search of Eve Wells' body. I'll send Doctor Meskins and her forensic crew out there. No need to involve the locals too much until we get our investigation completed on our terms. Good job, Vic. Keep me updated with what you find. Who knows, there could be more women buried on the property that we can mark off this list."

"Sure will."

"Hey, once the sheriff gets that warrant, I'm sure things will heat up out there, with his deputies wanting to get involved, plus news reporters wanting information before we are ready to give them any. Just remember, you are in charge. This is your baby to handle, not the sheriff's. They should have figured this one out years ago. It's our turn now to show local law enforcement how it's done."

"Got it."

Finishing his call to Special Agent in Charge Jesse Finch, Vic turned to Stan, "Stan can you show me where that little room is located? I don't need to see the whole farmhouse right away."

Agent Foster and Stan walked through knee-high weeds and stickers to the back of the house. Vic noticed this portion of the house was starting to show exterior rot, and if not fixed soon would need a major overhaul. A few of the second story shingles were broken and lay scattered in the weeds. He could see one of the windows from the second floor was broken out so there would probably be water damage to the floor up there, and possibly the wall and the ceiling below. Vic wondered how safe it was to enter the room if the ceiling or floor was rotten inside there. They would need to proceed with caution. Oh how Vic hated searching abandoned houses and buildings. The main thing Vic hated about doing searches in abandoned houses was the local poisonous snakes. Here in West Virginia, there could be dens of rattlesnakes or copperheads just waiting for someone to invade their territory. He had brought a handgun with him just in case. Normally, he didn't need to carry one for the type of assignment he was on.

Vic was still running scenarios through his mind around snakes, when Stan stepped in front of him, misinterpreting the agent's reservation and thinking Vic was concerned about going in the house before the warrant arrived.

"Here, let me get this since you don't have a warrant in your hand yet, and technically, I am named in the estates will as the owner." Stan raised his foot, slamming it midway against the weakened wooden door. The lock gave on the first kick. The rusty hinges ripped from their housing landed with a loud clank on the floor. Stan entered first. Pulling out the door, he leaned it against the side of the house.

"All these years, and I've never been inside this room. I'm kind of interested to finally see it." Stan's boots echoed through the room as he walked across the bare, dirty wooden floor. "Agent Foster, would you like to come into my Granny Maybe's office?" He waved his arm, leaning forward with a slight bow to the agent in mockery, thinking of his grandma and how she had treated him so many years ago.

Maybe's office consisted of just the one room. A twin-sized iron bed, caked with orange rust and attached springs, supported by dust covered wooden slats and ancient spider webs, lay naked. Vic wondered if they had burned the mattress long ago when they left the farm. He was sure it would have been stained brown or black with old dried blood. If it were found by someone else while out hunting, there would have been lots of questions from the local authorities. No one would have wanted to tell the truth about what had really happened inside these walls.

In some cities, places were raided regularly and people prosecuted for illegal abortion. Vic remembered reading that most people who performed them had no medical training. In fact, some were even bookies. Anyone with a hat pin, coat hanger and tape, or a douche bag full of lye or kerosene, offered his or her services to desperate women seeking help and putting their trust in complete strangers. Some women were even kidnapped, raped, robbed, or murdered; misplacing their trust while seeking abortions.

An oak farm table, scarred from years of use, was situated in the center of the room. This must have been where Maybe performed the abortions giving her easier access during the procedure.

Vic opened an inner door, finding it to be just a shallow closet with pegs. On the floor, were a stained white metal chamber pot, several rusted metal clothes hangers, and a cracked black hose. He shook his head in disgust, closing the door. Vic wished Maybe were still alive. He decided he would be happy to see her hand cuffed and led far away from this miserable, deteriorating farm. "No woman should ever have to be cared for in this manner," he murmured under his breath. He didn't blame her; he blamed the time period when women's rights were not a consideration.

Agent Foster bent to get a closer look at the wooden table. Blood soaked into the cracks would have been difficult to remove. There lots of deep dark marred areas. He noticed the wallpaper in the room was peeling quite a bit, with large pieces hanging down in strands. Vic could still make out the pattern on the dingy paper, elegant white vases bursting with pale pink hibiscus blooms. For some women, this wallpaper would have been the last thing they ever saw.

Stan kicked at a pile of trash on the floor, causing a dusky brown rat hidden under the rubble to bolt out the door from the disgusting room.

"I think I've seen enough here. Let's go check out the barn. Hopefully it's safe to go inside there." Vic quickly ushered Stan out, concerned he would lose his grip and out of anger start destroying evidence if they stayed inside the room any longer. He stood the door against the frame trying to reconnect it to where the hinges once hung. When it wouldn't work, he just leaned it up against the frame.

"I'm sure the barn is in a lot better shape than the house. Grampa Walter spent most of his time out there, and it's been sealed up tight," said Stan.

Vic opened the barn door himself by attacking the rusty lock with an old axe leaning against the barn. He shoved the big red door along its tracks, revealing an array of rusted old farm implements. Vic laughed, "This place is some antique dealer's dream."

There was a broken-down red tractor with flat, rotted tires in the center of the barn. It was covered with bits of hay that had sifted down from the loft above. In the far corner of the barn, he noticed the makings of what used to be a copper moonshine still, along with supplies to make the mash and plenty of glass containers for storing the moonshine. He knew instantly why Walter Imel spent most of his time in the barn. It wasn't caring for farm animals, which had been his original thought. The taste of moonshine was why he had taken such good care of this barn. The moonshine business must have been his real lively hood, not farming. Farming a few crops like corn was good for making mash, and probably kept the revenuer from discovering the hidden still. Perhaps this was how his son Stanley, and then grandson Stan, got started in the bar business later in town, making it into a legal business.

Stan saw Vic eyeing the copper still. Laughing he said. "I guess the Imel's had lots of family secrets, didn't they?"

Mad at himself for giving away so many confidential family details, Stan started to kick one of the foundation poles, but stopped in midair, fearing he would bring the barn down on himself and the agent.

He thought about his grandparents, *Grandma May had her business and so did Grampa Walter. They both broke the law in their own way.* One thing he knew for sure was his Grampa never threatened or laid a hand on him. *He taught me a lot about life and how to make a living out here in this barn.* Stan turned, leaving Vic to finish looking around. He had seen enough reminders from the past for today. So many dark rotten memories of this farm seeped into his thoughts. Stan needed to escape the memories haunting him, to breathe the mountain air and let the past disappear from his mind.

Vic made some quick notes on his iPad and took a few photos, just like he had done in the room. There was not much else to see in here. He was ready to see what secrets waited for them out back under the dirt.

He found Stan sitting outside on a turned-down, rusty, five-gallon Valvoline bucket. Stan pulled a cigarette from the pack he had in his jean jacket pocket and was attempting to light it with a trembling hand.

He took a long drag, blew out the white blue smoke, coughed, and took another quick drag, squinting as he did so. Stan welcomed the nicotine filling his lungs. He wanted to feel something else other than his anger for this farm and what ever happened to Eve. Stan forced himself to look at Maybe's little room one more time. Stan thought, *If only I had been there earlier that night. Perhaps, I could have saved Eve, somehow helped her get away from this farm. I was younger than her, but I loved my cousin. Eve was always kind to me.* Stan knew he would have done anything Eve needed to have kept her safe. She was long gone. He was left with the memories. Stan had managed over the years to push these thoughts from his mind. Now, this government agent was forcing him to remember things hidden in the past that just needed to be left alone. Memories like this needed to stay in the past. Stan needed a drink; the smooth burn of whiskey in his throat would hit the spot, but his bar was miles away. With his back against the barn, Stan leaned forward, dropping his forehead into the palm of his hand, as if he were trying to contain his thoughts, not allowing anymore to come to the surface to haunt him. He took another long drag of his cigarette before he flicked its orange embers, watching the dry ash scatter in the dust. The only other time Stan had visited the property since his grandparents' deaths was to bring out his chain saw and cut that willow tree down. Stacking the pieces up in front of the house, he had placed a sign for free firewood. After today, he was thinking of doing the same thing to the house.

Thirty minutes later, the sheriff arrived along with his two deputies whom Stan recognized immediately from visits to his bar, but couldn't make out the other passenger riding in the back seat. Behind the cruiser came a black van with a crew trained in the excavation of human remains.

The sheriff opened the door, and female legs exited the back of the cruiser. Stan watched with interest, trying to recognize the thirty-something female with cinnamon shoulder length hair. It was almost the same shade as Vic's. The way they greeted each other; it was apparent she also worked for the government. From what Stan could see from his perch on the bucket, she looked to be around five-foot-six in her flat black shoes. She wore a knee-length white lab coat over her skirt. He couldn't make out her facial features from where he sat.

"The rest of my team are in the van. What ya got for me this time, Agent Foster?" She was clearly letting him know she wanted their conversation to remain professional by addressing him so formally.

Vic noticed the tension in Doctor Sara Meskins forced smile. He knew better than to offer his hand in greeting. She wouldn't accept it anyway. That tiny gesture would make him look foolish in front of the officers, from whom he needed to command respect today. Vic took a deep breath before he pointed in the direction of May Imel's backroom business.

"Here is what I know so far; this farm was owned by Walter and May Imel from 1910 through October of 1969. They are both deceased, and the farm essentially has fallen into disrepair. No extended family including Stanley Imel, Sr., who is deceased, or Stan, his son, has come forward to claim the property formally. In my opinion, the family that's still living don't want to remember the past, with what really happened here. I suspect Stan sitting over there would rather it crumble to the ground," Vic stated, watching Stan as he suddenly realized he was probably the sole owner of the property since he never mentioned any other siblings.

"Okay, you've piqued my curiosity," said Sara looking into Vic's face. It was hard for her not to recall the last night they had spent together. She knew she had to stay focused, get her information and complete her forensic research. After all, this was the reason she had been called to the investigation.

"The wife, May, was known to have a small room off the house which she referred to as her office." Pointing toward the house as he walked up to the backroom and removing the wooden door, he carefully propped it against the side of the house. "This farm woman performed abortions in here. As far as I am aware, she was not a mid-wife. She had no special training by a physician to perform any medical procedure; which wouldn't have mattered anyway since abortions were against the law when she was doing them. Even medical doctors were arrested and taken to prison for performing abortions. According to her grandson,

Stan, the women who survived went on their way the next day after the procedure; a few women weren't so lucky." He rubbed his chin, feeling a light afternoon stubble beginning. Vic waited for Sara to take in what he had said and gave her a chance to step inside to see the room for herself.

Sara looked back at him to see if he was going to follow her into the dirty, uncomfortable room. When he didn't, she knew he was being respectful to her purpose there. This was her initial walk through of the crime scene, where she would get the overall feel and take note of potential evidence while touching nothing.

Agent Foster stood in the doorway, watching Sara as she moved slowly, taking her time in making mental notes.

She noticed several things that she could gather fingerprints from, along with potential DNA evidence, to determine who had visited the room. As an experienced scientist she could tell from the urine droplets possibly mixed with blood that had spattered against the wallpaper that May Imel wasn't very thorough in cleaning up after the procedure. This lack of cleanliness probably put her evening visitors at risk for internal life-threatening infections, even after they left the farm.

Sara was horrified at the thought of being one of those poor frightened women, just wanting to move on with their lives after they became pregnant through rape, incest, or other means, and coming here to put their lives and their trust in this woman to help them out of their predicament. Sara was disgusted at the thought of the maltreatment women in general received during that time period. But she also knew some women seeking abortions had been blind folded, robbed, or tricked into going places and either raped or killed by the person they thought was going to perform the abortion. At least this woman tried to help, but it was not a good situation all the same. Sara felt her stomach churn. It was all she could do to keep from vomiting on the trash-laden floor. She thought of her own sister, who just three years ago had been pregnant. Within a couple months, she found out she had cancer and needed to have lifesaving chemotherapy. She was glad that abortion was legal and safe in the United States today. Her sister didn't want to do it, but with a five-year-old at home who would be left with no mother, she had the abortion, followed by chemo and radiation, preferring not to have any of the three. Now, she was cancer-free and was trying to get pregnant again. She knew abortion was a hard choice just talking with her sister about her ordeal. She had told her sister she was glad it was legal and available, but didn't wish it on any woman that they would have to make that hard choice in their own life. She was glad her sister was alive and that her nephew still had his mommy.

Sara hoped focusing her thoughts on this room would keep her mind from roving to the handsome agent observing her. Unfortunately, this room just kept forcing her to think of so many things. She knew there had been a spark between them once upon a time. Perhaps there still was. *Vic had so much baggage,* Sara thought. *I'm just not sure if what we had could last. First, there was his drinking, and I could certainly understand why he needed that vice. It had nothing to do with his working for the bureau or his stint in Iraq, and had everything to do with what happened to his mom when he was seven. The nightmares of that experience shattered his young life.* Still Sara adored him and his flashy dress. Vic could be bold and brash, and very romantic in the way he held her, kissed her, and made love to her. It was hard to get this strong, yet vulnerable man standing there in front of her off her mind. It was just as difficult to let him go as it would be to keep him…. Sara scanned the room for more evidence, attempting again to get focused, stay professional, and complete this part of her assignment. She knew both she and Vic needed to move on with their lives, and she wondered if Vic had moved on without her in his life. It was difficult. Life was difficult. This thing, what she was doing here now, in this room, today, was easy, compared to other parts of her life.

"I think I'm done in here for now. What else is there?" She smiled, walking past him as she motioned her team to enter. This team would document the scene by taking photographs, drawing sketches, and identifying any evidence, without touching anything they saw. They would also videotape the entire room. Once that was complete, her team would collect all the potential evidence and tag it, log it, and pack it. Back at the forensic facility, the crime lab would process all the evidence. The table, plus the bed, would be broken down before packing. She was aware there could be hidden fingerprints under the edges of the table that could be missed if they weren't careful. For now, she would let them get busy gathering evidence. She planned to follow up with them later. Sara moved to where Vic stood waiting for her.

"The barn is over here," he said, pointing in its direction. "I can tell you this thing is full of stuff. It will probably take your team a full month to go through if you think that might be necessary. I know Special Agent Finch is expecting his missing women data before the end of the week, so don't get too caught up on the small stuff. The real kicker to this farm is out back, behind the barn. Stan told me he witnessed a hole being dug, which he thinks was for a burial, but I'm not sure of the specifics on that part yet. I have a feeling there are multiple bodies behind the barn. Some of them could be missing women from our list."

"Our focus will be on the room and the dig behind the barn. I don't want to get into the barn, unless a dead body turns up in the loft or under a bale of hay at this point. You're right; this needs to be quick and to the point like a scalpel in surgery. The local sheriff can go through that barn later, as far as I am concerned." Sara heard the motor from a backhoe as it lunged forward with its loader bucket slamming heavy metal teeth against the ground. Its force could demand to see what secrets were hidden below within seconds. She ran around the side of the barn, bumping straight into the Sheriff. He could barely hear her scream directly in his ear, but felt her slam against him.

"Please stop digging at once and get that thing out of here. This is a government investigative crime scene. We have tools, called shovels and trowels that we will use back here to excavate bodies, once we use our special ultraviolet cameras to find specifically where to dig. As of right now, this area is off limits to anyone who is not working for the government and for me," Sara ordered not wanting to offend the sheriff. She just wanted to get this day over with.

"I thought we could soften up the dirt back here for you. I didn't think we would dig that far down. I guess a backhoe might be a little too much."

"Sheriff, if you want to stay involved, I need you and your deputies to block off the crime scene out at the end of the road. I don't want any news reporters stepping foot on this farm while we are here," added Vic.

The sheriff dropped his half-smoked cigarette on the ground, crushing it with the sole of his shoe. He motioned to the driver to turn off the motor. They no longer needed his services to dig up the yard.

Sara stared at him, "Pick that up and take it with you, unless you want forensic to do DNA testing on you too," she demanded.

The sheriff hated being bossed around by government agents, let alone a woman. He picked up the cigarette butt and yelled for his two deputies to follow him. As far as he was concerned, that forensic witch could find her own ride back to wherever she needed to go. Halfway down the drive he flicked that butt out the window into the weeds. This was his county. They wouldn't even have a warrant to be here if he had not driven to Lily's Massage, interrupting the District Attorney's weekly visit. He expected to get credit for something with the reporters interviewing for the ten o'clock news. Smiling in the rearview mirror, he looked back toward the house; hoping reporters were starting to line up at the roads entrance. *I might just call them myself and get them out here for an interview from me first, if they are not here yet,* he thought.

Sara shook her head, "Locals, you meet all kinds on this job. What's that saying about a box of chocolates? You never know what you're going to get, and when you bite into one sometimes the taste is so bitter you just have to throw it in the trash and pick out another one."

Vic just laughed; Sara could hold her ground with anyone she was matched against. He liked that trait in her. He could see why his boss held her in such high esteem.

Seven hours later, Agent Foster watched as Sara's team place six sets of human skeletal remains in black body bags, zipped them up, and placed them on stretchers one at a time. They were loaded into an unmarked, black van. The remains were to be taken back to their special underground lab. That's when they would begin their research into the victims' identities, determine the time of death and the cause by utilizing deoxyribonucleic acid from their hair and bones. They could also establish the female bodies' height and weight. Blood samples from the room were identified by using luminol and ultraviolet light. They were scraped from the walls, floor, and table in the room using a scalpel and placed in sterile containers. Putting all this DNA together would help Sara identify who everyone was so they could notify the victims' families that their loved one had finally been found. Fibers from the corpses' rotted clothing would be matched against any fibers found in the house, proving without a doubt that this is where they had met their death.

Agent Vic Foster fully expected, before they began the dig, that they would find several women's remains beneath the dirt on this abandoned farm, based on his conversation with Stan Imel. What he had not expected, was that the last body, was the body of a male, not a female. His skeleton was not intact like the others, who were placed in the ground with some thought and care. Each woman was wrapped in a blanket, and a small bible placed on top of their remains. This body was not wrapped in anything; this body had been dismembered and randomly tossed into the grave, but not before cigarettes were smoked over the remains, as if in celebration of a task well-done. The filters were flicked in on top, presumably as a last act of power to humiliate and degrade the victim; or a last act of disrespect from the killer, or killers. Vic Foster knew from other cases, when victims were dismembered, there was lots of anger involved. The killer wanted to make certain the victim was completely dead, and was never coming back. The murder's goal, in this case, was to rid the world of this man's existence, putting him out of their sight permanently.

Agent Vic Foster had a hunch about this mutilated body, but had no idea as to his identity. Or he could be completely wrong, and it could be that the revenue man had finally found out about Stanley Imel's still. There were two distinct possibilities. Between his and Sara's investigative work, they would determine which was correct.

Vic left Sara at the van with her team. He needed to find Stan, who just up and walked away hours ago, stunned at all the bodies claimed back from the dirt. Vic figured Stan would have made his way back to the bar by this time. In fact, he could use a drink himself.

\*\*\*

Vic was on his sixth beer when Sara walked into the bar. *Just like always, she knows exactly where to find me,* he thought. He wasn't sure if that made him happy or sad, but he was here and so was she. *Now what,* he wondered. It didn't take long for him to find out. Vic fully expected Sara to put him in his place for leaving her out at the Imel farm. After that, he expected she would nag him about drinking too much beer while they sat there and threw back a couple for old times. Since she rode out with the sheriff, she might have expected Vic to offer her a ride. He probably should have at least taken the time to say he was leaving.

He was ready for her when she arrived at his table. He looked Sara right in the eyes with his blood shot baby blues. *Just give me your best shot,* he thought, half smiling with drunken bravado.

That's when Sara leaned forward and planted her lips firmly on his. Surprised at her action, Vic couldn't think. Sara completely caught him off-guard, leaving him dumbfounded. Sara grabbed his arm, yanking him up from the wooden stool. Vic staggered a few steps before he grasped hold of her shoulder, allowing Sara to lead the way.

*** 

## March 19, 2020

Vic awoke, disoriented to his surroundings, but it didn't take him long to figure out where he was since he was naked and in a bed. He heard water running in the shower and knew he wasn't alone. Vic pulled open the shower door. Stepping into the hot water, he wrapped his arms around Sara's damp form. Her red hair stuck in clumps to her shoulders and he smoothed it with his hands, noting how beautiful she truly was. He could tell by her eyes watching him that she still wanted him in her life, and at that moment Vic knew he would do whatever he had to do to keep her in his life this time.

# Chapter 15

## Lottery, March 19, 2020

At ten a. m., Agent Foster set out to find Stan. He was almost certain Stan Imel would have left the farm and gone straight back to his bar, but when Vic tried to find him there the night before Stan was nowhere to be found. Stan was his only living witness to the crimes on the family farm. Vic *needed* to find him.

Sandy had been working the bar instead. In fact, she was pulling a second shift and fully blamed Vic for having to be there instead of at home keeping an eye on Hayden. "Stan called here earlier. He sounded different than I've ever heard him. I could tell by his voice somethings really eating at him. I would ask you what all this is about but I'm sure you won't tell me. Just promise me you won't mess Stan up. He's a good man. He's done nothing but been good to me, and to this town." Sandy's seething anger kept her from spilling pent-up tears. Instead, she pulled Vic his first of many draught IPA beers and set it down in front of him. She walked to the end of the bar and began wiping it down.

"You should tell him," Agent Foster said after taking a sip.

"Tell him what?" asked Sandy. She moved closer to keep their conversation low, hoping the country music from the jukebox and dancers on the dance floor drowned out their conversation.

"Tell Stan that you're in love with him. If you're waiting for that meth-head son of yours to straighten up before you move on with your life, it might not ever happen. Why waste the years that both of you still have left waiting around when you could be with him right now? Its good advice you should take it," Vic raised his mug in her direction.

"I'm busy here, Agent Foster. If you're staying to drink, maybe you should find a table or go take your own advice about love. You don't know a thing about Stan and me. I sure don't know how much you know about Stan, but I have worked by his side for the past ten years. You spent one day with the man and you think you know him. Well you don't." Her hands shaking, she threw them up into the air as she moved on down the bar to take another order. "Men!" Sandy growled under her breath. That's how Vic had ended up drinking more than he planned; luckily, Sara had come to his rescue the previous night.

***

Back at the bar this morning, Vic wondered if Sandy was still mad at him today, or if he even really cared that much in the scheme of things. Luckily, Sandy wasn't working, or at least he didn't see her anywhere in the bar, so he didn't have to deal with her being irritated with him. Some women held grudges for days on end. He preferred a woman that screamed and yelled, and then made up all in one afternoon. Vic knew he always seemed to get too involved with his cases and some of the characters he came across on the job. It was in his nature to feel sorry for them. If he could, Vic tried to fix them in his limited interactions with them; instead of trying to fix himself, which was usually a mistake he just couldn't seem to help.

Sandy stood in the hall listening, she wanted Agent Foster to see her and know she was still mad. She muttered under her breath, "You just can't leave that poor man, alone, can you?" She thought about throwing the cast iron frying pan she was swinging ever so slightly at him, but she didn't want to get arrested, so she turned back to her prep work in the kitchen. The guys would be coming in soon to play cards, and they would want to order her special fried chicken livers to go with their beer. Agent Foster sat down on a stool at the bar, noticing the photograph of Stan and his Grandma May was gone, creating a dusty blank spot on the wall in its place. Stan was leaning against the other side of the bar from Vic, and there was a half empty bottle of Jack Daniels sitting in front of him. "It's not your fault, Stan, none of it. You were just a kid when all that occurred. You couldn't have stopped your grandma from doing what she did. She probably thought she was doing the right thing to help those women by performing abortions. She wouldn't have done it otherwise, knowing if she was found out she would go to prison for a long time. Years ago, women had few options when it came to abortion. You know it and I know it. Abortion was illegal and a dangerous practice, for both the woman and the person performing it, today it's not. Women have choices and times have changed for the better. If Eve's dad didn't think May could have helped her, Jim wouldn't have taken her there. Your uncle just wanted to give his daughter another chance to live her life. He didn't want her to have that baby around as a daily reminder of the trauma she went through in the woods. Watching that baby grow up with knowing it was a product of rape... Those types of decisions are hard to make my friend. Your grandma just wasn't a trained professional, and one look at that room would tell you it wasn't a very sanitary place. If nothing else came from you taking me out to the farm, you did a good thing yesterday; Eve was identified among the bodies we found buried in the yard. We matched her DNA to one of the bodies. As soon as this investigation is complete, we will release her body and she can be buried in the family plot by her mom. You also helped us identify several other women we were looking for, so I very much appreciate what you did."

As Stan raised his head, a tear slipped down his tanned wrinkled face. Relief appeared in his eyes. "Finally, that's all I've wanted for my cousin for all these years. I'll be able to visit Eve and put lilacs on her grave. She loved those flowers. The whole house used smell like them when they were in bloom." Stan lowered his head as his body trembled with sobs. He hated for anyone to see him like this. Maybe he should have just stayed home. "I guess I don't blame my granny on trying to help, I know as a bartender you hear all kinds of stories, and believe me, I have heard my share. It's the abuse that she put me and Eve through as kids that makes me the angriest with her. I am just so confused about the whole thing. Who was that guy's body out there? I know that me and Eve both were nosey kids. Many times, over the years I have wanted to go back there and see if I could find her body. I can't even begin to tell you how freaked out I would have been if it would have been that guy's body that I would have found instead of Eve's."

Agent Foster reached across the bar, patting Stan on the shoulder as he got up from his seat. Vic was done here. Sometimes nice people got hurt in investigations, when other people did bad things, and today the person left hurting was Stan.

Stan looked up quickly, "Where are you going now? You're not done here in town, are you?

"No, Stan I'm not," Vic said, not wanting to involve Stan any more than he needed to get the confession that was required before he left town.

"You're not going to ask me to go with you?" he questioned. Stan pulled a dry handkerchief from his pocket. Wiping his face, he waited on Agent Foster's reply.

"Not unless you feel up to it. Are you up to it, Stan? Think about this part long and hard before you answer me. Stan, I need to warn you, sometimes this part of the investigation goes badly." Vic waited to see what Stan had to say. He didn't want to pressure him, one way or the other.

"I'm not really up to it," he paused. "But I have to go. It happened, and it is never going to go away. He needs to know it was me that told. I'm not just going to sit here like a lazy coward this time. He needs to see me. Look me in the face and know it was me that told." Stan grabbed his ball cap, covering his messy, thick gray hair. He didn't yell to Sandy this time that he was leaving. He figured she was listening to their conversation since there wasn't any noise coming from his kitchen, and Sandy was always noisy, just like he was; that's why he liked having her around so much.

Driving down Main Street, Vic glanced toward Stan, "So, you know both reasons why I'm going to talk to him?"

"Yes, I figured that out last night. That's why I couldn't bring myself to come back to the bar. That bar holds too many good family memories. I needed to be alone to sort it all out inside my head. Try to make sense of the whole darn thing, which honestly makes no sense to me on so many levels." Stan fidgeted with the sun visor, not wanting it up or down since the sun was in that spot where no matter where you put the visor, it still didn't cover up that nagging bright light. He really wished he could just rip it off the darn hinges and throw it out the window, but it wasn't his car unless you counted that his taxes paid for it.

Agent Foster parked the agency car in the side parking lot marked 'visitor parking only' for Sunny View Nursing Home. Vic followed Stan's lead since he knew exactly where they were going. Passing the nurse's station in the center, Vic noticed there were four halls shooting off in separate directions labeled north, south, east, and west wings. It vaguely reminded him of something from his past.

Stan walked down the hall, marked over head as East Wing, stopping abruptly in front of Room 103. Out of habit Stan knocked on the door frame. The door was already open, as all the doors were throughout the day. Agent Foster noticed a frail, elderly, bald man glance in their direction for a second before focusing back on the television screen. His features were marred with wrinkles and age spots, from years of being out in the sun without sunscreen protection.

"Uncle Jim, it's your nephew Stan. Remember me? It's been a good while since I was last here, I know. Anyway, I brought someone with me today that wants to speak with you," He pointed toward Vic. "This is Agent Vic Foster; he's from the government, and he's here to talk to you about your daughter Eve." Stan could feel his mouth getting drier by the minute.

"Eve's dead," he stated gruffly, in a shallow hoarse voice. Jim Wells appeared perturbed with the interruption. He moved his attention back toward the television set again. A young woman in a blue sweater appeared on the screen as the commercial for a local law firm ended. She was just getting ready to announce tonight's Powerball numbers. Jim sat up as straight as he could, all his attention on the screen and the woman in blue. The cage was spinning, and the first white ball popped out. Jim didn't catch the number, she was too fast with her hands, he had lost his concentration at the last second. *Why do I have to have visitors right this second? Stan didn't even bring me anything sweet. What a waste of my time,* he thought. His ticket lay in front of him on the rolling nightstand. Jim was annoyed now he was going to miss getting the winning numbers firsthand. He would have to rely on the numbers from the nursing station and who really knew if they would be correct. Plus, at his age it was a long walk to the end of the hall. For the past twenty years, Jim had sat in his favorite chair, right here in this same room, waiting for the lottery numbers to pop out of that spinning contraption. Tonight, Jim figured he would either win that lottery money and get out of this hole or sit here in this same stinkin' spot and die.

"We know she's dead, Uncle Jim. The government men found Eve's body buried out behind the barn on grandpa's farm."

"Oh, yeah, well that's where me and your Grandpa Walter put her, alright. I wanted to bury her by her momma. My wife would have wanted it that way if she had been alive at the time, but Walter told me no... He said we'd get in trouble with the law. They'd take us all to jail. I think he was just afraid they would finally find his moonshine still. Your grandpa Walter was a stupid, senile old man, you know that? I never should've ever listened to him, not for even a minute. He deserved to get kicked in the head by that old mule. It hated him, too."

"Uncle Jim, they found someone else buried out there, too. They found a man's body. Do you know anything about that?" Stan held his breath, waiting for the answer that was sure to come. When Jim didn't respond right away, he goaded him. "You might as well say what you know because the government is out there searching right now, and they're gonna find out the answers whether you say or not, using that new DNA technology. I know you have heard about it on that television set of yours's. Uncle Jim, you can't hide what you know anymore, not from the law." Stan didn't know what else to say to get Jim to talk.

Anger and spit spewed from Jim's mouth, running down his wrinkled chin, "You didn't see what I seen, boy, the night I found Eve out on Dickens Run Road. She was a mess; all bloody and crying hysterical, she was so scared. She couldn't even use her hands right to tell me what happened to her out there. But I figured out who that fella was, and I killed him; me and your Grandpa Walter. We did it together. He was still alive while we took that axe to him. When we finished, we gathered up all the pieces and threw them in the hole we made him dig. Walter washed that axe off and stood it up by the barn as a reminder of what we'd done. Justice, that's what was done. It was the right thing to do. That fella got what he deserved, and a little more. He wailed like a baby, beggin' for his life and swearin' he never touched my Eve. But I seen him a watchin' her at the hardware store. I just knew it was him, alright; and he paid for his sins right behind that old barn."

At that point, Agent Foster spoke, "Mr. Wells, I understand your anger and how you must have felt when you saw your daughter after she was attacked. I knew this kid once, who saw his mom raped and murdered. I know the situation's not exactly the same, but the feelings you had at the time, I'm sure they were the same. However, the law's the law. You can't take a life just because you're angry, and you believe it's the right thing to do. You probably wanted to make that person suffer, like you were suffering when you met up with him. Neither could the boy I'm talking about, who was angry and wanted revenge. However, the accused in this country are considered innocent until proven guilty in a court of law. If they are guilty, they will be punished by the court system."

Jim was no longer listening. He didn't care what that government guy was saying to him. He picked up the lottery ticket and read the numbers again Three, twenty-one, nineteen, six, one, five. *Strange I never noticed that before, but the date Eve was raped has been lying right here in front of me on this lottery ticket the whole day.* Jim took that as a bad omen and turned the lottery ticket numbers face down.

Stan walked over, picking up the lottery ticket; he put it in his shirt pocket. "I'll be taking this just in case it is a winner; the winnings can pay for Eve's burial in a real cemetery this time. Disgusted with his uncle for violently killing a man without having proof of guilt and letting the law do their job. Plus, the matter of sending Eve over to Maybe's to get rid of the baby. Stan knew Eve would not have understood what was happening to her. It was more than Stan could bare. Stan turned his back on the old man. He walked out of the room, allowing Agent Foster to finish up the interrogation alone.

Agent Vic Foster towered over Jim Wells, reading him his Miranda rights. He cuffed his scabby, wrinkled wrist to the electric lift bed. Vic usually didn't carry handcuffs since he normally didn't do arrests; however, he made a point to pick up a pair just for this occasion. After everything he had seen the day before at the farm, he himself needed some type of justice.

Agent Vic Foster called the sheriff from his car, notifying him of Jim Wells' murder confession and requested he send a cruiser to come and do the official arrest. "Sheriff, I have a list of all of the identities of the women found on Walter Imel's property, so you can get in touch with their next of kin to have them arrange for their burials. Their names are Eve Wells, Joan Dickens, Elizabeth Markley and Penny Jean Hatley. According to forensics, they all succumbed from complications of the abortions performed on them, presumably at the hands of May Imel. The dismembered male body was also identified as Thomas Bane. Apparently, he worked at the hardware store. Mr. Wells confessed of this man's murder during questioning, stating he along with his father-in-law, Walter, did it together. They tortured the young man before he had been brutally murdered. Mr. Wells said he believed Mr. Bane was responsible for the rape of his daughter Eve Wells. However, that has not been proven to be fact yet. I will have to get back to you if we find any evidence, as far as DNA, that might suggest who that person of interest might be. Also, the murder weapon which was used on Mr. Bane was an axe which is leaning against the Imel barn, according to Mr. Wells. I believe it is the same one I picked up to break the lock on the barn out there yesterday."

The Sheriff couldn't believe his ears. The newspaper and television reporters would be flocking to his jail for statements with questions on all these homicides. He needed to be ready since he was up for reelection in November and couldn't afford any bad press. He glanced at his fresh cup of coffee and the Long John doughnut waiting on top of the white-paper-bag. The white cream icing oozed out the end just the way he liked, so he decided Jim Wells could wait a few extra minutes. "Thank you for the updated information, Agent Foster. I'll be sending a car that way just as soon as I can to pick up the suspect and another car to collect that murder weapon. I can't believe they left it in plain sight to be found. I'll start notifications to the victims' families right away." He picked at the end of the doughnut, saying, "Thomas Bane, now that name sounds somewhat familiar to me. I wonder if that was the same Thomas Bane my grandfather talked about years ago, that disappeared from around here. I guess I'll find out more about him soon enough. You just never know about some people. It's hard to believe all this happened right under their noses without anyone finding out what was really going on out on that farm. Absolutely amazing." He remembered the moonshine still and wondered if his grandfather knew more than he let on, and allowed the Imel's to do what they wanted for a few pints of the good stuff now and then.

The phone rang just as Agent Vic Foster pulled out of the parking lot. It was Sara, but he decided to let it go to voice mail. First, he would drop Stan back off at the bar. He needed a little solitude to clear his mind. He played back the message, "Vic, this is Sara. I did more testing on Eve Wells, and there is something very peculiar that we need to discuss. So, when you get this message, please call me back here at the lab as soon as you can. It's extremely important that we talk. I love you.

# Chapter 16

## Molly Lehman, March 23, 1981

Everyone leaves at some point in life. Molly decided several years ago she was no longer relinquishing that choice up to fate. Kismet had brought her too much heartache. Molly sped down the last stretch of highway. It was nine a. m. and the traffic going the way she was headed was crowded the first hour, but as soon as she managed to get out of town, she punched the gas just Eddie had taught her when she was ten years old. Now she was making good time. Two hours later she pulled into the park, leaving her Dodge Omni in the designated area for campers and hikers by the trail head. She was missing Hendrix already, but this just wasn't the type of hike you take an Airedale on. She couldn't deal with Hendrix, Eddie, and Patrick. That was just too many needy males all in one weekend for her to handle.

Molly laughed, looking over at the Chase and Sanborn coffee can. "Ready to make that last hike up the mountain, Cousin Eddie?" She pulled her camping gear from the trunk, strapped it to her back, and started up the mountain. The weight from the gear felt just right, and as she climbed, she was glad for the intense training she had put herself thorough over the past year in preparation. Eddie was a good teacher. He wanted her to learn everything she could to protect herself, regardless of the situation she found herself in. He taught her kickboxing when she was twelve and she continued to practice this art twice a week. She also lifted weights at the gym three times a week and ran between five and ten miles every day before class. She had her route set up so Hendrix could run with her part of the way. She circled around so he could go home and rest on the back step while she finished up.

Molly attended West Virginia University and was working toward a doctorate in human sexuality. She found it very interesting and used the tools from her degree in investigation for revenue. This weekend she was meeting Patrick, her last subject. After him she would finish her doctorate and finally be done with college. Thanks to her cousin, Eddie, she already knew the field she wanted to go into next. She would follow Eddie's career path, the one he had planned out for her.

*** 

Molly would never forget their last conversation. "First things first," Eddie had told her. "Now make sure you stay on the trail and follow the signs; they will lead you to freedom." That was the very last thing Eddie said before he closed his eyes for the final time. Molly never quite understood what he was saying in that last comment, until today. Perhaps he got just a small glimpse into her future. How could she have been so blind as to have let these two guys overtake her just as she was starting to break camp? She had panicked and not followed proper protocol. This was not the scenario she had practiced with Eddie many times. "Eddie, tell me what to do. Talk to me, Eddie. I need you more than ever before," Molly begged, looking up into the trees at the sun. The ropes around her wrists were tight, burning and cutting into her skin as he yanked on the rope pulling her forward. She almost lost her balance again. Her knees were already raw from stumbling multiple times.

"I thought I told you your boyfriend was dead. He ain't going to help you, so just shut up and keep moving, yah hear, or you ain't going to make it to my cabin. I'll just kill you right here and now." He grabbed her hair and yanked. "You wanna have some fun before you die, now don't you?" He put his sweaty face on her bruised cheek and licked her skin. "Hey, if you're nice to us, maybe we will let you live, well, for a while anyways. Now git moving and shut up, lest you want another little cut from this here knife of mine again." He yanked the rope again and it tore at the skin on her wrist a little more. Molly felt blood trickle down the back of her legs from the knife wounds she had already received from her attackers.

That's when she heard Eddie's voice in her head, *'Stay on the trail and follow the signs; they will lead you to freedom'*. Molly almost smiled. She knew what to do now, no longer did she feel lost; she could feel Eddie all around her. She would be ready for them when they let their guard down, which hopefully would be soon; she knew nightfall was coming fast and she would only have a few painful hours left to live.

# Chapter 17

## Molly Lehman Investigation, March 18, 2020

Driving to Morgantown, West Virginia, Special Agent Riley Harris turned in the drive at Tara Winston's two-story brick colonial. He pulled his brief case from the backseat of the car and went to the door.

"Mrs. Winston?" Agent Harris inquired to the petite older female who answered the door.

"Yeah, that's me and you are?" Observing the sharply dressed man carrying a black leather brief case, Tara thought he looked like an attorney, but he wasn't familiar to her. She waited for him to answer before she committed to unlocking the door to a stranger.

Riley opened his wallet, holding up his identification badge. "Good morning, Mrs. Winston. My name is Special Agent Riley Harris. I was wondering if I might talk to you about Miss Molly Lehman. I understand she was a friend of yours."

Tara looked him up and down before she opened the door. "Most people call me Tara, so you can too. Yes, I knew Molly very well. She used to live next door. Come on into the kitchen table and pull up a chair."

Riley followed her into the kitchen and sat down at the table. He could tell, walking through the house, that Tara was well-organized.

"Can I get you a cup of coffee or a glass of iced tea?"

"Coffee would be nice, if it's not too much trouble."

Tara poured Agent Harris a cup of coffee using her white teacups that she saved for only special occasions. She considered this a special occasion, if someone wanted to talk about Molly. She set a porcelain creamer and container of sweetener between them, along with some chocolate mint cookies she has just purchased yesterday from the local Girl Scout troop.

Agent Harris' smile showed his appreciation of her hospitality.

Tara noticed Riley had nice hazel-green eyes. In fact, they reminded her of Molly's. She thought he looked like he could use a good night's sleep. "Have you got news about Molly? Did they finally find her body after all these years?" Tara took a sip of coffee, waiting to hear what he had to say.

"I'm opening her case again, this time with the government, and I was wondering if you could tell me about her, so I can feel like I know her better than just the basics written in her file. Can you also tell me about the last time you saw her or talked with her before she went missing?"

Tara took a deep breath. "Well, first of all, she was raised by her older cousin, Eddie Lehman."

"Really, what happened to her parents?" Agent Harris had this information, but he wanted to see what other things this woman might add that wasn't gathered when she was questioned by the police.

"I never met them, but I was told her dad was a good-for-nothing drunk. He used to beat Molly's mom up all the time. Folks were always calling the police complaining about all the fighting going on at their house. One night he just pulled out a handgun, shot her in the head, then turned the gun on himself, knowing well that poor little Molly was just down the hall in her bedroom. Can you imagine? When she came out, they were both on the kitchen floor dead. I guess it could have been worse. He could have killed Molly, too."

"Wow, that's horrible. Is that how she ended up with Mr. Lehman?"

"Yes, it is. She was lucky that Eddie was able to take her in and got guardianship of her. He finished raising her right next door here." She pointed out the kitchen window, toward the back fence, but Agent Harris couldn't see a house from where he sat.

"So, her cousin Eddie raised her, but— why him?"

"They were inseparable as kids. Molly told me a story once when she was ten and Eddie was sixteen. She talked him into stealing his parent's car. It was a 1958 blue-and-white Chevrolet Yeoman station wagon. Molly said it was her idea; that Eddie just went along for the ride. Anyway, it took a week for anyone to find them hiding out in the woods living off the land and driving that big station wagon on any backroad Eddie could find with Molly behind the wheel."

"Well, I guess that's one way to learn to drive a car." Riley smiled taking a cookie from the plate.

"Yes, indeed," Tara laughed, raising her eyebrows.

Riley noticed that Tara could be quite animated with her facial expressions, and he enjoyed watching her talk, as he bet most people did.

"It was Eddie who taught her the love of the outdoors. Eddie was her one true north. He kept her on a steady path forward after all she had been through." Tara went into the living room still talking, but Agent Harris couldn't make out what she was saying. When Tara returned, she had several photographs with her. "Here is a picture of her and Eddie taken in 1979. They looked a lot alike. Their dads were brothers; of course, Eddie's dad was a lot older. I think there were a couple stillborn births in between the two brothers. Anyway, he didn't have much in common with his mom and dad. You know the type?"

When Riley didn't answer she continued.

"They were the parents that already had gray hair when their child entered grade school. I'm not exactly sure what Eddie did, but I know he worked for the CIA and traveled quite a bit overseas. That's kind of how we got to know each other, him asking me to keep an eye on Miss Molly for him while he was gone. So, I guess we sort of shared custody of her," Tara smiled a weak smile.

"Yes, I think Miss Lehman was very lucky to have the both of you in her young life." Agent Harris could tell from the way she held the photo of the two and made little moaning sounds as she gazed at Molly's image, that she really cared about the girl.

"So, where is Eddie now? What happened to him, or does he still reside next door?"

"Oh, my goodness, no; he passed away when Molly started graduate school here in town. He had Kaposi sarcoma. Are you familiar with that diagnosis?" She didn't give Agent Riley Harris time to answer but just kept talking. "I think he was one of the first cases that they diagnosed with AIDS here in town, poor guy. He was so handsome and brave. I think Molly got her bravery from him," Tara got a Kleenex to wipe her eyes. Tucking it in her pocket, she went on. "If he hadn't died Molly would probably still be living next door."

"How does Eddie's death, from an AIDS – related illness, relate to what happened with Molly?

"Several things actually. You know, you are the first person that has asked me that question. Remember when I told you they stole that car?

"Yeah, well that started both of their love for hiking in the wilderness. Every year, after she came to stay with Eddie, they went on weekly hiking trips out there in the Monongahela National Forest. It's a huge area; I think it was maybe over 900,000 acres of just forest. No wonder they didn't get found for a week, right? Eddie taught her survival skills, like how to live off the land with just a knife. He also taught her how to protect herself during an attack." Looking down at her hands Tara said, "But I guess that training didn't help her in the end, did it? She should have never gone out there all alone."

"What was she doing out there by herself? Did she tell you where she was going before she left, so someone would know where to look if she went missing?" Agent Harris wanted as much detail as he could get and decided Tara Winston was the perfect person to provide this information.

"I knew part of what she was doing yes. She dropped Hendrix off here for me to watch while she was gone. He was her three-year-old black and brown Airedale. Poor little guy, he waited right there in front of that door on the rug for her month after month. Even when I let him out, Hendrix would try to dig under the back fence, wanting to go home. He was such a sweet little dog. I think he died of a broken heart. He just adored Molly and she adored him, but she said he couldn't go with her that specific time."

"Did she think it was too dangerous to take him?"

"She was going camping on her own; I don't think that was the reason because Hendrix went with her most times. She told me she was going to take Eddie to his final resting place somewhere out there. I think she said she was going to bury his ashes up on Bald Knob Mountain. Does that sound familiar to you?"

"Yes, I have been hiking up that way myself, but I have to admit I have never hiked that far alone. I think it's safer if you take a few friends. You never know what you might run into in the dense forest."

"Well, that's where he told her to put him before he died." She frowned, saying "I wish she had never gone, at least not by herself. Maybe if she had told that new boyfriend of hers, he would have gone on that leg of the trip with her. I watched her pack her hiking gear; the last thing to go in the car was that cream cloth bag containing Eddie's remains in that Chase and Sanborn coffee can. Eddie had loved that brand of coffee, so Molly put him right in the can as a joke between them. He told her to spare no expense on his funeral, but what he meant was don't spend a lot."

"That coffee can idea sounds like something he would have approved of; I hope she told him that before he passed so they both could have enjoyed knowing about it. Now, just to back up a little in your conversation, you briefly mentioned Miss Lehman had a boyfriend and it sounded like she was meeting him somewhere along the way. I believe you said 'that leg of the trip.' Can you tell me more about that? I didn't see anything about a boyfriend in the file when I read through it. That seems like a pretty important piece to leave out."

"Oh, he was new. She had only been seeing him for a couple months." Tara whispered as if someone might hear what she was saying, "Actually, he was one of her professors. She was a bit closed mouth about their relationship. Personally, I think he was married. I know for a fact that he didn't leave any messages on her home phone after she disappeared. Probably afraid the police would pay him a visit at home and the wife would find out. I think the whole thing is a little strange. He must not have cared all that much about her in the long run." Tara's eyes were darting back and forth as she thought about what she had just said.

"Do you by any chance remember her mentioning his name, at all?" Agent Riley Harris asked, feeling he might finally be getting somewhere.

"I don't. But it's probably in her diary, well sort of a diary. She was working on her dissertation for grad school, and it had something to do with her experiences with men, of all things. Human sexuality, I believe was what she studied," Tara's cheeks glowed bright pink. "I hate to say anything bad about Molly, you know, since she's gone, but Molly was pretty much what you would call a free spirit these days. She was looking for adventure, and she was not the type that wanted to settle down. I believe she got her open-minded thinking from her cousin Eddie, and, of course, what happened to her mom. I am sure that played a big factor as well." Tara didn't like talking about Molly's love life to a stranger this way, even if he was working for the government. She had protected Molly when the police questioned her and never mentioned her dissertation notes. She didn't want Molly's name drug through the mud. She felt more comfortable discussing Molly with Agent Harris and was finally ready to let a stranger see who Molly really was underneath.

"Where is this collection of papers she was working on? It's probably not around anymore is it?"

Tara's eyes lit up, "Yes, it's right next door. Nothing in the house has been touched since the day she disappeared. I went over and cleaned out the refrigerator, and that sort of stuff, after the police looked around. I took a letter that Eddie had written to me years ago, giving me permission to be responsible for Molly if anything should happen to him on one of his trips, to their attorney. So, under the circumstances the attorney told me to watch over the house until Molly either came back or her body was found. Would you like to see it?"

Riley smiled, "Absolutely, if it is not a bother."

Tara shook her head, "It's no bother at all. Maybe you can find something over there that would be helpful with her case. I don't know, but you certainly are welcome to look. I can show you her dissertation that she was working on, if you are interested in seeing it too."

Agent Harris and Tara walked next door to the Lehman residence. The living room furniture was covered with white sheets. There were a few cobwebs gathering in the corners of the living room ceiling.

"I used to come over here about once a month and dust the place, but it just got to be too much, so I just covered everything up. I probably haven't been in here for at least six months. Once the money runs out for the upkeep, I'm not sure what the lawyer intends to do at that time. When I asked, he said maybe a museum. I think he was making fun of me. I'm just glad it's not going to be me throwing someone else's memories away. He can handle that when the time comes."

She pulled a sheet off the couch for Agent Harris to sit down. Then she went up to Molly's room and brought down her folders. Agent Harris started reading her entries. Blushing, he looked up at Tara.

"I know; you don't need to tell me what she has written in there. She was young and wild, but she was also a beautiful, strong, and intelligent young woman, and didn't deserve what ever happened to her out in those woods."

Agent Harris noticed an entry scribbled to the side in the margin: *meeting Patrick Sherman in Cass 3/23/1981.*

"Got it!" Agent Harris closed the folder replacing it in the box with the other things Tara brought downstairs. "This is a lead that the police did not have in their report."

"So, you think that might help you?"

"Well yes, if I can find this guy, he might be able to tell us if he did meet up with Molly on whatever the last leg of the trip was, but probably not, so don't get your hopes up too much. Molly has been gone a long time. Who knows if this guy is still alive or if I will be able to find him. Those two men that were charged with her abduction changed their stories so many times. I need to go back and read the transcripts from the hearing again. But I am going to try to track this guy down, too."

\*\*\*

Back at the Colonial Arms Hotel, Agent Harris pulled out his laptop to read the transcript from the hearing on the two men that had been arrested related to Molly's case. The report read that some hikers found an abandoned camp site which appeared to be in shambles, and the camping gear appeared to belong to a female, so they reported their concern to a park ranger. The park ranger called the sheriff's department, believing there had been a possible abduction or at least a missing woman in the woods. There was blood found on the side of the tent, so it was thought she might be injured. The sheriff and the park ranger searched the area; approximately five miles from the camp site, they found Molly's backpack, along with her purse, driver's license, and her keys. They were able to locate her abandoned red Dodge Omni parked in the lot by the opening of the trailhead. Nothing was found in Miss Lehman's car to lead the sheriff to believe she had been back to the car since the day she parked it. The two men in question finally admitted they had surprised her at the camp and planned to have some fun with her at a cabin about twenty miles from Deer Creek. It was there that she pulled a knife from her pocket and cut one of the men's arms. She jumped in the river and started to swim. They said that was the last they saw of her since neither of the men could swim, but it just didn't add up to Riley. Both men failed their lie detector tests, though the test weren't allowed in court.

"So," Agent Harris said to himself out loud, "What happened to you out there, Molly Lehman? Where did you really go?" Agent Harris' phone rang, Tara Winston's number popped up on the display screen. "Hello, Mrs. Winston. Did you remember something else?"

"No, but are you planning on going out there to the forest where Molly was taken, as part of your investigation?"

"Why are you asking?"

"Because I need to go and can't get there by myself. I didn't tell you when you were here that when they found Molly's stuff out there, that Chase and Sanborn coffee can was still full of Eddie. I need to try to at least take him to the area where Eddie wanted to spend eternity since Molly couldn't fulfill her promise. I also have a small box full of Hendrix. I think they should be buried together, don't you? Will you help me to do this for them?" Tara begged.

Agent Harris took a deep breath. How could he say no to such a request? "I'll pick you up in the morning. Dress warm and wear hiking boots. I don't want to have to carry you any of the way is that clear?"

"Clear as a bell, thank you, Agent Harris. I'll see you in the morning with hot coffee and a packed lunch."

# Chapter 18

## Eddie's First Burial of the Week, March 19, 2020

Instead of parking at the trail head, where Molly's car was found, Agent Harris went off road in a camouflage-painted Outfitter 4x4 UTV he had borrowed from the ranger station. As they entered the forest, Tara saw red spruce, hemlock, and yellow birch trees. Agent Harris was an experienced driver, which Tara soon found out as they sped under canopies of pines, white oaks, birch, and mountain ash. *At this speed, I might be home for lunch*, she thought

Tara was grateful for her seat belt and the metal grab bar beside her that she could hold onto when he drove up and down the hills. She found herself yelling so Agent Harris could hear her above the roar of the powerful vehicle. "I can't imagine hiking up and down these hills. You know, Molly trained with weights for a year, so she could handle the extra weight on her back in order to manage carrying all that camping gear. Most women would probably cower at the idea of hiking alone, but this is how Molly preferred living her life — alone and out on the edge. She said it gave her more time to think and to write."

"Oh, yeah, well I would think most women might be scared off by the thought of coming across black bears, coyotes, or foxes, not to mention those eastern screech owls at night up in the trees."

Tara laughed, nodding her head in agreement. "You wouldn't catch me out here after dark." Her voice vibrated as the vehicle hit several bumps in a row.

Reaching the top of Bald Knob Mountain, Tara found the perfect spot to bury both Eddie and Hendrix's ashes. He would be able to watch the sun come up every morning. Tara believed Molly would have approved. The pine trees and plants this high up were typical of the Canadian wilderness making the whole area beautiful and interesting. She understood why Molly and Eddie loved coming up here.

"Even the rabbits look different, up this high in the mountains," noted Agent Harris. He pointed one out to Tara saying, "The mountain cottontails have short, rounded, black-tipped ears, unlike the eastern rabbits seen below which have the tall, slender-pointed ears that we are used to seeing."

"How do you know so much about the wildlife up here, Agent Harris?"

Agent Riley Harris laughed, pointing to the park brochure he had picked up detailing the specific wildlife which could be found in the area. He pulled out the map with the forest trails marked along with his compass, to get his bearings before they started out again. He drove onward toward the river, taking extra time to go through the mountain gap. Agent Harris looked at the map several times so he could figure out the best way to get down several steep grades they came across without rolling over.

At last, they made it to their next destination. The Greenbrier River lay just in front of them. "This was where the two men reported they parted ways with Molly when she jumped into the water. Look how strong the current is and that white water just ahead. I bet anything that goes into that area is sucked directly to the bottom; so that water would have pulled her under. I just don't think she would have risked going in that direction, not with the training she had from her cousin Eddie." *What if they were lying about what happened here? Where would she have gone when she got to this area?* Agent Harris wondered. He pulled the map of the area out again, to take a closer look, that's when he saw the answer right in front of him.

In the meantime, Tara got out of the vehicle. She had held her breath and white knuckled her door handle until they safely reached the bottom of the mountain and arrived at the riverbank. She was relieved for her feet to be on solid ground for a few minutes. She needed to stretch a bit and take a look at the river. Thinking that this was probably the last thing Molly had seen; she wondered if those two men lied about her getting away, and thought it more likely they probably drowned her close to where she was standing along the river.

Riley motioned for Tara to get back in the vehicle. He was ready to go, now that he knew their next stop.

"Agent Harris, are you going to try to drive back up the side of that mountain? It was exhilarating, I have to admit, but I sure hope you have found us a different route to take on the way back."

"We aren't going back, not just yet anyway. I get the feeling Molly didn't stop here for good. I think she made it a little farther than was reported. If she did, that means those two suspects accused of killing her lied in court. If they lied, what were they really hiding?"

"Well, don't most criminals lie on the witness stand? I would suspect that none of them want to be found guilty, especially for something like that since they know they will be going to prison for a very long time."

"Mrs. Winston, I think you are probably right."

Agent Harris gunned the motor, turning east as fast as they could safely travel. When the vehicle turned a bend in the road, he saw the sign, *Welcome to Cass*. Agent Harris stopped abruptly, getting out of the UTV. "Just wait here. I need to make a call; I'll be right back." He walked several feet away to create distance between himself and Mrs. Winston. Riley pressed speed dial on his cell phone. "Jesse, it's me, Riley. I don't think Molly Lehman drowned in the Greenbrier River. I can see how it forks off, right here where we are parked, and turns into Deer Creek. Deer Creek runs right alongside the town of Cass according to this map. If you ask me, I think Molly Lehman made it to Cass, looking for help."

"It sounds like you don't believe she was drowned in the river."

"No, I don't. Will you do me a favor? I don't have access to my laptop, to check any records. Take a look in the computer files there for Cass, West Virginia and tell me if anything happened, out of the ordinary, the day Molly went missing, and if so, where and what was reported to the sheriff's office in Pocahontas County?" Riley paced back and forth, waiting on Jesse to come back to the phone. He could see Tara watching him in his peripheral vision, so he waved at her to let her know she need not be concerned over his call.

Jesse pulled up the information from the sheriff's office in Pocahontas on the computer. After quickly scanning the sheriff logs, reports, and arrest sheets for March 23, 1981, Jesse picked up the phone and stated, "Riley, it looks like there was a murder reported to the sheriff's office. It was at a house on Main Street in the town of Cass."

Riley grinned. He wanted to do a high five but none of the other guys were around, "Great! What was the house number?"

"It was at 113 Main Street."

"Who was killed, a male or a female, and were they identified by any chance?"

"No, they were not identified, the victim was male. The guy is still listed as a John Doe." Jesse was intrigued. *How did a male victim listed as John Doe being murdered in Cass have anything to do with the Molly Lehman's case?* he wondered. *And who was Riley with?* He didn't have time to ask due to Riley interrupting his thoughts.

"Okay, now do me another favor and run a check on a missing, Patrick Sherman, possibly from somewhere across the border in Virginia. Cross-check the two; see if we can find a match between a missing Virginia adult male, around that time period, and the John Doe in Cass." Riley crossed his fingers as he waited on Jesse to get back on the line.

"It looks like it's a match. His wife reported him missing from Elkton, to the sheriff's office in Rockingham County, Virginia. So, your John Doe, or rather Patrick Sherman, was an English professor at James Madison University. Does that help with the case I assigned you to work on? You're not straying off the beaten path, are you? Who are you with, by the way?" Jesse was fully aware that sometimes he had to pull Riley back to the task. Riley was used to doing things his own way out in Arizona. "Don't forget, I need your report on Molly Lehman, not on some English professor."

"Yes!" Riley raised his fist in the air, pleased with matching the John Doe, and only partially listening to his boss on the other end of the phone. "Don't worry Jesse. I'm staying on task. I promise it all relates. You will see when you get my report. I am going to take Mrs. Winston home. She wanted to ride out here with me today, so she could keep a promise Molly Lehman made to her cousin Eddie. By the way, he was one of us; I will tell you about him later. I'm going to visit a couple convicts in the state prison, who lied in court. Call you tomorrow." He didn't wait for Jesse to ask him anymore questions. He could see Mrs. Winston was getting restless, and he was on tenterhooks waiting to hear the convict's story.

# Chapter 19

## West Virginia State Prison
## Interview, March 20, 2020

Agent Riley Harris' car entered the prison gates after stopping to show his identification. He was routed to the superintendent's office by a security guard. Agent Riley Harris explained he was following up on another case and needed to question a convict who was there for the kidnapping and murder of Molly Lehman. The superintendent was happy to assist Agent Harris in setting up a room for his interrogation.

"I'm afraid Convict 48452, Daniel Monroe is not available to interview today, but you are still welcome to interview Convict 48451, Dexter Roberts, and we can arrange for Monroe to be here a different day if you don't get the information you're looking for today and need to come back another time."

"I'm on a tight schedule, so I'll just meet with Roberts today. If I don't get the information, I need from him, I'll call ahead next time to make sure the other convict is available before I drive all the way here."

Agent Harris was shown down the corridor into a small interview room to wait while the cell block was notified to bring up the prisoner he requested. The interview room consisted of a heavy steel table and two metal chairs. The table was anchored to the concrete floor with bolts to prevent prisoners from using it as a weapon. Riley began by setting up his tape player while he waited. Fifteen minutes later, two guards accompanied the prisoner to the interview room, cuffing him to the chair before they left him alone with Agent Harris.

Convict 48451 sat across from Riley in cuffs and leg irons. He was dressed in a dingy, crumpled, orange jumpsuit and black vinyl shower slippers. He was unkempt with greasy, black, curly hair hanging just below his ears. Agent Harris noticed when the convict entered the room, he had a spider web tattoo on his elbow, and he knew the meaning behind that one, was prison bars.

Dexter Roberts had no idea why he was in this room, but the man across from him looked important so he thought he must be a new attorney. He sat there with his head down waiting to be addressed.

"My name is Agent Riley Harris. I'm here from the government."

Dexter slumped down in his chair further. He was disappointed, having hoped to get a new attorney since he felt the attorney he had was not doing him any favors in working on getting him out of prison.

"I'm here today to talk to you about the young woman you were charged with abducting in the woods, Miss Molly Lehman. Do you remember her?"

"I didn't kill her if that's what you're askin'," the inmate snidely remarked.

"Yeah, I understand that's what you said in court. I know this will be a surprise for you to hear, but I think I might believe you. I just have one question to ask you about that day. Did you kill Molly Lehman's boyfriend, Patrick Sherman, first? Then what happened? You just accidently ran into Mr. Sherman's girlfriend, Molly, in the woods that very same afternoon? Is that how it all went down?" Agent Harris sat quietly, staring at the prisoner, waiting on his response.

Dexter smiled, thinking if he gave this agent the information he asked for, maybe he could get his current sentence lessened; and he wanted out. "That's more than one question, but I guess they are related in a way. It wasn't me. Well, it was, but it wasn't. It was the guy that was with me. We were casing cabins in Cass, looking for things we could hock to make a few bucks to buy some coke. That's when we saw this guy you mentioned. He was gettin' things out of his car. You know unpackin' stuff for the weekend, I guess. Anyways, he leaves the front door open as he goes in, which is kinda stupid if you ask me. So, we follow him inside."

"So, once you are inside the house, what happened next?"

"Dan, the guy with me, tries to take this dude's money, but instead of givin' over his wallet, he decides to put up a fight. Which was totally stupid trying to fight two guys, am I right?" When Riley didn't answer he continued his story. "Well, the next thing I see is Dan sticking him like a pig with a switchblade. The guy falls to the floor, and Dan just rolls him over and takes his wallet away from him. He pulls that dudes head way back and slits his throat," the inmate closed his eyes tight, shaking his head to try make the thought of the blood spurting from the guy's neck go away. His breathing became rapid, "Listen, all I done was follow Dan Monroe into that house. My intention was to steal enough stuff to buy a little coke, not to kill anyone. I mean it. I didn't do nothin' to that dude; never even laid one hand on him during the whole incident." He pushed his hair away from his eyes, giving Riley a pleading look to believe his story.

Agent Riley Harris showed no emotion, "So, what happened to Molly Lehman? Did she make it to the house when she got away from the two of you?" He had no pity for the convict. This guy got himself into the mess he was in by the decisions he chose to make.

"We surprised that girl at her campsite. She put up a good fight, but in the end, we got control of her. After we tied her hands, we figured she wasn't getting' away. I don't know where Dan thought he was going to take her. He was enjoying himself tormenting her, that's for sure. He had tied a rope to her, after he tied her wrists together, and was pulling her along. She tried to make it hard on him by grabbing the rope and yanking him backward. He hit her a couple times, with his fists in that pretty little face of hers. After that she knew he meant business and she started to get more scared, I think she did anyway. Then, she started talkin' to Eddie, whoever that was. She was begging him to help her, to tell her what to do. Dan got mean with her and told her he was gonna kill her right there if she didn't shut up, so she obeyed, and she never mentioned that Eddie guy again.

"When we stopped to rest, he pulled out that dude's wallet to count the money he stole, and low and behold, there was a picture of her right in that wallet. It was nice and sexy, too. Dan couldn't believe it, and of course he had to stick it in her bruised, bloody face and brag about what he had already done to her boyfriend. Since he knew that guy was dead, he decided his cabin would be a good place to take her for whatever he had planned." He took a deep breath. "Anyway, there was no controllin' her after that. Somehow, she got out of that rope around her wrists, kicked Dan straight under the chin, knockin' him up in the air. When he hit the ground, he was out cold. She grabbed me by the hair and yanked me forward. I lost my balance and she slammed my whole face right straight into the bark of a big tree and broke my nose. She had a good runnin' start by the time I got Dan on his feet, and she was in real good shape, which we hadn't realized until she showed us just what she could do. We tried our best, but we just couldn't catch her. Dan kept yelling at me, as if I could run any faster without breakin' my neck, sayin', 'We gotta catch her cause if we don't, she'll tell the Sheriff what we did, and we will both go to prison.' He stopped for a moment to reflect on what he had just said. "Well, he was half right. Here I am, sittin' here talkin' to you."

Agent Harris asked, "So, what happened to Miss Lehman after that?"

"You wouldn't believe me if I told you," he said rubbing his forehead; the stress of recalling that day was giving him a headache. His fingers trembled.

"Try me; I have a pretty open mind. Tell the truth so you can finally get it off your chest. Otherwise, you know it will eat at you once you go back to your cell. I won't be here later. This is your final chance to make things right." Agent Harris waited on the inmate's response.

He sat quiet for several minutes. "Okay, here goes. You can either believe it or not, but what I am sayin' is finally the truth. It was startin' to get dark when we made it back into Cass. I'm sure she could still see her boyfriend's light silver Camaro parked in front of the cabin. I saw her as she turned into the drive. She had picked up steam and ran full force into that house. I figured we would catch her in there with that dead body. If we did, I knew for sure Dan was gonna go crazy on her. I was purdy mad myself about the gashes she gave me to the head, not to mention my broke nose. I have to admit I was ready to slap her around a little, too." He suddenly became quiet, thinking he didn't want to get himself into more trouble.

Agent Riley Harris just listened while the recorder tape went around and around, gathering this new evidence. Both convicts would be going back to court for a new trial on the murder of the college professor.

"I wasn't sure if I wanted to be part of anything else Dan had planned in his crazy head, and I was tryin' to figure out a different scenario of what would happen once I got in the house with the girl. All at once, I heard this weird sound outside somewhere, like it was all around us or maybe overhead. I can't even explain it very good."

Agent Harris sat up straighter in his chair. This was the part he had waited patiently to hear. Finally, he would get the answer of what really happened to Molly Lehman. He could finish his report and move on to the next assignment.

Dexter thought for a few seconds before he responded, squinting his eyes, "Maybe like a tape recorder or a VCR movie on rewind, a high-pitched horn sound could also be a possibility. It's all I know to describe the noise. Anyways, this bright blue beam of light shot down from the sky along with little bits of sticky stuff like spider webs which stuck all over my clothes. Hearin' all that weird noise first, and then that intense flash of light which blinded me for a few seconds, was just long enough to make me trip over a big tree root in the yard. I fell hard to the ground, knocking with wind clean outa me. I scraped up both of my hands in that stupid gravel and slammed my chin into the dirt, which knocked out two of my bottom teeth." He looked at his palms remembering how the bits of stone had stuck in the dried blood and he had to pick each piece out. He pulled his lower lip down to show his missing teeth to the agent.

"You still haven't answered my question. What happened to Miss Lehman? Why are you stalling? Just tell me what I want to know so I can leave, and you can go on back to your cell," Riley's voice was rough, demanding the final answer.

The convict became angry at Agent Harris' *I couldn't care less what happened to you, you brought it all on yourself attitude.* He thought he was giving agent Harris plenty, and a little empathy back would have been nice. In fact, most prisoners would have just sat there with their mouths shut and stared at the wall until they were led back to their cell.

Agent Riley Harris glared at him impatiently while tapping his fingers on the table.

"Okay, when we went in the house, that girl was nowhere to be found. I'm tellin' you, she just wasn't there. We got a flashlight out of that dead guy's car and searched around the house outside. We found nothin'. She wasn't out there either. I don't know where she went. We just didn't want her telling the police what we did. I wanted to get outa there, but Dan said he was stayin for a while. He seemed to think she would be back and was just outside somewhere in the woods hiding." He sat silently, waiting for a response from the agent sitting calmly across the table. When none came, the convict became frustrated, tired, and wanted to go lie on his bed in his cell. He said emphatically, "I guess I only have one question for you, Agent Harris, and I promise you it will be only one. Afterwards, you can call the guards and send me back to my cell. "Do you believe in aliens? The reason I'm askin' you that one question is because after that night out there, I sure think I do."

Agent Harris never responded to the convict's question. He gathered the tape recorder and left the room. Outside in the car, he ran the tape back, deleted the last part of the conversation, put the tape in a manila envelope, and dropped it off at the guard station for the warden on his way out of the prison.

# Chapter 20

## Lehman Family Secret's, March 20, 2020

Agent Riley Harris went back to the Lehman house to get more answers. This time, he waited until Tara Winston left. He didn't want her to know he was snooping around.

Tara had kept things tidy over the years, but under all these sheets Riley really couldn't see anything and wasn't sure what to look for. Still he knew there had to be a reason the attorney was keeping this house from the market and not letting it deteriorate either, and that comment about turning it into a museum just didn't make sense to him at all. He decided to remove the sheets off each piece of furniture one room at a time and then replace them, after he got a good look at everything. That way Mrs. Winston wouldn't be the wiser. With her not there, he also wouldn't be distracted from his mission.

Riley remembered Tara told him Eddie Lehman was in the CIA, but he had searched for Eddie's records in their database and he never found a spook with that name. Eddie was either lying to her about what he really did for a living, or he was deep under cover, even more so than Riley and Jesse's investigative team.

Riley started to bypass the kitchen, with it's a poppy red appliances and black and white waxed tile floor. He couldn't imagine finding anything in this room, except for maybe some very expired canned food. However, when he opened the cabinets, everything was neat, clean and in its place. No expired canned food or spices of any kind were on the kitchen shelves, only the bare minimum of dishes needed to make it look like a kitchen. Perhaps the attorney was preparing it for that museum look after all, but for what reason?

Riley quickly moved on to the living room, uncovering a burnt orange velveteen sofa with matching swivel chairs. A large macramé tan owl stood guard on the wall behind the sofa. Riley could feel the solid plastic black eyes following him around the room. He opened a long cabinet revealing a mahogany stereo console, Gloria Gaynor's *I Will Survive* was the last album left on the turntable. On the other side of the living room, Riley uncovered a 1930s Victorian flame mahogany writing library table. Two stylish brass double-frames held photographs of an older couple in one set and in the other framed set the photographs appeared to be of the same couple, however, they were much younger, possibly in their early thirties. Riley wondered if these were photographs of Eddie's parents. Perhaps at one time this house belonged to them, since it appeared from the outside to have been built in the early 1920s. Riley pulled the chain on the overhead amber swag lamp to get a closer look, realizing there was no electricity on in the house. He wondered if Mrs. Winston had the lights set on a timer, and decided that going through the desk was probably a waste of time. He quickly moved on to Eddie Lehman's bedroom, wanting to finish before afternoon shadows overtook, what he believed, would be one of the most important rooms in the house.

Eddie's room was elaborately decorated in foil wallpaper of solid red with gold braided diamond shapes. The room was finished off with 1970s dark brown walnut bedroom furniture. Riley grunted in frustration at all the drawers he would need to rummage through; his only hope was perhaps either Tara or Molly had seen fit to empty out most of Eddie's belongings after he had died.

Unfortunately, he realized very quickly opening the first drawer that was not the case. Riley mumbled, "What's with these women?" Bored after the fifth drawer, Riley eyed a bookshelf in the corner and sauntered over to see what might be stacked on there. He pulled out a photo album, sat down on the bed and began looking at the photos and news clippings. It appeared this was an album featuring Eddie's family. "No wonder Eddie's parents were older when they married and had him," Riley said as he turned page after page. "His dad was a physicist. He apparently worked on the Manhattan project during the war. Humph, very impressive indeed."

Riley found news clippings of Eddie's mother. She was a war reporter and photographer for *Life* magazine during the same time period. Riley wondered if that was when the couple had first met. Perhaps she had interviewed her future husband for a news article. Well, no wonder, they were older parents as Mrs. Winston had put it. They had awesome lives to live before they were ready to settle down and start a family.

Next, Riley looked inside the closet. Since all of Eddie's things were still there, he had a hard time moving around and finally started pulling things out, placing them on the bed. Once the closet was empty, he looked for places there might be a secret compartment by patting and pounding on the floor and the inner walls. A leather belt was lying on the floor, so he picked it up, hanging it on the forked silver door hook. The pressure from his hand on the hook caused it to tilt downward, and a large panel in the back of the closet slid open. Riley laughed out loud in relief. "Alright, now let's see what we have here," he said as he rubbed his hands together.

Hanging on the inner wall were multiple handguns. In pull-out drawers, Riley found passports with different male names, and by the ink stamps inside, Riley could tell Eddie had been overseas and in lots of dangerous places. Another drawer contained different hair pieces, mustaches, and beards in various shades of black, brown and blonde. Another drawer held several pairs of non-prescription glasses and sunglasses.

The last things Riley found were Eddie's jock strap medals. They were called that because medals presented to a CIA officer were almost always awarded to the recipient secretly, due to the classification level of the operation he had performed. The officer couldn't ever display them, or even acknowledge he had received a medal publicly. But here they were, and Riley was proud to have found them. He put all the medals back in the drawer, except one. It was the Distinguished Intelligence

Cross; Eddie had been given that one by the Central Intelligence Agency for his extraordinary heroism. This medal Riley put in his own pocket. He decided he was taking it to Eddie. That medal shouldn't be locked away in a closet; it needed to be buried with the brave man who had earned the privilege of receiving it.

Riley's last place to search in the house was Molly's room. The attorney who was caring for this house received money from somewhere, and Riley wasn't satisfied yet with his search. Perhaps Eddie saved a lot of money, or was left money by his extraordinary parents, but Riley felt like something was still missing; and he was determined to find it. He wanted all the facts when he presented his case to Jesse. He could still hear his boss specifically telling the team before they left to leave no stone unturned.

Riley opened Molly's bedroom door, and there, gawking back at him from the opposite bright pink wall, hung two posters. One was a poster of KISS advertising their 1979 hit, and the other was an oversized poster of a young Robert Redford wearing several red lipstick kisses on his face, seemingly from Miss Molly Lehman.

"Well, Molly Lehman, this is a surprise. So, you liked KISS and Robert Redford. What else will your room tell me about who you really were?"

Riley noticed Molly's papers, the ones Mrs. Winston had brought down for him to read. Tara had left them on Molly's bed. Riley now passed those by; he felt he had read enough of her dissertation on sexuality. He noticed a photo of Molly and a dog stuck in the mirror on her dresser; Riley thought that must have been the infamous Hendrix, Tara had spoken of. He looked through her cream-colored dresser drawers and came up with nothing that announced her being any different than any other young woman who came of age in the 1970s.

Riley noticed a trunk at the bottom of her bed. It was a Lane cedar chest to be specific. He remembered most girls during that time called them Hope chests. Riley opened it to see what Molly had in hers, and she surprised him once more. Her chest was not filled with linens, china, doilies, or other household items, which he fully expected. He wouldn't have even been surprised if she had simply filled it with forty-five albums, single playing records. But that was not what Miss Lehman had hidden away for anyone coming in her room to visit and not see. She must have had over thirty paperback romance novels neatly wrapped in thin tan paper for protection, but from what he didn't know. He noticed they were all written by the same author, Miranda Hawkins, so she must have been a big fan of her work.

Riley noticed that none of these books appeared to have been read. Usually paperback covers were scraped up, worn, and dog-eared from being read and shared with friends, but not these paperbacks. No, they were just stored neatly in this trunk. Riley thought that seemed very strange for a teenager, until he pulled a sheet of paper from one of the books almost tearing it in half. Reading it, he realized it was a check stub from a royalty check made out to Molly Lehman with her pen name Miranda Hawkins, and the cash amount was quite staggering, to say the least.

Now it all made sense. The attorney involved with the house wasn't Eddie's as Tara had suggested. Molly's attorney was using her royalty checks to care for the house until, as Tara said, either they find Molly's body, or she comes home. Riley had all the answers he needed from the Lehman house for his report. He put everything back and left the house before Mrs. Tara Winston returned home.

# Chapter 21

## Blue Powder on Bald Knob Mountain

Agent Riley Harris parked his black M5 series BMW at the park ranger's station. He was glad he had called ahead, catching the ranger before he went off duty, so the key to the camo-painted Outfitter 4x4 utility vehicle he had borrowed the day before would be waiting for him under the seat. Riley just needed to remember to drop the key in the office door mail slot when he was finished using it for the day.

He sat in the open vehicle, staring at Eddie Lehman's silver Distinguished Intelligence Cross medal, turning it over in his hand. He knew there was no one in Eddie's life, such as a significant other, that would have appreciated or even understood the sacrifice this agent went through to be recognized by the agency in this manner. The right and only thing to do was to bury it with Eddie. No one else would ever need to know that Riley took the medal and what he was about to do with it.

Riley started up the engine with a turn of the key. Pressing his foot hard on the gas, he sped out of the parking lot and down the access road, leaving a trail of gravel and dirt behind him. It was the middle of the week; he noticed there was barely any traffic on the park roads which to him probably meant there wouldn't be very many campers or hikers in the woods today. After all, it was still late March, and, in the mountains, it could get quite chilly, especially at night. Riley was glad he had remembered to grab his jacket and leather gloves from his trunk when the morning wind blew against his face. Riley just wanted to get this done as quickly as he could, since it really wasn't job related, and Jesse had stressed that they were on a tight schedule. If Jesse knew, Riley would probably get in trouble for going off task yet again, but he believed what he was doing was worth getting in trouble for. He felt guilty about taking time to do this one small thing, but was sure if he did not take the time today, he was fully aware he could at any moment receive new orders and be on a plane to any state or country in a matter of hours. Things changed quickly in the espionage business. He went wherever he was ordered and did whatever he was ordered to do. If he hurried maybe he could be back in his hotel by midday and finish the last part of his report on Molly.

Riley noticed it had rained during the night causing the ground to soften on the trails and adding another element of treachery to the already dangerous trip, so he had to slow his speed down to twenty five miles per hour in some spots to keep from tipping the utility vehicle over.

Finally, Riley came to the bottom of Bald Knob Mountain, looking up at it he knew with the steep inclines there was no way this thing would safely take him where he needed to go. Riley parked the utility vehicle in a safe open area where he would be sure to find it on his way back down and proceeded to hike the last two miles of the rocky terrain.

About halfway up the mountain side, a red-tailed hawk with its fifty-six-inch wingspan was soaring directly at him. If he didn't dive out of its way, they were on a direct collision path. Unfortunately, that took Riley over the edge, where he found himself rolling sideways downhill, approximately a hundred yards, before he managed to grab hold of a small tree trunk and stop his rapid descent into the rocky ravine. In the process, he realized he lost his gun. When he reached the top again, there in front of him stood the hawk, still ripping at the brown and black timber rattlesnake that Riley had not realized he was sharing the trail with. At first, he wondered why a rattler would be out this early in spring. Then remembered reading that as season temperatures increase earlier due to global warming, snakes are one species that will be seen earlier in the season, and further north from the equator. He really had not thought much about it when he read the article online, but now looking at this dead rattler, he decided he was not much of a fan of snakes unless they were behind glass at a zoo. Adding southern copperheads and coral snakes to the already poisonous snakes in the Midwest would keep many hikers off the trails, including him.

Riley marked the trail with some rocks so that when he came back, he could look for his gun. Hopefully, it wouldn't be too far down the hill and the hawk would be gone.

Finally reaching the top of Bald Knob Mountain, Riley located the spot where Eddie Lehman was laid to rest. He dug up the ground with a trowel, opened the coffee can, and placed the medal on top before he buried Eddie for the second time in a week.

As Riley started hiking back down the mountain, he saw something of interest, just for a second, that piqued his curiosity, making him turn in a different direction instead of where he needed to go to find the utility vehicle. Riley quietly slipped down through the trees in the direction he and Tara had gone the day before.

Once he reached the bottom, he quickly sprinted across the open field and slipped into the white pines. From his vantage point, he watched as four dwarf sized forms descended from the saucer on a platform lift. Once they reached the ground, the lift retracted rapidly back up into the saucer. Riley was keenly aware of the unnatural stillness of the forest, even he was trying to hold his breath, not sure of the beings' acute ability to hear or detect his presence. It was especially difficult trying not to breathe after covering so much ground so quickly.

This distinct type of spacecraft, he noted, was silver which had brought his attention to it up on the mountain. Now that he was so close, he could see it was dome-shaped with perplexing hieroglyphics inscribed into the metal. Some shapes he was familiar with, but unsure of their specific meaning when it came to this craft. The three windows that he could see from where he was crouched were small and oval. If he could climb up into one of the trees, perhaps he could peer inside the spaceship, but he didn't think if he tried to do that now he would be able to stay hidden for very long. Riley watched quietly as the bald humanoids gathered samples from the sphagnum bogs growing in the area, which knew were quite similar to the bogs normally found in arctic tundra. *Could these aliens be assessing the changes in climate change on Earth on this mission?* Riley wondered. Becoming more curious in attempting to figure out what they were doing with the samples they were collecting, he miss-stepped, causing a fallen, dried branch to snap directly under his feet and bringing all of those overly large, black, shiny, slanted alien eyes right in his direction. That's when he heard their clicking chatter and knew he was in deep trouble.

Riley turned, running as fast as his legs would go. Simultaneously, he noticed a blue chalky substance floating in the air around him. He remembered something similar from his past, when he'd run in a ten-kilometer color run in Columbus, Ohio ten years prior with an old college friend. There was blue chalk and other colors floating in the air around him that day too, whatever made him think of that he had no inkling. *With so many memories stored in the human brain, at least it was a pleasant one that chose to emerge,* he thought.

Agent Harris soon realized he was no longer running through the forest attempting to get away. His legs continued moving, but when he glanced down, his feet were not touching the ground. Instead, Riley was floating inside the spaceship. There was an echo booming in his ears, causing him to feel disoriented. It was difficult to comprehend what was happening. He could hear voices around him; at least he thought they were speaking. Whatever the language was, he did know that no one of human origin, or otherwise, was speaking by moving their mouth.

Riley's body moved in slow motion as he continued to observe the aliens meander around the saucer's cabin doing their work, unconcerned, as if he didn't exist. They no longer cared now that they had captured him, and he was inside their vessel. He was no longer a threat to them since he was under their complete control. As far as they were concerned, he was free to roam, or so it seemed to him.

Riley floated down a small corridor, noticing other small dome-shaped rooms, one after another, each filled with specimens in jars, boxes, or odd shaped containers that the aliens had collected or brought with them from somewhere else in their travels. Some required refrigeration: others were freeze-dried or changed into powder or liquid form before they were stored. He watched as the aliens in the room changed mushrooms into powder. Riley decided this must be some sort of scout ship, but he had no proof since this was the only ship, he had seen first-hand. It was not the big one that he had heard about that had landed in the field close to the military base. *So, where was that one?*

Riley remembered having a conversation earlier in the week with his friend Sergeant Anderson, who told him in confidence about what happened at the base and of what he saw when he was in the tower. He swore Riley to secrecy and told him not to speak of the incident with anyone. Sergeant Anderson said he originally saw multiple blips that registered in patterned flight of the extraterrestrial spacecrafts. After seeing this craft, Riley decided Sergeant Anderson must have been correct in his initial assessment, and that the other smaller crafts had disappeared off his radar field due to their incredible acceleration and their other assignments in the area had nothing to do with the delivery of females to the base. Riley determined this was one of those beam ships Sergeant Anderson told him about. Jesse only told them about the one ship, so he wondered why Captain Jamal Bryant was not giving Jesse and the team all the information unless he wasn't concerned about the other ships or didn't see them when he arrived in the tower. *The mother ship must be concealed somewhere above the clouds. Where are the other three, or four, beam ships Sergeant Anderson saw, and what were they doing? Did they each have a specific assigned scientific duty?*

Riley was amazed and confused at how calm and relaxed he felt. It was that feeling you get right before you go under anesthesia, when the doctor says, 'just relax and count back from four for me please.' There's no time to freak out unconsciousness happens in seconds. Riley was astonished that no one was stopping his exploration of the spacecraft. He decided he would take advantage of the situation and try to gather as much intel as he could while they weren't paying attention, hoping at some point, they would let him go. *When exactly would that be?* He had no idea.

The rooms in the craft looked like individual igloos which reminded him of a time from when he was a kid. He was with his mother at an antique store built from large wooden igloos. There was old stuff stacked everywhere, even hanging from the ceiling, at that store and it was the same inside this craft. It had the same familiar feel and smell. *Why am I having all these weird memories of days past?* Riley wondered. *Maybe the aliens' computer is extracting information from my brain and I am just feeling it as it passes from me to them, I better not think about the agency while I am here. Crap! Double crap!*

Riley passed by what he would call the main operations room, assuming he was looking out of several windows, but soon realized these were access screens. One view was of the planets Mars, Jupiter, Saturn, Uranus, Neptune, and Pluto. These weren't faraway views like Riley had watched on the History channel. These close-up views made him feel he could reach out and touch each planet. Then he realized he was watching another spacecraft, such as the one he was currently on as it raced past each planet at time warp speed. *Where was that alien ship's destination if not Earth? Home?* Another access screen showed a blue and neon-green planet, which Riley was not familiar with from the astronomy class he had taken in college. *Was this their home?* The last access screen, which he only got a glimpse of, was a screen with aliens and humans going about their day, but the landscape did not appear to be that of the planet Earth. The structures were more mid-century modern architecture. He wanted to go in and get a closer look, but for some reason he couldn't get his feet to cooperate, so he just floated on down the corridor.

Riley decided the humanoids on this ship reminded him of carpenter ants with their pointed skulls and acrocephalic shaped faces and solid large black eyes. Maybe it was the angle of their oversized, expressionless coal-colored eyes, or the fact that they had no auricles, only ear canals, or that they had no external nose, only small external nasal passages. Their mouths were merely straight slits, exhibiting no labium oris or outer pigmentation for lips, which made it difficult for Riley to read their emotions. He did notice their teeth were tiny, neither dark nor light, but apparently extremely sharp. He watched one alien eat bits of unidentifiable food with a spear-shaped utensil. Some aliens had sage-colored skin, appearing thick but smooth, resembling a gelatinous texture with no prominent blood vessels. He wanted to touch their skin to see how it felt, but didn't want to create an issue of disrespect or aggression, since he felt he was being treated more like a guest aboard the ship than a threat to them. As Riley floated to a different room, he realized he was not controlling where he was going; it was the aliens aboard that were moving him from place to place. A little boy around six years old with blonde hair and blue eyes was sitting on a stool. Riley noticed he didn't seem scared either. In fact, he was laughing. The little boy ignored Riley, not even trying to communicate with him. A humanoid arrived carrying a beaker with brownish green thick liquid in it and handed the glass to the little boy who immediately drank it without being forced. He smiled up at the creature, "Umm, that was good." Poof— the little boy was gone from the room.

Riley realized he had been left alone with the tall alien. Taking a closer look at it, Riley realized this one had more human characteristics in its appearance. This one was much different than the rest on board. Its eyes were smaller; they more of a blue color than black, and he could definitely see a very small pair of ears, a nose, and lips on this alien. It smiled, handing Riley a beaker of the same liquid. Riley noticed this alien only had four fingers on each hand. All the fingers were the same length and diameter. They had no little finger which in humans is very important as it gives the hand more strength. Riley started to put the beaker to his lips to drink, but the alien held his arm. It didn't speak to him, but through some type of telepathy, Riley could hear words circling in a rhythm inside his head. Riley repeated the sentence over out loud, twice, not sure exactly why. Perhaps it was to make sure that he wouldn't forget due to the importance of the message.

The alien nudged on his arm, so Riley would know to drink from the beaker. He drank the liquid. It was thick and sweet. No wonder the little boy seemed to enjoy it so much.

*** 

Hours later Riley awoke sitting in the UTV in the dark. His lost Glock-27 was lying on the seat beside him. He had no idea how he got there, but was glad he was no longer aboard the spacecraft. Riley wondered if the craft was still in the forest. If it was, he was not going to look for it again, not by himself. Riley remembered most of what he had seen on board; and it seemed to him that there was something else he needed to remember, but for now he wanted a hot cup of coffee and a note pad so he could make notes of his time aboard the craft. This information also needed to go into his report, which meant he would now have to tell Jesse he took Eddie's medal up to Bald Knob Mountain.

# Chapter 22

## Jesse's Women, March 18, 2020

The farther down deep inside the mountain, it seemed to Jesse, the cooler the temperature. Perhaps they had to keep the climate controlled to a certain range for the scientists to work on their delicate specimens. Anyway, he was glad to put on the knee-length, long-sleeved white lab coat hanging in the hall, before entering the next corridor.

The walls were painted plain white, matching the marble tiled floors. It was easy to get lost in the maze of offices and laboratories, and there weren't many signs to point visitors in the right direction. They preferred it that way. If you belonged, you knew where you were going. If you were lost, you probably didn't belong, and you were easy to spot and redirect away from things that needed to remain out of sight.

All sections were air locked. Card, fingerprint, voice recognition, and retina scan were required to move from one section to another. Through the computer security system, Lucia had the ability to authorize or forbid entry. Lucia could be friendly, firm, insistent, and provide deadly force if necessary, to protect the integrity of the inner base. She had the ability to interface with any computer component inside the base and surrounding area. She was both computer and robot with human emotion to a point, but not enough that it would affect her final decision for destruction if that were needed. Even though security was tight, occasional reporters pretending to be lost hikers tried to sneak onto the base, but they would never get this far without an intruder alarm sounding on the elevator and total lock down occurring.

Jesse knocked on the steel door. Military guards stood one on each side with an M-27 Rifle at his side. The door alarm beeped, displaying a green light. The automatic door opened, allowing him to enter the first entry way where he stood as positive pressure ions bounced off him, destroying any airborne pathogens, so as not to contaminate any laboratory top secrets. Once the air stopped blowing, Jesse smoothed his hair. The next steel door swished opened automatically. Jesse hurried out the exit, quickly turning down the left corridor.

He was there to meet with Doctor Charity Armstrong. She was the CIA's top scientist in the division of Quantum computer technology and artificial intelligence; she was also Lucia's mother figure and her creator. Lucia had been developed from intelligence recovered from the Roswell crash in 1947. She was destined as a collections officer in making specific decisions on the development of a new alien race in the new world they were developing. Being on the craft wrecked in Roswell gave her vast worldwide networking opportunities. Lucia, the primogenitor of her kind like Adam and Eve, who represented the beginning of the human race, Lucia was many centuries old. She also had a mind of her own with developed sentience, personality, and super intelligence. She followed her, Dr. Armstrong's orders in completing projects now on Earth. As the expert in her field, Jesse was anxious to hear Doctor Armstrong's and Lucia's thoughts on the women the soldiers had brought in to be studied and examined.

Jesse tapped on the door before entering. Charity looked up smiled, put her pen down, and motioned for him to take a seat opposite her at the desk. Charity looked the same every time Jesse met with her, wearing her white lab coat, white linen blouse buttoned down the front, black slacks, and black flat shoes. She never swayed from her professional demeanor. Her hair on the other hand, had a mind of its own. She tried to control her long, thick, auburn ringlets by pulling her hair up in a Boho-style updo, showing off a little bohemian and hippie flare, but her red locks always appeared to be escaping their bonds. The style framed her face well and brought attention directly to her smoky eyes and soft smile.

Doctor Armstrong reached for Agent Finch's hand, "I had a feeling you would be stopping by soon to check on our female visitors. How are Bette and the kids?"

"You know Bette, she always thinks something's going on. She doesn't understand the hours I keep and how important our work here really is, and not just to this nation. Of course, I can't tell her what I am doing, so it's really a catch twenty-two. Has Lucia weighed in her evaluation of the women yet?"

"I haven't notified Lucia of having the women here, yet. It's kind of a sticky situation. You know what I mean. They have been kept somewhere by aliens for a long time. Lucia was part of an alien ship. I am not sure what will happen when we introduce them to each other, or what the consequences will be for us on Earth. I need to weigh all this information for our safety." Changing the subject, she said, "Well, is Bette, right? Are you having an affair?" She picked up her lipstick, reading the color label to herself before she looked up at him.

Jesse was silent, just looking off into space to avoid her eyes. "What's the name of that lipstick? I bet Bette would look good in that color."

Uncomfortable with the conversation she herself had begun, she whispered, "Its Knockout Nude." Embarrassed with his question, her cheeks flushed.

"I'd say that is just about right," tapping his fingers on the desk, Jesse smiled.

Charity laughed nervously. Pulling out her desk drawer, she dropped the lipstick in her Calvin Klein purse to get it out of sight. Pressing her mouth together, she could still feel the smoothness of Knockout Nude across her lips.

Jesse could tell his teasing was bothering her and that he should change the subject back to work. "How are they doing now, the women, I mean? Have they settled in, started asking questions about where they are, or where their families are? Anything like that?"

"Believe it or not, no they haven't asked any question about family or anything for that matter. There's something very odd about these women. I think we should take one thing at a time, and maybe just talk about one female at a time. That will give you time to take notes and brief your men on them later this week. Speaking of your men, are they having any luck with finding any family or friends that are still around, to talk to about the women? If they do find them, what then, are you going to bring them here? It could be dangerous in numerous ways. This is going to have to be a wait and see, one day at a time, thing for everyone."

"I'm not sure yet of what to do. I think I am going to leave it all up to you with regards to these women. They have been gone for a long time. We have no idea, at this point, if they are friendly or dangerous. What kind of capabilities have they developed? We know Rose has been gone since the 1940s. What's she been doing for the last seventy-eight years and why hasn't she aged a day since she left? I guess I am mixed on telling any family, or reintroducing them to people they haven't seen for years. How do you tell someone that the world has moved on without them? Since these women were abducted, things in our world have drastically changed. Earth is not the same, and neither are they. It would be a giant culture shock for them, even more so than when you hear about when convicts are released after being in prison for decades. At least prisoners have other humans they can get information from about the world outside. Plus, they have television to watch. But these women have no knowledge of what has happened here on Earth since the day they were taken. Just think about all of the technology that has been developed from the 1940s to 2020. It is totally mind boggling for someone to have all of that science thrown at them in one day."

"Yes, can I see your point with that and certainly agree, but think about it this way: With all the women we have down here, Rose would have information from Earth up until the last twenty years, with the span the aliens have taken the women. She is not completely in the dark. Who knows? We are probably the ones in the dark as far as technology goes. You know they are light years ahead of us, just from what Lucia can do, that we are aware of.

"So, back to the women here, tell me in general what are they saying or doing?"

"The doctors and scientific staff basically kept them up all night. First, they had to decontaminate them before bringing them down here. Then, they did complete head to toe physicals on all of them. We reviewed lab work for malnutrition, and DNA for identification. After that, they were taken to the showers and shown how to operate them. The women just stood there, the female assistants had to assist the women and put them to bed like children. When they finally went to sleep, they were still in the same shocked state as they had been when Captain Loch found them out in the field. Maybe it takes a while for them to get over the shock of being on a different planet. Speaking of which, what happened outside to the men that witnessed this whole thing? I am sure they are full of questions."

"Commander Bryant met with all the men on the base and stated this was a top-secret project, and absolutely nothing was to be spoken about the episode. If they did, they would be court martialed and sent to prison. He made everyone sign a consent form agreeing to top secret clearance, and giving up any hope of a pension if the information leaked to the press, from them or a family member. I believe that part is contained. There have been UFO rumors all over the world and so far, the public either thinks they are silly, or we have debunked them with information proving that the event never happened. You know the old balloon, meteor, satellite, flock of birds, or swamp gas story. One always seems to work, especially when we get a story put in the *National Enquirer*. Most people read those big titles in the grocery aisle then just tend to forget and go on with their busy day."

"Yes, that's true. Good, I'm glad that's taken care of, but still a few of the soldiers may need to have some counseling. Our computer system has a list of soldiers in the data base who already have issues with post-traumatic stress disorder. I will send those files to the psychiatric staff today, and make some recommendations for soldiers in Sergeant Loch's squad to have a chance to process the event. With suicide in the military over PTSD issues so high, it is better to make sure they get what they need to process and heal than to ignore it, especially after they developed the condition by putting their lives on the line for their country."

"I agree with that. I will make sure and add this information in my report to General Kearns. He is always looking for positive things to help his soldiers."

"So, tell me what else is going on with the women?"

"When they woke up, they started wandering around the room — just pacing. Not engaging with the staff that brought in food or even with each other for that matter. I'm waiting for one to finally step forward and be the mouthpiece for the rest of the group. We know they have the ability to speak, so I'm hoping that will happen soon."

"Interesting. Maybe it's a trust issue instead. Are they in a room where they can be observed from outside? I would like to see them for myself."

"Oh, sure. I have their names and DNA identification for you now, so here's that list to match up against your list of missing women from the Cass area. The last thing I did before I went to lunch was to leave some art supplies in the room with them. I thought maybe they might want to express themselves somehow, if they weren't ready to talk yet."

Charity stood up, "Would you like to go see what they've done with the paint or if they even touched it?" She came around the side of the desk.

Agent Finch smiled saying. "Charity have dinner with me tonight at seven and bring that Knockout Nude lipstick with you." He patted her hand and walked out the door ahead of her, so she could gain her composure before joining him. *How dare she ask him if he was having an affair. He would never cheat on Bette.*

They walked down two short halls and turned left. Everything was quiet except for their footsteps on the tile, which echoed loudly through the halls. Agent Jesse Finch and Doctor Charity Armstrong stood outside the one-way window, watching the three women move around the room.

"This is what I wanted to show you, and not tell you ahead of time"

Agent Finch noticed the women had sorted the colors of paint, putting the red, yellow, and orange hues in a stack over by the door, and only the blues, greens, and violets on the table.

"I will be interested in what they are doing with just those colors. Isn't that odd?" She asked a staff member, who had arrived to drop off snacks, to turn the easels around so they could see the women's paintings.

"Charity, everything about this is odd."

"Odd is the new normal today. Look at those."

Two of the women returned to the canvas paintings. They were using broad strokes with paint brushes loaded with acrylic purple, blue, and green paint. Once they completed a painting, they removed the canvas from the easel and stood the painting against the far wall to dry. Jesse stared at the paintings to try to figure out the meaning, or if there was a meaning. Some paintings had large circles of blue and violet. Others had shapes like triangles, and they were painted in green and blue. Some were painted solid and others were deliberately left incomplete, or incomplete in Jesse's eyes.

Jesse moved over to the window, pressing his face on the glass trying to see closer. He wanted to get a better view of the women and the room.

A woman with long dirty blonde hair and blue violet eyes quickly approached him on the other side. Jesse was sure she couldn't see him and hoped she moved out of his way. Instead, she turned to face him at the last minute, putting her outstretched hand across his forehead. Jesse was stuck in a bent position against the window. His body was shaking violently, and his hands pressed against the glass. He started screaming in pain, or so it seemed to Doctor Armstrong.

She was terrified and started to put her hand out but was afraid to touch him for fear he was somehow being electrocuted. She didn't want to be killed. Charity began screaming, "Lucia, help Jesse break free," then she yelled for the guards. If Rose did not let go of Jesse, she would have no other choice than to have them shoot her through the glass.

Within minutes, they were on the scene, but not in time to help Jesse. His body slump to the floor. One of the soldiers did CPR on him, and he started to come around. From there, they put him on a gurney, and rushed him to the infirmary to be checked out further. Doctor Armstrong ordered all personnel out of where the women stood, now facing the window, listening. "No one is to be with the women alone.

Everyone should be escorted in and out with an armed guard. We need to consider the women non-friendly and dangerous, and no one is to touch or look in the glass window," she instructed the guards.

Doctor Armstrong followed Jesse to the infirmary after she spoke to the staff. By that time, he was undressed, a nurse was placing a heart monitor on him, and he was receiving oxygen. "This is completely unnecessary. I am fine; I just need to get back to work," Jesse kept insisting.

"Agent Finch, you need to be quiet and stay in bed for a couple hours to make sure your heart is stable. The guards had to resuscitate you. Your heart stopped. I will not sign for you to be released just yet."

Charity bent down close to his ear. "Jesse, are you okay? What happened back there? That was some scary crap. Did Rose do something to you, or is there an electrical short in the window that I need to get taken care of immediately?"

"Yes, very scary crap. No; not the window. It was the woman. So, that blonde-haired woman was Rose? I thought it was from her photo."

"She's the one they said who was standing in the field. The other two were lying down behind her. Rose Jackson went missing in 1941 from Cass. I'm betting Rose is the leader. I don't expect any of the others to interact with us, at least not for now, since she has stepped forward."

"She didn't seem to like you very much. She must have heard about your reputation," Charity smiled.

Jesse blushed, "That Mrs. Jackson used telepathy on me in a very painful way. She wanted my full attention, and she most definitely has it. I need you to keep everyone else away from the window. Cordon off that hall. Get an electrician down there, and after he is there for a while, have him report that he repaired a broken switch. I don't want anyone else but you to know what really happened. Tell no one. We can't let that leak out, okay? Also keep those guards with guns out of there; I don't believe they will harm us now."

"Okay, what did happen, Jesse?"

"I can't tell you right now, too many ears, but I will. Believe me, it is not good."

Charity turned to go.

"Are you leaving?"

"Yes, I have things to do, but I'll be back in a few hours to check on you. Try to rest, or at least pretend to, or that doctor will never release you."

"Well, in that case, kiss me so I have something good to lie here and think about. Every time I close my eyes, I see what Rose Jackson put in my head."

"Only because I thought you were dying, Agent Finch. You are a married man and I am only twenty-six. You know if you talked to any of the other women around here like this, they would report you for workplace harassment. Now, promise me you will behave yourself the rest of the day, or I will have to call Bette. You know I am serious, and I have her number."

Jesse shook his head. "Yes, you certainly do." She had him dead to rights, but he enjoyed teasing her.

Charity leaned in pretending she was only going to kiss him on the cheek, but instead kissed him full on the lips. "Consider that from Bette, since she is not here right now to comfort you after you almost died." Then she slipped behind the curtain and left the room.

Charity had finally paid him back. *Man, that girl could kiss, besides being the best scientist in the field of artificial intel.*

Jesse couldn't get Charity off his mind; she had gotten him good. Maybe it was time he stopped teasing her. She was probably right about the harassment thing. For some reason with her it made him feel like she was one of his gang when he teased her, but there was nothing more to their relationship, except their harmless banter back and forth. He was too old for her and married to the love of his life already. Perhaps he could fix her up with Agent Bilodeau. Charity needed someone besides her work, and that ugly grey cat, Herschel, to go home to at night. Jesse wondered… *if he himself even has time, now since rose has opened my eyes to what is coming next.*

Jesse lay there with his eyes closed, thinking about Mrs. Rose Jackson. He wanted to know more about her ability to communicate directly to him by touch. No one else had heard their conversation. He wondered if this was how the women communicated amongst themselves. *Maybe they no longer needed to express themselves through speech.* Rose Jackson most definitely got his attention, in an immensely painful migraine way. What she revealed to him through their telepathy session frightened the life out of him. Jesse couldn't wait until his team was back together so he could get the full background on these women. He wanted to see their faces when he told them what Rose Jackson knew. Now, Jesse was even more curious as to why the women chose the colors they did and painted those canvas's with only those specific shapes.

# Chapter 23

## Herschel's Replacement

Doctor Charity Armstrong yanked back the thin tan curtain, "Miss me?" she asked, then smiled, seeing he had taken her advice for once.

Jesse opened his eyes and stretched. "I can't believe I fell asleep after you left."

"Well, I can. Whatever Mrs. Jackson did with those mind games probably sucked the energy right out of you. You, poor man."

"Charity, stop placating me. I know you enjoy seeing me in this bed, standing over me and ordering me around. I've decided I'm not going to pretend to chase you anymore."

"Oh, really? You mean I finally knocked some sense into your think head on the harassment thing?"

"No, I now have other plans for you. I need to get you to fall head over heels with just the right man. You're much too intelligent to find someone on your own. You need to be having fun."

"I suppose you have that man already picked out, do you?" She laughed. "Well, good luck with finding someone that will put up with the hours I keep."

"Maybe you wouldn't keep long hours if you had a good man to go home to at night."

"That's possibly true, but I wonder what Herschel would think if I brought another male home?"

"You need to toss that stinking cat out of the bedroom."

"But Herschel is so cuddly. I love the way he curls up on my lap and purrs."

"There you go. See, you're getting me started again. You should be the one purring, not Herschel. Anyway, let's get out of here and go somewhere we can talk so you can bring me up to speed on our young ladies."

Once back in Doctor Armstrong's office, Jesse moved his chair up, closer to the desk. Charity pulled one file out at a time, reviewing each test result so Agent Finch would understand the health of each female. So, what you are saying is they probably have not aged one day since the day they were taken. How is that possible?"

"Maybe, suspended animation? Who really knows? We certainly don't have that ability here on Earth. But none the less, they have not aged. They all have scars on their bodies so I am assuming they have had multiple surgeries done. It is possible the aliens wanted to know how their bodies functioned. It looks like they had their middle fingers removed at one time, which is kind of weird; unless they wanted to make them more like themselves."

"But the aliens we have stored here all only have four fingers on each hand. They could have attempted some type of mutation then decided to reverse it."

"Rose has a large scar on her left wrist; I wonder if she tried to attempt suicide after they took her. The women all must be able to transmit their thoughts to each other, and probably communicate with the aliens in their telepathic language. We found a small device like a coil embedded into the cochlea behind their right ear. I don't know if that is related to telepathy, or if it might be a tracking device of some sort."

"If it is a tracking device, and they are still monitoring them, then the aliens know where they are in here, and probably know their dead alien friends are here as well. Now that I said it out loud, it sounds sort of scary. I think the scar on Rose was from an injury. I read in her police file there was blood all over the kitchen and glass everywhere, so she may have cut the artery in her wrist before she was taken, and possibly it saved her life when they abducted her."

"Their radiation readings were slightly above normal; however, it doesn't seem to have affected them one way or the other. No hair loss, radiation sickness, or cancer of any type. The last thing medically found about all of the women, is that not one of them has a follicle left in her ovaries."

"What are you talking about? Do they still have their ovaries?"

"Yes, they're intact. I am just saying they can't bear any children due to the fact they no longer have the follicles to produce a child. They are all young in their twenties and should still be of childbearing age."

"That's very odd for all of them not to be fertile."

"Yes, I agree. Women are born with one to two million follicles, and by the time they reach puberty they have approximately four-hundred left. If Rose would let us question her, maybe she could give us some answers to our questions. So far, she has been cooperative unless you are around. You seem to set her off."

"I wonder why that is?"

"Maybe she has heard about your reputation around here, or maybe it is those piercing, dark brown eyes that got to her, or that aura of confidence that surrounds you."

"Yeah, right now who is harassing whom?"

"I know; you're right. All I can say is thank goodness Bette knows me and what kind of nonexistent relationship we have. She puts up with it knowing how I love to tease you. Anyway, enough about me, what were you going to say about Rose Jackson?"

"I have a feeling she knew, somehow, I was in charge, but how would she know that? She is an interesting character. If she doesn't start communicating verbally, we may have to put her under aggressive hypnosis."

"Do you think that might work?"

"We have done it with soldiers to help them remember, so it could work. Right now, it is the most effective method to unlock forgotten periods of time that we have. We've also done some telepathic communication experiments using energy lines, so we may try that tomorrow and see how far we get. Listen, when any of this stuff with hypnosis or telepathy is tested on the women there needs to be limited staff present."

"I understand. The other thing I would like to suggest is seeing if Rose would communicate with Lucia?"

"Don't do that just yet. We don't know what her capabilities are. What if she were able to gather all the data Lucia has stored on her and use it against us?

"Okay, yep, terrifying. Keeping them apart for now."

"Do you have a pen and tablet I can borrow?"

Doctor Armstrong handed Agent Finch some paper and a pen.

He wrote, *not for Lucia's ears in large letters.*

Doctor Armstrong nodded agreement.

Agent Finch then wrote to her what he saw when Rose put her hand on his head. Then he handed her the pen.

*Is OMG enough of a response for now*? She wrote back.

He nodded.

Doctor Armstrong started to put the files back in the drawer then pulled them out again. "Jacqueline has multiple scar puncture wounds on her legs, which would lead me to suspect that she was bitten by more than one poisonous snake, at the same time. I wonder when she was in the woods next to her house, if she by any chance came across a den of poisonous copperheads or rattlesnakes just before the aliens found her. Molly Lehman had multiple wounds to her back, like stab wounds, they are different lengths and angles as if she were moving when the knife met her skin. I think she was being attacked with a knife as she was running, maybe when she tried to get way. From the looks of all of these injuries, they could have all died from their wounds had it not been for the medical care they received from the alien abductors." She put the files back in the drawer, locked the cabinet, and put the key in her jacket pocket. Looking at her watch, she realized just how hungry she was. "Is that dinner offer still available, for the cafeteria? I have my lipstick in my purse and will even put some on if you want to buy me some food."

Jesse laughed, "You better leave that lipstick where it is. I will buy you dinner in the cafeteria, since you asked."

"Good. You can tell me all about this man who you think might try to take Herschel's place on my bed."

What Doctor Armstrong didn't hear, was Lucia say in her soft voice, "These women sound very interesting. I need to review their files. They may be who I am looking for. Uploading data, now."

***

The cafeteria was doing heavy business, so Doctor Armstrong and Agent Finch stood patiently in line until it was their turn to make the circle around the room, piling food on their plates. From there, they started looking for a quiet place to sit, which Jesse was beginning to think they would never find. Finally spying a spot when a small group of soldiers got up to leave, he motioned for Charity to meet him there. Suddenly someone came up fast behind Jesse, brushed past him, and took the table. "Hey, Agent Bilodeau, when did you get back?"

Colin smiled, "Oh, did I take your table? I'm so sorry."

"No, you're not, so don't even go there."

"Okay, I'm not really. Is that Miss, excuse me, Doctor Charity Armstrong with you? She looks to be coming in this direction."

"Yes, she is, so be on your best behavior when she sits down."

Colin smiled, showing his gorgeous white teeth. "You know I will. She is one hot woman." "Yes, she is and single, too."

"She sure has pretty eyes, and that hair of hers. I bet it looks nice hanging down around her shoulders."

Jesse thought, *Well, maybe half of my job is already done.* "Doctor Charity Armstrong, this is Agent Colin Bilodeau. I think you have probably seen each other in one of our meetings.

"Yes, you do look familiar to me. Please, call me Charity here during dinner. Won't you stay and eat with us?"

Jesse looked at his watch, "Colin, I completely forgot I told Bette I would call her and the kids. Would you mind keeping Charity company for me? I really have to run." Grabbing his food, he left the cafeteria before either one of them could say a word.

Colin said, "So, I hear you have a cat named Herschel. Are you a fan of that zombie show?"

"I've seen a few of them, but not really. Maybe you could come over sometime and watch an episode, if you like the show, and meet my Herschel. Or better yet, how do you feel about music? I personally enjoy listening to Sir William Herschel's concert music. I find it can be very exhilarating under the right circumstances."

"What are you doing tonight? I have to be on a flight to South Carolina in the morning, but I'm free until six a. m."

"Six a. m., huh?" Charity tapped her manicured nails lightly on the tabletop, thought about the note Agent Finch wrote to her about his vision Rose gave him, and then picked up their plates, placing them on the kitchen conveyor belt on their way out of the cafeteria.

# Chapter 24

## Greasy Spoon Confessions, March 20, 2020

Vic parked outside Marty's Café. It was his and Riley's favorite greasy spoon. He didn't know if any of the other guys ate there or not, but he always seemed to run into Riley about this time, when they were both in town. In fact, as he got out of the car, he noticed Riley was just being seated in a booth right in front of the big picture window. That meant he would have no wait time, since Riley was already seated.

Vic's first words to Riley were, "What's today's special?"

"Fried chicken or meatloaf and coleslaw. I can't decide. Both are pretty good."

"No, I mean what is the pie for the day? Once I get that figured out the rest is easy."

Riley laughed, "Vic, I honestly forgot to ask."

"Really? Okay, what's up? I know you too well. The first two things you always ask when you come in here are 'What's the pie for the day'? And number two, 'Is Tanya working'? So, if you didn't ask either of those two things, what's going on? Hard week? It's only Wednesday." When Riley didn't answer, Vic waved his hand in front of Riley, "Earth to Riley. Hey, you're in luck. That sweet little Tanya with the long black hair, and hourglass shape, is headed right toward our table."

"Hey guys. How's your day a goin'?" The waitress pulled her pen and pad out, ready to take their order.

"I'm doing great, Miss Tanya. I think I will have the meatloaf special, and what kind of pie do you have today?"

"Cherry, lemon, and coconut cream, my favorite," she waited on his reply.

Vic squinted his eyes, "What, no blueberry?"

"You know what? I think there might be one piece of blueberry left. I'll put it back just for you, Vic." She smiled at Riley, "Now what can I get for you today, sir?"

Riley's mind was not on the here and now. He was on his phone, on the Internet looking something up, and didn't even hear Tanya speak to him.

"Riley will take the fried chicken special, and I happen to know he likes coconut cream pie, too, so put that down for him. He's a little stressed right now."

"Stressed? That's my middle name, today. See that guy over there in the red shirt?" Tanya said, rolling her eyes to the right trying not to turn her head.

"Yeah, what about him?" asked Vic.

"Well, I don't know who he is, but he's been following me for the last three days. Everywhere I go I see him, and it's starting to scare me a little, like I might have a stalker following me or something. You just never know these days, what might happen. I've got my mace, but that won't help if someone sneaks up from behind. You know what I mean? Anyways, I don't need to bother you all with my problems. Let me go get this order put in for you real quick, before that pie disappears." She hurried toward the kitchen.

Riley got up from the table, walked over to the guy in the red shirt, flashed his badge, and the guy stood up from his seat. He hurried toward the front door with Riley trailing right behind him. Once they were outside, Riley shoved him up against the side of the concrete building. "I know you've been stalking that black-haired waitress. I just want you to know you are being watched, and if you come within twenty feet of her again, you will have to answer to me. Do you understand what I am saying to you, boy? Just nod if you do." Riley stood with his fists clenched, wanting to use them on someone today. He didn't really care who.

The guy nodded before he ran toward a blue truck with Riley still right behind him. He jumped in and drove away.

Vic and Tanya both watched from inside the cafe. When Riley returned to his booth, Tanya stood on tippy toes and kissed him on the cheek, "Thank you, Agent Harris you have made my day."

Riley smiled, "I don't expect you will be seeing him again. I put the fear of God in that one. He won't be coming back around you."

After Tanya left the table, Vic said, "Did you get his plate?"

Riley opened his computer, plugged the plate numbers in, and then called the local highway patrol, "Sure did." The dispatcher answered his call, "This is Agent Riley Harris. I need to report a sexual predator who has been stalking his next victim for the past three days. Could you send a cruiser out to meet him? He is heading east on Route 60 toward Meadow Bluff. He needs picked up for breaking his parole. I would search his truck good. I am sure he has his tools of the trade in there, he was probably ready to pick his victim up after her shift today." When Riley hung up from the call, he muttered, "I wish everything was that easy."

"So now that you're talking, where are you headed next, or have you not finished your first assignment yet?" asked Vic.

"Yeah, I'm done, finally. The last couple days have been more than crazy. I am going out to good old sunny California. Where are you off to next?"

"Roswell, New Mexico, of all things," Vic laughed. "At least it will be nice and warm out there. Who knows? Maybe I'll see a spaceship while I'm out there." Vic joked, but when Riley didn't laugh, Vic decided Riley must be thinking about his kids today.

They ate their lunch, paid, and went outside. "Hey, I've got a few minutes. Why you don't jump in my car and let's shoot the breeze a few more minutes, before we go to the airport, or are you packed?"

"Sure, I'm ready." He followed Vic over to the car and got in.

Vic pulled up the messages on his phone, "Crap! Sara called me yesterday, and I didn't see her message until just now. She's probably fuming. Just when we finally got back together."

"You mean Sara took you back again? You'd better call her and apologize before it's too late. So, how did you guys even manage to speak after that last time you messed up?"

"She got assigned on the same case. My missing girl turned out to be dead, unfortunately, and we found more bodies. It was crazy. One male was murdered, and the other five were females with abortions gone bad. She and her team were there on the scene all day. Later that evening, she tracked me down at a bar and dragged me home with her. So yeah, we are — were back together again; unless I screwed it up already. I can't screw it up again Riley; I am crazy in love with that woman. I have a feeling this voice mail was her giving me one last chance. I can't even bring myself to listen to it. Sometime things just aren't easy. Too much baggage, mostly mine not hers."

"I know what you mean, with everything you went through as a kid," Riley picked up a paper straw off the console and bent it back and forth. "Vic, if I tell you something, will you keep it to yourself?"

"Of course, I will, unless you tell me you robbed a bank. If that's the case, I might have to turn you in, especially if there's a big reward. What's going on buddy?"

"This last assignment that I was on, the cousin to the girl I was looking for, was one of us. I mean, as in he worked for the CIA, and I helped bury his ashes twice this week."

"Okay, that's kind of weird. Why were you burying his ashes at all? Does Jesse know about this? He doesn't, does he? Never mind, just go on."

"No, Jesse doesn't know, but that's not the point. Anyway, I helped someone bury him, and then later I found his medals in his closet. He had received the Distinguished Intelligence Cross medal, so I decided to go dig him up and put the medal in there with him. Don't tell Jesse He will write me up for not staying on task."

"Hey, I have done plenty of stuff to get in trouble. Trust me, he will never hear it from me. So, is that all that's bothering you? That sounds pretty minor."

"No, that part was fine. It's what happened after the second burial that has me in a weird state of mind, and I need to snap out of it so I can do my job."

Vic sat silent, waiting on Riley to talk.

After a few minutes, Riley began. "I've always been a little skeptical when I have interviewed abductees. You just know some are lying through their teeth and others can be very believable. Well, after I buried Eddie out on top of the mountain, I was starting back down, and I saw something, so I went to check it out. It was a spaceship." Riley waited to see what Vic's response was. If he joked around, he wasn't going to tell him the truth.

Vic's face showed no emotion. He wanted to let Riley get whatever he needed to say off his chest.

"As soon as I realized what and who they were, I was already caught in their trap. This blue dusty stuff came down around me, and the next thing I knew I was already on board the thing. It was so weird. I was floating about a half-foot off the floor, so I couldn't get away, and I didn't have any strength to try to fight them off. When I realized they weren't going to hurt me, I relaxed and tried to look around to gather some intel about the technology they had on board. It was far more advanced than what we could even dream of inventing. They had screens in there where I could see planets up close, just like I would if I were on a NASA shuttle, probably even better than that, honestly. You know the photos we have in the office of the dead aliens we have in storage? Well, I can tell you, not all of them look like that. There was another giant screen, which they were using like we would use Skype, and they could bring up aliens from their home planet and communicate with them from that far away. Can you even imagine that capability? I could see the planet, and even aliens on the planet and some of them looked very advanced, not like the photos. In fact, they looked more human than alien if you asked me. The planet was amazingly beautiful, more like where I would envision my wife and boys would live if they were in heaven."

Vic jumped out of the car, went over to a vending machine, bought two cold waters, and returned to the car, handing one to Riley.

Riley opened his immediately and drank it halfway down before he started talking again. "Thanks, I needed that. A couple of the aliens on board took me back to an exam room. One of them pushed a button on the wall and a steel table appeared. I think they had me under some type of anesthesia but I don't remember getting injected with anything The next thing I knew, I was getting dressed and being led to a different room where an alien was visiting with a little blonde-haired kid, and giving him this weird liquid to drink. The kid drank it all and said it was good, so she— the alien, I think it was a she, handed me a beaker of the liquid and I drank it, too. The next thing I knew, which was about ten hours later, I was sitting in the dark in a vehicle I had borrowed from the park ranger. How I got there, I have no idea. Oh, and get this, I had fallen down a hill— well I guess it was part of the mountain– earlier and lost my gun. I had planned to look for it on my way back, but it was there, beside me on the seat, and I know I didn't put it there. Do you think I am crazy or what?"

Vic put the cap back on his water, "Riley, my friend, welcome to my world of crazy. I believe you, and I will tell you why, but this conversation stays between friends, just the two of us. My dad was a pilot. He died when I was five, when the plane he was flying hit the side of a mountain in the fog. My mom and I lived in Elkins. She was a telephone operator for Bell. One night, an intruder broke into our house; I heard my mom scream, and ran out in the hall just in time to see her being attacked. She screamed for me to run and hide as he dragged her into the bedroom and slammed the door. I could hear her screaming, over and over, and then it was quiet. So I knew he must have killed her. I climbed out the second-floor window to hide on the roof, but I lost my holding and fell to the ground. Luckily, I didn't break anything, but when I looked up, the man was standing at my window and he saw me on the ground. He turned from the window, and I knew he would find me in the backyard, so I jumped up and started running across the field behind the house. I heard him break the lock on the back gate by kicking it with his foot. I figured he would find me if I didn't hide in the woods. He already knew I had seen his face. He couldn't afford to leave any witnesses. Anyway, the next thing I knew I was aboard a spaceship, and I wasn't afraid anymore. They saved my life. Several days later, the police found me walking along the side of the highway. I told them about my mother, no one had found her body yet. I described the man I had seen. Luckily, he had a record. I was able to identify him from a photo, and he went to prison. After that, I was in and out of several foster homes before my aunt and uncle finally took me home with them. They made me go to counseling over her murder, but I never told anyone about the aliens. I knew better than that. So, when you tell me you were aboard an alien spaceship, my thoughts immediately went to the kid, not you. I wonder what kind of situation they rescued that kid from?

"This is what you haven't told Sara, right? I wish I could tell you to just spill your guts and tell her, but I must admit I'm having a hard time wrapping my own head around what happened to me. Wait, I almost forgot the most important part. They told me something and made me repeat it twice, so I wouldn't forget it, but you know how things are when you dream. I keep racking my head for the answer, but the only part I can recall is something about water and a triangle, or possibly the Bermuda Triangle. I'm not keen on going to the Bermuda Triangle; there have been too many people, planes, and ships that have disappeared in the Devil's Triangle. I keep hoping it will come back to me before I find the person I need to give the message to and can't remember it. You're not expecting me to tell you something delivered by aliens, are you?"

"No, I wouldn't know what to do with any secret alien message. You're thinking too hard about it. Just relax and try to forget about it, and soon, in your sleep, you will remember again. When that happens, write it down right then. If you wait and go back to sleep it will disappear from your memory again." Looking at his watch, he said, "We both better get to the airport before we miss our flights."

# Chapter 25

## Annette Young, March 23, 1967

Annette sat in her wheelchair listening to *The Rolling Stones*. Her mother would never approve of the music, but she didn't care. Her mom wasn't home. She spent most of her days alone. She had no outside friends. Getting polio when you're seven sucked. Most days as a child were spent in bed. Her bed was her playroom, her classroom, and her dining room. Four walls and a bed, that was her life, and her prison. Now that she was older, at least she was able to use her wheelchair to get around the house so she could watch television. There was a ramp on the porch, which gave her access to get to the car when her mom took her to the doctor, church, or a rare trip to the store. Annette longed for adventure, for friends, and for companionship. She had seen on the news that young people her age out in California were living in communes. They were tanning themselves on beaches, swimming in the ocean, playing beach ball, and dancing with boys. These were all things she would never experience in her life.

Annette knew her future already. She and her mother had already planned it out; she would live here until her mother passed away. Then she would contact the attorney to sell the property, and Annette would use the money to go to an institution where she would live out the rest of her days. She was terrified at the thought. Surely this was not how her life would end. If that were the case, she didn't want to live anymore.

Not like this helpless to protect herself from others that would want to take advantage or cause her harm.

Annette opened the front door and rolled her wheelchair down the ramp. If she hurried, and the ground remained solid, she might make it to the forest before her mom got home. Twenty minutes later she was across the field and a hundred yards further she would disappear into the pines. Her plan was to find a ravine and roll over into it, hoping she would die before she hit the bottom. As cold as it was today, perhaps if she didn't die from the fall, maybe hypothermia would take her, and she would just fall asleep and never wake up. All Annette knew was she no longer wanted to live, not like this, helpless to protect herself from others that would want to cause her harm. There was no way she was going to be put in an institution after seeing the movie *The Care Takers*.

# Chapter 26

## Annette Young Investigation, March 20, 2020, San Diego, California

The jet landed on the runway with a bounce as the pilot braked. Overhead the intercom light came on, and Agent Riley Harris heard the airline stewardess announce, "Welcome to San Diego. The temperature today will be sunny and sixty-seven degrees. Thank you for flying South West Airlines. We hope to see you again soon."

Agent Riley Harris pulled his black carry-on bag from the overhead compartment before he got in line to exit the plane. It was almost lunch time, so he began to look for a restaurant inside the terminal. He would just grab a quick chicken sandwich or wrap inside the busy terminal before going to rent a car for the day.

Arriving in downtown San Diego, Riley found a parking garage just around the corner from his destination. He pulled up the file on his laptop, to review the information again, on the next missing female from Cass. Riley was still amazed at the technology for the new face recognition software on his computer. He loved how just by scanning in a photo, the software could generate enough information to age the photo to whatever year he needed. He could run it through the national registry, and within minutes he could find a match. Riley was surprised where he found this missing female, and that he had to travel clear across country to meet and speak with her. But according to his information on the screen, she had gone through the very red light he was looking at just a few hours ago.

Annette Young, born in 1950, was reported missing from Cass at the age of seventeen on March 23, 1967 by her mother. Looking at home photo from 1967, her jet-black straight hair hung almost to her waist. She had blue eyes and a dimple in her thin chin. Annette Young was listed as being five-foot-five and weighing one hundred twenty pounds on the missing person stat sheet. Riley logged onto the California License Bureau to see how much she had aged over the past fifty some years. Riley could see that she had taken good care of her health. He checked the license for any driving restrictions and was surprised that none were listed. Now he was confused on two counts. How did she get so far from home and how was she driving with no restrictions or any handicap capabilities built into her car? He studied the missing person stat sheet again. According to the record, Annette contracted polio at the age of seven years old. She was wheelchair bound from that time forward. The information didn't make sense. Riley thought, *Perhaps this was not the Annette Young I'm looking for at all. Jesse will not be pleased if this turns out to be a wild goose chase. On the other hand, there is someone else I could make a quick visit to see, if this does not pan out.*

Agent Riley Harris got out of the car, walked a block to the end of the street, and turned the corner past two store fronts. One was *Amelia's Books,* a used bookstore with a witch hat and broom decal below the name. The other was called *The Ocean Reef,* displayed a large marijuana leaf in its window. This store sold a variety of marijuana products for medical and recreational use. Finally finding himself standing in front of *Journey's End Boutique,* Riley opened the artistically painted purple door to go inside. Fragrances of amber, musk, vanilla, and white sage incense drifted past him. He nosed around the shop for a few minutes while he waited on Annette to finish waiting on a customer. The glass shelves were lined with fragrant goat's milk soaps, soy candles, natural food snacks, organic honey; these were just a few things for sale. Multicolored hippie art decorated the walls of the store.

Agent Harris noticed a sign leading customers into a different room where a yoga class was just beginning. Riley only peeked in for a second, just to see what was going on. He heard the instructor say, "Alright class, for our next move, feet apart and with your arms at your sides, breathe in slowly and deeply," that was enough yoga for Riley, who went back to the main part of the boutique.

"Annette Young?" Agent Harris asked in a polite voice to the woman standing behind the counter. She was wearing colorful hand-painted bangle bracelets, a black flouncy blouse, and a tie-dyed ankle length skirt. He also noticed she still had her long hair from her teenage years. Now, there was a lot of gray mixed through at her temples. Today she had it pulled into a loose braid, which draped over her left shoulder.

The woman turned with a startled look, putting her hand on her heart, "No one has called me that for years. My last name has been Costello since I turned eighteen. Who are you and how did you manage to find me?"

"I'm Agent Riley Harris. I work for the government and am clearing up some old missing person cases. I was able to identify you using our new facial recognition software. I am here to speak with you, Mrs. Costello."

Annette, still surprised, said, "I see. Well, I'm certainly glad that technology wasn't around when I ran away from home, or my dear old mother would have found me for sure. I can't begin to tell you how very happy I am she never found me." Annette looked down at the gold wedding band on her finger; she had worn it for so long that it left an indentation in her ring finger.

Riley laughed, "So, do you have a few minutes so we could go somewhere and talk. I'd like to hear how you ended up clear out here in California."

"Sure, let me just go get one of the girls and have her watch the shop. We can go back to my office and speak without being interrupted." She motioned for her young assistant before she led Riley to the back of the store.

Annette poured them both a cup of organic white tea before she sat down in her chair, waiting on Riley's questions. She was not sure how she would answer some if asked. Annette could hear her heart pounding against her chest and wondered if Riley could hear it, too. She adjusted her thick turquoise and silver necklace, feeling all at once, that piece of jewelry which she loved was either too heavy or too tight. She smiled awkwardly in Riley's direction, wanting to take it off, but felt the task to be too telling of her uncomfortable state.

When Agent Harris didn't speak right away, Annette clasped her hands together nervously, "Well, as you can see, I am still alive, not really missing anymore. In fact, I am happily married. My husband Gilbert and I have three wonderful adult children, two lovely granddaughters, and a grandson."

Riley noticed she never asked about her mother as he opened his file, "So why California? Why did you run away clear across country? And most importantly, how did you manage to get all this way?" He knew that was a lot to ask her all at once, but wanted to get the answers he needed.

Annette took a sip of the hot tea, "I left because my mother was smothering me. She treated me like an invalid for years. I always felt she needed me more than I really needed her. You know, to fill the void of having no man in the house. It got to the point that she was abusive with all her neediness. Then, she told me she was going to go see her attorney since she was getting older and she wanted to make sure that he would take care of my placement in the sanitarium once she was gone. Those places don't even exist anymore, thank God, but back then they sure did. Any child with a disability, whose parents' couldn't deal with, could discreetly place their child out of sight of society's vision. Then later, deinstitutionalization came along and put those same kids, now grown up, right out on the streets to fend for themselves. Anyway, back to how I decided to come out here. I was watching the news and they were interviewing someone who was talking about a commune; it was out west in California. The area looked so pretty, so I just made up my mind that was where I was going to go live. I am so glad that I came to California. Coming out here was such a good decision. It completely changed my life."

"Really? The file I have here says you contracted polio when you were seven. You are listed as disabled requiring a wheelchair, is that not correct?"

Annette took another sip of her tea, "Yes, that information was correct. I spent most of my childhood confined to my bed. But a miracle happened, and I no longer needed to be in bed or restricted to that chair anymore. I packed a few of my things in a bag, and sneaked through the woods finally, coming out next to the highway. From there, I hitched a ride with two young men in a truck going out to Indiana. I found another truck driver at a diner that was going to California, and he agreed to give me a ride the rest of the way."

"You were lucky you weren't killed, hitchhiking with strangers. So many young girls during that era had bad luck when they attempted that sort of thing."

"I know; I certainly understood the risk, but I was willing to take it. What can I say? I had to get out of there by any means necessary. When I got to San Francisco, I was alone and hungry. I remember sleeping on a bench in the park. There were several other young people there at the time, boys and girls. That's where I met Gilbert. He was lying on a bench in his green camouflage pants and jacket. His dog tags jingled when he turned over. He said he had just returned from Vietnam. For some reason, he didn't want to go back home to New Jersey. Some of the other young people were talking about the commune I had heard about on the television. They said it was just north of San Francisco Bay, so a couple of the guys put their money together and bought an old 1950's Volkswagen camper. We bought several buckets of paint to cover the rust, and when we were done painting it looked beautiful tie-dyed in all those psychedelic colors. One of the girls painted love and peace on the sides. It was so cool. Anyway, we made it there, and all eight of us lived together for the next two years." Annette began smiling, thinking of those first years with Gilbert.

Agent Harris brought Annette back from her memories when he asked, "I remember hearing about that place. Wasn't that commune connected in some way to a scientist that was into ufology?"

"Yes, I believe you are right, he was interested in UFO's. We did a lot of star watching at night. Agent Harris, what part of the government did you say you worked for again? I don't remember your saying." Annette asked.

"The US Department of Defense, I work out of the defense department in Washington. So, this miracle you mentioned with your polio and your disability, how did that happen? I don't remember seeing anything in your file like a surgical procedure, and it looked like your mother didn't think you could manage getting very far, being in a wheelchair."

Annette finished her tea, "Are you really sure you want to know the whole story, Mr. Harris? Perhaps that's the real reason you are here. Am I right? Not here to just close out my old missing person case, but to investigate something else altogether, something maybe of the unexplained type. What do you think about ufology, Agent Harris? Is that subject of interest to you and your agency, or do you think it's just silly made-up stuff?"

Annette had just ignited Riley's interest, and he was most definitely open to hearing more of this type conversation. "I find ufology very interesting; to the point of having had an unbelievable experience myself. I would be most interested to hear anything you might have to tell me about any experience you have had in the past as well. Especially if you experienced an incredible event before you left Cass. Did you have something happen to you when you lived in Cass by any chance?"

Annette put her hand to the side of her forehead, *so her thinking was right, this was the real reason Agent Harris was here.* He must be working for the Central Intelligence Agency. She had heard rumors that the CIA investigated UFO sightings and interviewed abductees. Now she understood it to be true. "You have to understand, I've never spoken to anyone about this event ever in my entire life. I will tell you about it once, however, I will not repeat it to anyone from your office ever again. I don't want my husband to know this about this part of my life, or that this ever happened to me. Do you agree to my terms?"

"You have my word that no one will contact you, or your husband, after today. So, what happened to you in Cass?"

"My mother was gone for the morning, as I previously said, to see her attorney. I was home alone, I was bored in the house— no, I was distraught at what she had told me she was going to do with me. I wanted to die, to kill myself. But I didn't want my mother to find me right away, so I wheeled myself outside, headed towards the field, and from there the ground was still solid, so I just kept going across the field toward the pines. It took about twenty minutes for me to get across the field and another hundred yards or so to reach the pines. Mother would have never let me go that far from the house. I heard this soft, low horn type noise, so I started to turn my chair around, but it wouldn't budge. That's when I realized someone, or something, had hold of the handles on the back of my wheelchair, and they were pulling me backward into the forest. Pine needles were smacking me in the back of the head. I started yelling, but no one came to help me. My voice must not have carried very far. When they turned my chair around, I saw I was being pushed right up the ramp and straight into that silver spaceship. Once the door closed behind me, I knew there was no one coming to rescue me. I sure couldn't figure out how to get back out, even if I could have made it back to the door. There were no knobs or handles on the inside. In fact, the door just seemed to melt into the wall, becoming part of the wall. All the inner surfaces were completely smooth.

"That must have been terrifying for someone in your condition. What happened to you after that?" Riley couldn't wait to hear the rest.

"They took me down a small corridor into a room where they did exams, I think. Anyway, there were several aliens of various heights. I guess that's what I would call them aliens. They were all surrounding me. Most had on gray one-piece jumpsuits, but there were two of them who seemed to be doctors, maybe. They both had on white one-piece outfits. There was an exam table, but they didn't seem to want me on there. They started to undress me, and I tried to fight them, but it was useless with all those hands coming at me at once. It was terrifying. Somehow, they lifted me into the air, without even touching me, and they spoke to me, without speaking. I can't explain it any better than that. But I understood they had a gift — something to offer me — a cure they said, but also at a cost, and told me if I wanted it to just shake my head. So, I shook my head, not really understanding what I had agreed for them to do. I just didn't want them to kill me. Isn't that weird? Only just an hour before that I was rolling that chair across the field to kill myself, and here I was now, not wanting to die, at least not by them."

Annette got up, fixed another cup of tea for herself, and checked Riley's cup, which was still half full. "I was floated over to a tub of some sorts. I remember it being cream colored and formed in length long enough for me to lay completely flat inside. A hose connected to the tub and when the tall, thin alien female turned the knob, warm thick orange liquid began pouring in, covering my entire body. I was terrified that I was going to drown as these aliens watched me take my last breath. Maybe I did die, I don't know. The next thing I remember was being taken off their ship and pushed back to the outer edge of the forest. I heard one of them say not to tell what had happened to me inside of the ship, and that if I wanted to, I could just push that chair on wheels instead of sitting in it from now on. So, I stood up, said okay, and I pushed it as fast as I could run across the field. Once I got inside the house, I sat down in it again, and pretended I still could not walk. I was afraid to tell anyone what happened to me inside that spaceship. I also knew, I didn't want to pretend all my life that I couldn't walk. So, that is when I decided to make a plan to leave Cass and go to California." Annette put her hands on her lap and waited on the agent to respond.

"Wow! Thank you for your honesty with me, Annette. I believe everything you said. Look at you; no one would ever know you ever had polio. So, what did they take from you? You said something about them wanting to trade you a cure for something? What was it?"

Annette shrugged her shoulders, "I'm not sure; unless that was the real reason that I couldn't have babies of my own."

"Whoa, wait a minute, I thought you and your husband had three children?"

"Oh, I did say we had three wonderful children, but I didn't mention they were all adopted. To me, that part is not important. They are still mine. When we found out that I was barren, my ovaries had produced no eggs, so we decided to adopt."

Agent Harris put his hand to his mouth, "So, they traded you the ability to walk for your future offspring." *I wonder what they did with all those eggs*, he thought.

Before he left, Agent Harris thanked Annette for speaking with him, and again assured her their conversation would be kept confidential.

# Chapter 27

## Grandpa's Secret's

Once at the airport, Agent Harris decided to get a connecting flight with a layover in Scottsdale, Arizona. He very seldom got to see his mom, and he knew she would welcome a visit from him.

"Mom, you shouldn't have," were Riley's first words when she opened the door. He could smell fresh-baked chocolate chip cookies wafting down the front steps from the house.

Rosalind Harris stood on her tiptoes to kiss Riley on the cheek. "You just keep growing taller every time I see you, son."

"Mom, I haven't grown an inch in the past five years. I hate to break it to you, but you might be getting shorter." Laughing and feeling her love surrounding him like a soft warm blanket, Riley followed her into the kitchen.

"What, that's a terrible thing to say to your mother. Maybe I should just give these cookies to the neighbor kids," she said as she picked up the cookie plate.

Riley grabbed the glass plate from her hands, "Don't you dare. You know how much I love these cookies. I was just teasing you. So, what is that mean sister of mine up to?" Riley sat on the stool at the kitchen bar, looking at the cookie dish to determine which one might be the biggest before he chose his from the pile.

"Your sister is pregnant again, so you're going to have another nephew to buy Christmas gifts for this year. She swears this is the last one. Four kids are plenty enough for anyone, if you ask me. I'm glad they were able to buy your grandpa's house, since it has those extra bedrooms. It's nice to still have it in the family, too. Plus, she kept some of his stuff, so I didn't have to do too much over there."

"That all sounds good, Mom. I'm excited for her."

"Now that you have had a cookie, can I ask you if you are dating anyone yet?" She cringed a little after she said it.

Riley was quiet for a few minutes, "I still think it's too soon, Mom. I'm just not ready yet."

"Riley, Cheryl and the boys have been gone now coming up on three years. They are not coming back. It's time for you to find a nice woman and settle down. You know Cheryl would not want you grieving forever. It isn't your fault they're gone. It's the drunk driver that hit them, and you can't even take your anger out on that poor girl either, since she died, too. Why people have to drink, or text, and drive is beyond me. But I am just a short little woman from Arizona who loves her big tall son and wants him to be happy." Rosalind took a small cookie from the plate.

"I know you do, Mom. I promise I'll work on it before the year ends, okay?"

"That's good enough for me," Rosalind smiled, patting Riley on the shoulder before she left the room.

Riley walked over to the refrigerator to examine the new photos of Melinda's crew of two girls and two boys, all under the age of five. They looked like Melinda's husband, Scott. They had the same blonde hair, same brown eyes, and same big ears. Oh well, at least they were healthy, and the girls could hide their ears, if they wanted to, with longer hair when they got older.

Rosalind yelled from the living room, "Riley, bring your cookies in here. I have some stuff to show you that I found over to your grandpa's house."

Riley carried in the plate, along with his glass of milk, which he placed on the coaster his Mom quickly slid his way. In front of him were lots of photos, some with all the family and others were just of his grandma and grandpa. There was one photo of his grandpa when he was young in the middle of the pile.

"Look at this one, Riley," Rosalind picked up the one of just her dad. "I still can't get over how much you look like your grandpa. I swear, you two could have been twins if you had been born to the same mother.

"Yeah," Riley smiled, looking at the photo. "You're right. We sure do look a lot alike. So, these were all over to the old house?"

"Yep, I found most of them in the top of the bedroom closet. In fact, I almost missed them. But here is the thing I really wanted you to see. And I was so glad when you called today and said you were stopping by for a quick visit." Handing Riley an envelope she said, "Here, look at this. I want you to read this letter your grandpa wrote."

"Who did he write the letter too? Maybe it's personal. It feels a little weird to be reading it without his permission. You know how secretive Grandpa was about certain things."

Rosalind smacked her leg, "Riley, my son, you certainly hit the nail on the head with that one, it is a little weird, but not how you are meaning it to be. The letter was written by your grandpa and he wrote the letter to us, his family, but mostly to you. He had something he wanted all of us to know, but apparently not until after he was gone, which annoys me to no end that he got the last word."

Riley reached for the letter, "Okay, you have piqued my interest. Now give it to me, so I can decide for myself if it is weird or not." Riley read the letter from front to back. After that, he read it again, just to make sure he didn't miss anything in it the first time. "Jeez, just when I thought I knew the answer to who am I, Grandpa goes and changes the whole scenario with a one-page letter. Then just like that, he up and dies without getting to put our two cents in. What kind of crap is that anyway?"

Rosalind took the letter from him, "Exactly."

"Has, sis, read the letter yet?"

"Nope. I just started looking through this stuff today, right before you called me. She'll be over tomorrow; I'm watching the kids while she goes to her prenatal visit. I'll tell her about it after she gets back."

"Mom, you have to promise to call me and tell me what she says," Riley laughed. He glanced down at his watch, "It's time to get back to the airport, I can't miss my flight. Can I take this picture of Grandpa with me? I'd like to frame it."

"Of course, you can, son. Just give me a minute, and I will put some of those cookies in a little bag for you to eat on your flight back east."

Riley put the photo and the letter in his briefcase, along with the chocolate chip cookies and drove to the airport.

# Chapter 28

## Lucy McCallister, March 23, 2014

Lucy Chavez spent most nights lying on a wooden picnic table in the back yard. From this vantage point she could scan the whole sky, but not for planets, falling stars, or constellations like most people. No; she was looking for something else altogether. Tonight, marked the second anniversary of her newfound life and she wanted to share this heavenly view with her newborn daughter, Zarita. Lucy wrapped Zarita in a thick warm blanket once she was certain Antonio, her husband, was asleep, and then slipping quietly outdoors into the backyard. She curled up on the picnic table with her daughter, pointing to the starry sky spread out above them. "Zarita, you are the only one that your mother can tell her secrets to because you are a baby, and I know you can't tell." She kissed Zarita's tiny cheek and ran her fingers through her infant daughter's thick dark hair. "Two years ago, tonight your momma came from somewhere up there and landed here. We are not alone in this universe, Zarita, as some would like us to believe. Someday they may come back for me. I want both you and your dad to meet them, too. Maybe they will take us with them." She kissed her tiny daughter on the cheek again. Baby Zarita stretched her little arms and legs inside the woven blanket. Just waking, Zarita blinked several times before she opened her eyes to see the sky above her. Lucy carried Zarita back into the house, not wanting to keep her outside too long, she tucked Zarita in her warm soft bed.

Lucy crept over to the bed where her husband slept. Carefully, she slipped in next to him. Antonio rolled over, pulled her close to him, and whispered in her ear, "Lucy, have you been outside again?"

"How do you know I have been outside, Antonio? I thought you were asleep. I'm sorry I woke you."

Antonio sighed, "A soldier that has been in battle never truly sleeps once he is home. There are too many nightmares hidden inside my dreams. I try to keep them buried, but sometimes it is hard." Before she had a chance to comment, he changed the subject to something light, not wanting to talk about war. "Also, my wife, no matter how quiet you think you are, you always come back to bed with such cold feet." Antonio pulled her close to him, running his hand across her cheek before he kissed her.

Lucy giggled, moving her feet even closer to feel his warmth. "Someday our daughter will love the night sky as much as I do. Antonio, thank you again, for falling in love with me, and giving us such a beautiful child. She will have bunches of your beautiful black hair by this time next year." When he didn't answer, she assumed he had already drifted back to sleep. This was the first time Antonio mentioned he had nightmares about the war. He kept that part of his life to himself, and she never saw a reason to bring it up. But now that she lay there thinking about him, she wondered if some of the sadness she saw around his eyes when he thought no one was looking had to do with the terrible things he had seen. What had he been like before he was a soldier compared to his personality now? She couldn't really have a lengthy conversation with his mother, since she was still learning to speak Spanish and only knew enough of the language to get by. They understood how grateful she was for their hospitality though; she could see the love they showed her reflected in their eyes.

When his parents' old red truck stopped in the early morning, two years ago, they could hardly believe their eyes that a young girl her age would be walking alone. She remembered his mother saying that Lucy was *un regalodel cielo,* a gift from heaven. They had motioned for her to get in the back of their truck. Lucy remembered seeing a male in his mid-twenties, dressed in camouflage attire, asleep, and a duffel bag lay beside him, so she hesitated.

The short woman kept repeating, "*Mi hijo es un buen hombre*," encouraging her to climb on in, but no matter how loud the woman got, Lucy could not understand what she was saying.

Antonio sat up hearing all the commotion. "My mother is saying to hop up here in the back of the truck and not to worry. Her son is a good man." Smiling, he extended his hand to her, but she did not budge, "I am Antonio Chavez, and this is my family. You are all alone out here. It is not safe, too many wild things around here. Can we offer you a ride into town?" He reached for Lucy's hand again, and she accepted, not knowing where she was, but clearly, she could tell she was not in danger, and no longer in West Virginia. The language being spoken to her and the country's terrain were both so much different from what she had grown to know.

Once the truck started again, Antonio pulled out a long-sleeved shirt with Sgt. Chavez stamped on the pocket handing it to Lucy. "Here, put this on, it will help shield you from the cool morning air."

Besides realizing her dress was no longer torn from her uncle as she put the shirt on, she saw his last name, rank, and the letters *USA Marine Corp* stamped in black ink on the pocket. It must have been repaired when she was aboard the spaceship. "Can you tell me where we are going? I'm afraid I have lost my bearings." Lucy said, feeling as if she were yelling due to the noise of the truck tires on the highway.

"I am going home to my parents' house. I am on leave from the military; I just got back from Afghanistan a few days ago. This is New Mexico. My family lives just outside Roswell. Does that help you any, in recognizing where you are now?"

"Not really, I'm from the Midwest. I hitched a ride with some people, and when I woke up, I was here. I need to find a job and a place to stay."

"Don't worry. My family will give you a place to stay. It is just their nature to help others in need. You can take your time finding a job. Maybe we can both look together. I have sixty days to decide if I am going to reenlist. *Mi mamà*, of course, would like to have me here at home." Antonio looked at his parents sitting in the front of the truck. He had missed them, too.

"I seemed to have lost track of time being on the road. Is it still March of 2014, by any chance?" Lucy was worried about how long she had been gone. Was anyone looking for her? If they were, she didn't want to be found, not yet anyway.

Antonio looked at her with concern, "You should be more careful with who you accept rides from, it's dangerous for young women. I'm sure you have heard that before, right? It is March 31, 2014, have you been gone long from your home?"

Lucy looked away, not wanting to tell him a bold-faced lie, knowing now she had disappeared seven days ago, "Only a few days. I guess I got here faster than I originally thought I would." Lucy watched the sunrise over the desert as colors of orange, red, yellow, and green flowering cactus dotted the backdrop of the mountain range. Lucy wondered, *Eight days. Where have I been? Why can't I remember?* She already knew the answer to who she had been with, well sort of anyway.

Antonio was five years older than her when they first met. He was a hard worker, a good provider, and she knew he loved her and would protect her with his last breath. Lucy closed her eyes, but she knew she would not sleep no matter how hard she tried. It was well after midnight, so it was now March 20, 2016. The anniversary date of her abduction March 23rd was getting closer.

***

Morning light filtered through the thin lace curtain of the bedroom window. Lucy could hear Antonio packing things he would need to take with him on his new assignment at Kirtland Air Force Base, where he was to begin teaching special forces classes. He told Lucy the project he was working on would probably take a month. He hated being gone from Lucy and Zarita for that long, but at least he was here in the country most of the time and not stationed overseas like before they had Zarita.

Lucy looked at herself in the bathroom mirror. Maybe green highlights weren't the best idea she had ever had for her hair, but where she worked the tourists seemed to enjoy interacting with her as being a part of the oddities on display, and she enjoyed talking about aliens. She raised her arm again, looking at her right breast in the mirror. She didn't even need to feel for the lump. It was prominently there, calling out to her for attention. Lucy understood now how her own mother felt when she first found out she had the Big C, cancer. She couldn't think of it in any other terms yet, except she was definitely planning to kick its butt. After her appointment this morning she would know more, but by that time Antonio would be gone, and there was no way she was telling him this before he left. There would be plenty of time to talk to Antonio about her diagnosis once he returned, and she would know more, and have a plan. No way was she leaving this world without him or Zarita. Lucy quickly dressed then went to prepare their last breakfast together before her husband left.

***

Antonio, dressed in civilian clothes for his first meeting of the day, carried Zarita out to the car and placed her securely in her child car seat, planning to drop her off at the day care center on his way.

Lucy leaned inside the car for one last hug and kiss from Zarita, who was holding out her arms to Lucy. Looking at her smiling dark-brown eyed four-year-old, Lucy couldn't help but feel how just one smile from Zarita could warm her heart so much. After their final goodbye for the day, Lucy handed Zarita her little stuffed giraffe before closing the car door.

Antonio put his things in the trunk, along with Zarita's diaper bag and snacks. He kissed Lucy one more time. Looking into her eyes smiling he said, "I miss you already. Stop looking so sad. I will be back in a month. I promise. When I return, let's start looking for a bigger house." He winked, "You know Zarita would like a little brother or sister to play with."

Lucy half smiled, hugged him with all her strength, and then quickly turned before he could see the worry set upon her face. She walked up the steps, closing the door behind her. There were so many unanswered questions in her life this morning. The only thing she knew to do was to put one foot in front of the other, and get ready for what was coming at her next.

***

Sitting on the exam table, Lucy heard the oncologist say, "Breast cancer." His words echoed through her head. He handed her a paper with information about chemotherapy treatment for her to read at home later. She could call him with her decision, but he also told her not to take too long.

Lucy slowly walked to the car. Still stunned, she sat there for ten minutes before realizing she had not left the parking lot. If only Antonio were there; she knew what he would say so she looked in the rearview mirror at herself. "Get a grip. You have been through a lot, and you will get through this, too. Keep moving forward. Never look back." Lucy laughed hysterically at the irony of it all as she backed out of the parking space. As manager of the museum, work was waiting, and since she had the only key, her coworker would be waiting for her to unlock the door so their day of tourist entertainment could begin.

# Chapter 29

## Lucy McCallister Investigation, March 20, 2020, Roswell, New Mexico

Arriving at the Roswell International Air Center, Agent Vic Foster hailed a cab, "114 North Main Street."

The driver clicked the taxi meter prior to pulling away from the curb, thinking most of his fares wanted to go to their hotel first before hitting the popular sights in the area. "First time to area? Staying long?" He liked having conversations with his passengers.

"Hasn't everyone been to Roswell one time or another?" Vic wasn't in the mood to give out information. His assignment was to gather it from others.

The driver nodded in the mirror, "*Si, señor.* Some days it seems like it is very busy for me."

Vic pulled up his laptop computer again, reviewing the information on the missing person he was there to find and interview. According to the information from the local law enforcement in Cass, they seemed to think she was dead. They had searched the woods, under old brush, and down a couple abandoned wells, but her body was never found. The only person found dead on the farm the day she went missing was a man listed as Justice P. McCallister, age forty-eight, who was found in a field face down in the dirt. His death photo was ghastly; with open mouth, no eyes, just sockets, and parts of his body completely gone, from animals who had claimed him during the night. After DNA identification was completed, it was filtered through the database and four rape victims' reports were matched to the dead man's DNA. Vic attached this evidence to the side of the profile of the missing female he was working on, in case it was pertinent later. Finding this evidence made Vic a little less sympathetic toward Mr. McCallister's demise and grotesque crime photo.

The cab pulled into the side parking lot of the International UFO Museum and Research Center. The large stucco structure was painted cream in color with a silver metal spaceship mounted over the entrance. A large cutout figure of a green alien had been erected in front of the building, for visitors to stand behind to get their own alien photo taken. Once inside the museum, Agent Foster noticed a woman pointing out a sign to the three children she had with her, it read, "Caution! Unattended children might be taken by the next passing UFO." She apparently was pointing out the museum rules. Vic got in line behind them to wait while she finished her transaction, purchasing tickets for the next guided tour.

Behind the ticket counter an office the door was partly ajar, and he could see a young woman talking on the phone. She had long brown hair with thick highlights of dark green mixed through. When it was his turn at the counter he said, "I don't want a ticket. I was wondering if Lucy is working today?" The older woman turned toward the half open door, "Lucy, there's a customer out here to see you. She'll be out in a minute. Please wait over there," pointing toward a silver metallic spaceship suspended overhead. "Next."

Agent Foster stepped out of line and walked toward the exhibit, hoping he didn't have to wait too long. He was reading an article about owners of the Wilmont Hardware Store, who claimed to have seen a spacecraft, when a female voice interrupted his thoughts.

"What can I help you with?"

"Are you Lucy McCallister, from Cass, West Virginia?" Agent Foster quietly inquired.

Lucy stepped back, creating distance between them. Her pulse quickened, and she could feel a lump starting to form in her throat, "And you are?"

Agent Foster pulled out his card, placing it firmly in her hand, "Is there somewhere private that we can talk for a few minutes?"

Lucy looked around, feeling a little dizzy, "In my office, I guess." She slowly walked behind the counter. Agent Foster followed her and closed the door behind them. Lucy leaned against the desk not sure what to say.

"Why don't we have a seat, Ms. McCallister, so we can talk," Vic could tell by the way she was standing that she was ready to bolt out the door. He didn't want her to make a scene.

Lucy walked over to her chair, holding onto the back of it; she hadn't decided if she wanted to sit or not. "I'm not going back there, if that is what you are here for, to take me back after all this time. Look, she held out her left hand, "I'm married, now. I'm not a McCallister anymore. My last name is Chavez. No one can make me go back to that place. Besides that, I'm of age now and can make my own decisions."

"Have a seat, Mrs. Lucy Chavez; I am not here to take you back. I'm investigating cold missing persons cases; clearing them off the docket, and am pleased to see you are no longer missing, and are still alive. I do have a few questions for you, as part of my job with the government, just so I can close your case."

Lucy rolled out the chair and sat down, motioning for Agent Foster to sit down, too. "It's been five years since I left home." She smirked, *Home,* she thought. *How could I even refer to that place as home? Wasn't home a place of safety*? Lucy sat in silence. Of all things to happen to her on a day like today, this was the last thing she could have imagined.

"I know for some young people, sometimes homes aren't true homes. They are just places that happened to be born. Is that how it was there for you? Is that why you left when you were sixteen? Did something happen to you to you to make you want to leave? What brought you way out here?" Agent Foster asked Lucy multiple questions, hoping one would hit the right button for her to answer. He waited in silence for her reply. Noticing her hands were trembling, he excused himself from the room, returning in seconds with two cold bottles of Coke. He opened one and set it in front of Lucy.

She raised her head, allowing her blue eyes to meet his, "Thank you. Have you ever had a day that just keeps getting worse by the second?" Taking along drink, she set it down on a rubber coaster on the desk. She didn't really expect an answer. "You're right about some homes not being loving homes. That's how I saw Cass the day I left. You know how teenagers are, they can't wait to be their own boss. My mom started getting sick when I was around eleven. I took over most of the household duties so she could concentrate on getting well, but that never happened. I am truly at home here. My husband, Antonio, and my three-year-old daughter, Zarita, together, they are my real home." Lucy took another drink of the cold soda. "I have never told my husband how I got here. Some of it he would understand because he has had a very hard life growing up. But some of it he would just think I was telling a lie. Either way, he loves and respects me, and that is how I want to keep my life with him."

"Lucy, I want to know everything that happened to you on March 23, 2014, when you disappeared. Whatever you tell me will be kept confidential. He doesn't even need to know that I was here today, unless you decide on your own to tell him."

She picked up a paperclip, tapping the end on the desk. "Okay, I guess it won't hurt to tell someone besides Zarita if it stays confidential. I just don't want to be hounded by news coverage that Lucy McCallister has finally been found, or some crazy magazine wanting to splash my picture on the cover like they do when other people are found from kidnappings and such. That's not what happened, and I just couldn't handle the craziness of it seriously." Lucy held up her hand, "Before we go on, you need to know I was not kidnapped. That's not what happened to me back then. I also didn't just wake up one morning and decide I was running away. It's a little more complicated than that, and maybe not even believable by some. Overall, my parents were very good to me. I found myself here and things started working out. One day, soon after I arrived, I was at the library looking at want ads on the computer and found myself curious to see what was said about me in the paper back home. That's when I found out my parents didn't make it back home from Mom's appointment. Something must have distracted Dad. Maybe Mom was sick in the car, who knows. Anyway, I saw they got hit by that train and they were gone. I was better off being here, around people who seemed to care, and did not pressure me with questions. That's what I needed during that time — unconditional love, and I found a family who gave that to me."

"Okay, I wondered if you were aware of your parents' fate. I'm sorry for your loss of them. I'm very interested in hearing your story." Agent Foster opened his laptop, pulled up Lucy McCallister's file, and entered the time and date. Looking up, he encouraged her to begin. As she told her account of the events on March 23rd, he took notes.

"Well, as you mentioned before, it was March 23, 2014. My parents had gone to Lewisburg. My mom was scheduled to see an oncologist early the next morning, so she could start another round of chemotherapy. Dad didn't want the trip to be exhausting for her, so they planned to spend the night in a local motel. I was home by myself, which was fine. It was just a boring Sunday afternoon— until he showed up and ruined everything." Lucy's voice trailed off, thinking of that day.

"Who showed up, Lucy?" Agent Foster knew from the file, but wanted to hear it from her.

Lucy pulled her hair back and began loosely braiding it down one side. "My dad's younger brother, my sleezy uncle, Justice McCallister. I always thought he was sort of creepy. Even his own daughter warned me not to be alone with him. Can you imagine that? His own daughter. She didn't say why at the time. Now, I think she was probably too scared or embarrassed to say, but wanted to alert me just enough to put that idea of *creepy* inside my head." Lucy walked over to the door and listened. She could hear talking outside at the counter, so she knew her coworker was not eavesdropping on their conversation.

Agent Foster added, 'Justice McCallister, Cass, West Virginia', to the computer file noting his death date as March 23, 2014. He pulled that information over into Lucy's file, since she also mentioned him as being on the property. *He died the same day as she went missing. There seemed, from her conversation about him so far, a definite connection between the two.* "So, Justice McCallister showed up at the house and you were alone. Did you let him in the house, or what happened next?"

"He let himself in the house. He was one of those types of people who never knocks, wherever he goes. He just assumed he was always welcome, and had no reason to believe my dad was not at home."

"Or possibly, he knew you might be there by yourself, and thought he would take advantage of the situation. You never know. Sometimes things happen just that way."

"True. Dad always kept his truck parked in the big barn, so his brother wouldn't know it wasn't there. Dad could have even asked him to come over and check in on me. Anyway, I had just gotten back from mid-morning church, and had not changed yet into my work jeans. I had chores that Dad left for me to do on the farm, but when he showed up, I had to wait to go get changed. He asked me where dad was, so I told him and turned to leave the room. That's when he grabbed me by my wrist. I lost my balance and he pulled me down on his lap. His gross disgusting hands were everywhere within seconds. I grabbed his forearm and bit him so hard blood squirted everywhere. He yelped, jumping up and throwing me off his lap. Then, he decided he was going to hit me. 'To put me in my place,' were his words. It gave me a chance to run. I made it down the hall, to the kitchen. My heart was beating clear out of my chest. I was so terrified of him my body literally shook, and it was hard to breathe. We made several circles around the kitchen table, with him getting closer with every step. He was getting tired of that game I could tell, and I saw he was planning to just throw that table to the side. His adrenaline must have been on over drive. I bolted out the door, but he caught it before it slammed shut so I knew he was only just a few steps behind me. I frantically started running across the east field, hoping to gain some headway. I wasn't sure where to go, or where to hide with him so close behind me. He kept yelling for me to stop, saying he didn't mean it, wouldn't hurt me for anything. No need to be afraid. No need to tell since he was just teasing me. I knew he was trying to come up with any lie he could to get me to slow down and wanting to trust him, to forgive him for scaring me the way he did. If I didn't rely on my fight or flight instinct, it would have given him just enough leverage to catch me." Lucy stopped talking. Her whole body was trembling from the thought of what he could have done next. She was certain he could not have left her alive after what would have happened next. He would have crushed her skull right there in that field, right after he raped her. She dabbed at tears forming at the corners of her eyes, trying to make the tears stop that had wanted to flow for years, to acknowledge what had happened to her. Now they refused to be buried. She couldn't hide them anymore.

Agent Foster took a deep breath and rubbed his chin not knowing what to do to make Lucy feel better. He handed her a white tissue from the box on her desk to wipe her eyes, and gently, he reached over to touch her hand. Lucy held on tight to his hand, trying to pull herself back together and calm her emotional state.

"Just take your time, Lucy, it's okay. He can't hurt you anymore."

Lucy was relieved Agent Foster was not pushing her just to get his information. Closing her eyes, she took several deep breaths. Blowing air out of her lungs through pursed lips, she could feel herself becoming less anxious. Her head still down, she said in a muffled voice, "That's when I saw it. The flying saucer, it was close up against the tree line, and three of the aliens were coming down a ramp from the ship." She raised her eyes to look at Agent Foster for his reaction. Would he believe her or think she was now avoiding the truth and was telling him a lie, but he was stone-faced, so she continued. "Surprised by the closeness of being caught or seen, they looked up when they heard my screams and recognized I wasn't running away terrified but straight toward them. I bumped into a tall thin alien just inside the craft, and it held me in its arms. I remember just begging over and over help me. When I looked back toward my uncle, he had stopped running. You should have seen the shock on his face. Seeing those aliens was not what he had expected that day."

"So, what happened next? Did he get in some kind of fight with them, or try to get you off the space craft?"

"No, one of the aliens outside pulled out some type of weapon, pointing it at Justice as a warning. They could sense from my reactions he was a definite threat. The weapon didn't shoot bullets. It wasn't a gun like we have. It looked like a bolt of lightning, maybe. It just came from its hand. I'm a little confused on that part, since it all happened so fast. Anyway, that bolt hit Justice straight in the heart. It knocked him up in the air a couple feet. I saw his body slam, forcefully, face first into the dirt. He never got back up. I was happy he was dead. I hugged every alien I could find on that ship. They saved my life that day. While the ones outside finished gathering whatever they were looking for from the farm, I waited by the door just to make sure he was dead. I hate to say this part because it makes me look bad, but I think they may have taken his eyes when they were finished gathering specimens. I didn't care. They could have done whatever they wanted to him, and I honestly would not have cared."

Agent Foster smacked the desk, making Lucy jump in her seat. "That's awesome, and you never told anyone? I see here that the autopsy on Justice McCallister appeared to be a heart attack. He had several animal bites, too, before he happened to be found the next evening. The coroner said his eyes were missing, but seemed to think that was just from animals. So, what happened after that? How did you manage to make your way clear out here?"

"My dress of course, had been torn by Uncle Justice when we were in the house. I remember trying to fix it, still crying over what had just happened with him chasing me. One of the aliens dressed in white, I think might have been a doctor, or maybe not. I just associate that color with the medical field. It took me back to one of the cabins and handed me a container with grey liquid in it, and encouraged me to drink it all. I did, and the next thing I knew, I was standing out on Clovis Highway just outside of town here. It was early morning; I just started walking and a Spanish speaking couple in a red pickup truck stopped to offer me a ride. I had no idea what they were saying. The woman kept trying to get me in the truck. When I wouldn't get in, her son woke up. Realizing what she was trying to do, he introduced me to them and himself. It was Antonio, the man I am married to now. He was just returning from Afghanistan."

"So, you stayed here and never went back. You have that big farm just waiting for you. Why not go back and claim it?"

"At first, I was hoping the aliens would come back for me. They kept me for seven days. I still look for them at night sometimes. I just wonder why, of all places, did they choose to drop me off here. I keep waiting to see if they will remember and come back for me. I want the three of us to go with them to wherever they are out there. Some people fear aliens. You know how they portray them sometimes in movies, but they are different from us, so peaceful, so much more than the so-called human race that we know. That's the only way I can explain my time with them."

"How many would you say were on the spacecraft that you were on?"

"I believe around eight or ten in all. I only remember bits and pieces of what went on, but I remember I was never afraid. They have a direct purpose for studying us, and it felt like they were light years ahead of us here on Earth, so it makes me wonder even, why they bother coming here. I am glad they saved me that day. I hope they can save me one more time."

"Are you in need of saving? Is there something else you want to talk about while I am here related to your safety?"

Lucy shook her head, "I'm not worried about my safety. It's something else that only a doctor can help me with. I'll be fine. It's just been a stressful morning all around." She tried to smile so he would not question her further.

"Well, I wish you luck with your health issue and want to thank you for your time today, Lucy. I appreciate your honesty and am glad to have been the agent to interview you."

"You must have met them, too, since you have accepted and not questioned what I had to say." Before he could, or would, answer her question, Lucy's cell phone rang. She noticed it was the daycare. She raised her hand, "Don't leave yet. I need to take this call. My daughter is at this daycare. I will walk you out. Hello, this is Lucy. Is something wrong with Zarita? What do you mean she didn't get dropped off? Antonio was on his way there with her this morning, Darla. What! Do you think they got caught up in that raid? So other children are missing too? Oh my God, this can't be happening! How can this be happening today?" Lucy laid her phone on the desk, put her hands over her face, and cried. Then frantically, she was on her feet. "I have to go. I have to go right now and try to find my husband and daughter. I think they have been accidently taken by ICE, the Immigration and Customs Enforcement, to a detention center, probably over in Otero. Antonio was dressed in civilian clothes when he left the house this morning, and he is a DREAMer. He was born in San Pedro Sula, Honduras, and his parents brought him here when he was two years old. They have already been deported. We haven't heard from them in over a year. My husband is a United States serviceman and a teacher at Kirtland Air Force Base. It could be days or months before he is processed and either shipped back to Honduras, or released, and what about my baby, Zarita? She is a US citizen. She is only four years old, just a toddler. I can't lose them. They are all I have left in my life. Please, help me get them back, Agent Foster, please!

Agent Foster grabbed his laptop and briefcase. "Do you know where this detention facility is and how to get us there?"

"Yes."

"Let's go. Can we take your car? I will drive." They ran from the museum without telling her coworker what was going on. They didn't have to, since Lucy bumped her with the door on their way out. She knew Maria had been listening after all.

# Chapter 30

## Earth's Humans

At the Otero Detention Center, Agent Foster convinced Lucy to wait for him in the car. He was concerned she would become hysterical and then she might get arrested, making things even more complicated than they already were. After showing his identification, Agent Foster was taken to the director's office to wait. On the way there, he saw lines of Hispanic males, females, and children standing with zip-tied hand cuffs waiting to be processed. A van drove up, and twenty more detainees moved to the back of the line. The sun was high in the sky and the day was more than just warm. From a distance you could see the heat rising from the hot pavement.

"How long are these people supposed to stand in the hot sun, waiting to get processed, before they are offered water or a place to sit down?"

"As long as it takes. They're illegals. They're used to standing in the hot sun," said the guard firmly.

"Some may be used to working in the hot sun, like construction workers here, but not standing on hot pavement with no water being offered to them, or a place to sit in the shade for a break. They could easily have a heat stroke, dehydration, or even go into acute kidney failure without water. What about food? Shouldn't they be given some type of protein snack in case some of them are diabetic or have other health conditions? Would you want your children or nieces and nephews standing out there with no water? What about your dog, if you leave it outside tied up and no water? You could be looking at severe dehydration or even death." They had reached the office at this point, so Vic had to yell after the guard, who by that time had walked away shaking his head. "Hey, just so you know, not every human being standing out there in that line is a hardened criminal. In fact, I bet none of them are criminals. They are humans just like you. They are Christians just like you. Show some humanity."

The Director was sitting at his desk talking on the phone. He motioned for Vic to take a seat. Agent Vic Foster slid his government identification across the desk, and the director ended his call abruptly.

"What can I do for you, Agent Foster? As you can see, we are quite busy today processing this new round up of illegals?"

"The raid you ran this morning in Roswell accidently picked up an American child and a military instructor at Kirtland Air Force Base in civilian clothes, and he is needed at work. He is heading a special project that can't be started without him. His wife is an American citizen. Their child was taken as well. I need them released to me now," Vic waited for an answer.

"Agent Foster, there are several hundred detainees waiting to be processed. I really don't know what I can do to find one Hispanic man and one little girl that probably looks Hispanic like her daddy. Unfortunately, there is nothing I can do. If he is a DREAMer he will be processed just like everyone else. Those are the rules. I am sure once this is done the child will be returned in the coming weeks."

"How can you be certain the child might not get lost in the system, or sent to another state? I am not leaving here without them. That little girl's mother is right outside in the parking lot, waiting to take her family home. What should I tell her? Your practices here are unacceptable. These people are not animals; they are human beings just like you and me. They get up every day and try to make a living for their families. They came here to seek a better life, to keep from starving in their own countries. Some of them are seeking protection from being raped, killed, or forced into the sex slave business. Now I understand why the German people turned a blind eye on the extinction of the Jews during the Hitler era. They were told the Jews were mean, nasty, and taking jobs from the Germans. So, the Germans decided it was okay to round up the Jews strip them naked, torture them, gas them, and throw their bodies in mass graves. All I can say is shame on my government. America should be better than this... You should be ashamed of what you are doing here. at least offer your captives water, food, a bathroom, and shade before you steal their children from them." Vic knew he had overstepped his bounds, and he would get nowhere with this guy on his own.

"Agent Foster, I have told you there is nothing I can do. Now I have a very busy day in front of me, so I will need you to leave now. Please leave the premises, or I will have to have you arrested."

Vic stood up, "I will leave your office, but we are not done here by a long shot. We, — you and I, will be speaking again very soon. I can promise you that." Vic returned to the car in a huff.

As soon as Lucy saw him without her husband and child, she got out of the car screaming hysterically and ran toward the line of detainees, frantically searching their exhausted faces for her family. "Antonio, Zarita, where are you? I am here for you. I am here to take you home."

Vic quickly grabbed Lucy, dragging her back toward the car, "Listen, I need you to calm down; this is not over. Do you hear me? This is not over. We are not leaving here without them. You need to trust me, okay? I need you to calm down so I can make a very important call."

Lucy tried to calm herself, still whimpering; Vic could see her fingers tremble. He was worried she might go into shock from all the stress. He put her in the car and turned the air conditioning on high, letting the air hit her face.

"Jesse, I am here at the Otero Detention Center with Lucy McCallister. She was taken and returned from alien abduction, and has a very interesting story. Her husband and four-year-old daughter have been arrested in a raid. He is an instructor at Kirtland Air Force Base; I tried to get them out, but the director here is throwing his weight around. Can you make a call? I cannot and will not leave here without them."

"Yes, I will call General Kearns right now. Just stay there at the detention center and try not to make any trouble. I will get back to you soon."

"Jesse, I may have said a few angry things to the director, comparing him to a Nazi working at the Jewish concentration camps, but you should see the inhumane things they are doing down here; it's shameful."

"Just let me handle it here on out; don't say any more to them. I'm serious, Vic."

Thirty minutes later, Antonio walked down the front steps of the facility. He was carrying Zarita. He had no idea what was going on. he only knew that he was told to take his daughter and get out. They were met by a smiling Agent Foster and Lucy.

"I don't know how you managed to get us out of there, but thank you."

Lucy spoke up, "Antonio, there are many things we have not talked about since your family found me on the road that morning. I think this is the time we need to talk about what really happened to me." Vic was driving them all back to Roswell as Lucy started telling Antonio her story. "I have a farm in Cass, West Virginia that I would like to take you to see. I also need to tell you I had to go see an oncologist this morning. I need to be treated for breast cancer. I was going to tell you when you got back so you wouldn't worry about me while you were gone."

Antonio kissed Lucy's cheek, "Please promise me you will not keep secrets, I can't help you otherwise. I am not leaving you while you are getting this treatment."

Agent Foster looked at Lucy in the rearview mirror and their eyes met. Now he had the whole picture of this amazing, strong young woman.

"Agent Foster, I wonder if there are any seats left on that flight you are going to be on tonight. If so, maybe we could meet you at the airport?"

He pulled over at the next exit, opened his computer entered some codes and then smiled. "It looks like three seats right in front of me just opened up. Can you be ready by six?"

"Absolutely. I want my family as far away from that ICE detention center as I can get them today. Hopefully they will be safe on my farm in Cass."

"I will have Jesse contact General Kearns, and he will handle Antonio's absence from Kirtland."

"Thank you for doing this for us today. Somehow, my Lucy always has an angel around when she most needs one," said Antonio.

Vic laughed. That was the first time he had been referenced as an angel. "Most of those people don't belong back there in that line, being mistreated like that, I wish we could have had all those families released."

"I know."

"Today, I could only help you and your daughter. The government needs to find better, more humane ways to process and treat humans coming to America."

*\*\**

At three a. m. they landed safely at the Greenbrier Valley Airport in West Virginia. From there Agent Foster drove them to their farm in Cass. "You will hear from me again this week. Don't go getting yourselves arrested in the meantime."

# Chapter 31

## Reports, Details and Accounts of All of the Missing, March 22, 2020

"I've brought you all back in to the office today, since I feel our time is running out, not just in finding the missing women, their families, and helping us make sense of the details you have uncovered, but several things have occurred here at the facility, which are very ominous to say the least. I will have each of you here present your cases. As each agent ends their part of the investigation, Doctor Meskins and Doctor Armstrong will discuss their findings, and then I have several things I need to add. I am sure that I don't need to stress how top secret our discussion is today. Some of our jobs, perhaps all of them in fact, could be on the line when I am finished. Do you understand?" Special Agent in Charge Jesse Finch looked out at the small crowd seated in the meeting room as each one nodded in understanding of the seriousness of their work.

"Agent Foster, you are up first please; bring your information to the front to present to the group. Also, let me remind everyone else to wait until the agent has completed his thoughts on the specific case prior to asking any questions. Agent Vic Foster, take us through what you have found." Special Agent in Charge Finch took a chair in the back of the meeting room so he could observe along with the rest of the staff.

"Good morning, everyone. The first case I am presenting is that of missing female Eve Wells. She was born deaf-mute. Most of the information I obtained about her was through her younger cousin, Stan. Her grandfather, Walter Imel, had an active moonshine business and her grandmother, May Imel, sporadically performed illegal abortions, some of her 'patients' died there on the farm. Mr. Stan Imel, her cousin, reported to me that he saw a grave being dug late one night on the property. Doctor Meskins and her forensic team recovered the bodies of Joan Dickins, Elizabeth Markley, Penny Jean Hatley, Eve Wells, and Thomas Bane. Jim Wells confessed to the brutal murder and dismemberment of Thomas Bane. He believed Mr. Thomas Bane raped his daughter, Eve. It is believed Miss Eve Wells hemorrhaged, and subsequently died, from a botched abortion. Mr. Jim Wells has been arrested for murder and abuse of a corpse for the death of Mr. Thomas Bane." Agent Vic Foster looked at Jesse to see if he had any further questions before he moved on to his next case.

To Agent Vic Foster's surprise, Doctor Sara Meskins stepped forward as she gave him a "why did you not return my call" look. Vic flushed, sitting down, giving her the floor. "Through extensive DNA testing we were able to identify all the missing women; they were all from the Cass area. We have returned all the remains back to the families for proper burial. "There is one piece of evidence that I have, which I am sure you will all find very interesting. The fetal remains were not completely removed from Miss Eve Wells. We checked the DNA against Mr. Thomas Bane, and it was not a match. The young man in question did not impregnate Miss Eve Wells. We did, however, find a match by utilizing Lucia's extensive data base in our search. It was a 99.9% match to the DNA we have here in the lab, which was taken from the aliens that are in storage from the Roswell incident. So, it appears Miss Eve Wells was involved in an encounter of the fourth kind, and apparently impregnated by an alien, then either returned or somehow escaped." Sara glared at Vic before she took her seat. Vic now understood why Sara had attempted to reach him. He was sorry he had not taken time to even listen to her voice mail.

Vic took the floor again, "Lucy McCallister went missing from a farm in Cass on March 23, 2014. During our interview at the Roswell Museum in Roswell, New Mexico, she reported her uncle, Justice McCallister, was attempting to sexually molest her when she was rescued by aliens. They killed Mr. Justice McCallister before leaving the area, taking Miss McCallister. She reported they also took Mr. Justice McCallister's eyeballs with them, but didn't say why or what they did with them once on board the ship. Miss Lucy McCallister stated, seven days later she found herself wandering along a deserted stretch of highway, in the early morning hours, just outside the town of Roswell. I was able to match her uncle's DNA to four female rape victims in the surrounding Cass area. I believe with hypnosis she could most definitely tell us more of what happened aboard the ship in the seven days she was with them. I was unable to get any more information from her the day of the interview, due to an emergency involving her spouse and child. She is married to a DREAMer, Mr. Antonio Chavez. He and their four-year-old daughter were arrested in an ICE raid and transported to Otero by Immigrations and Customs Enforcement for detainment. Mr. Antonio Chavez was born in Honduras and is a United States Marine Special Forces instructor at Kirkland Airforce Base. I accompanied Mrs. Chavez to the detention center in attempt seek the release of her husband and daughter, but was unsuccessful and had to call Jesse so he could enlist General Kearns' services and intervene on their behalf. They were released. She has had a fourth kind encounter. She was just diagnosed with breast cancer and is supposed to begin treatment very soon." Vic sat down, waiting on questions or Jesse's response.

Special Agent Jesse Finch stood up. "I would like to say well done. General Kearns on the other hand is not happy, due to someone from the detention center complaining that the CIA was there demanding that a detainee and a child be released into their custody, comparing the facility and them to Nazi concentration camps. The President is nosing around, wanting to know why the CIA is getting involved with ICE detainees. The General is trying to come up with a cover story, but mumbled under his breath to me that it might just be time to finally shut the whole alien thing down."

"What? He can't be serious. We're finally getting somewhere after all these years. What did he say exactly that is worrisome to you? Should I go to him myself and explain the situation I was in?"

Jesse raised his hand, "Please don't say anything, and that goes for everyone in this room. I am not sure how much we can even trust General Kearns with the information we have. He also mentioned that we may have to quietly just make the women that were brought back on the spacecraft just quietly disappear. Saying, 'After all, they're already missing and assumed dead, according to the rest of the world.' Only a small few of us in the government know otherwise. Listen up; we could all find ourselves reassigned anytime General Kearns feels it is for the good of the country. In the meantime, Agent Riley Harris, can you give us briefings on what you have discovered with the missing women you were assigned to investigate."

Agent Riley Harris greeted the group as he laid the files in front of him on the desk, "Good morning. Miss Molly Lehman went missing from Cass on March 23, 1981. I wasn't unable to find a direct relative to interview about her, due to her parents both having died in a domestic violence episode when she was young. She was raised by her cousin Eddie Lehman, who was an undercover operative, however, he unfortunately died early during the initial AIDS epidemic, but not before he was awarded the Distinguished Intelligence Cross. I was able to interview her neighbor, Mrs. Tara Winston, and she walked me through the Lehman house, which is just right next to her home. In doing the latter, I found a treasure trove of information and a multi-faceted young woman. I believe Miss Lehman just happened to be in the wrong place at the wrong time. She was not a native of Cass. She went to Cass that weekend to accomplish several things. First, she promised Eddie before he died that she would bury his ashes. The second part of the trip, she was to meet up with a college professor whom she had been seeing. I believe she was using him as part of her project for her dissertation toward a doctorate in human sexuality and was planning to follow in Eddie's footsteps with joining the Central Intelligence Agency. She was putting herself through college by writing romance novels under the pen name of Miranda Hawkins. Somehow, she was surprised at her camp in the wilderness, and taken hostage by the same two perpetrators who, by happenstance, had murdered her professor boyfriend the same morning. The information came from Daniel Monroe, one of the convicts now serving time for her abduction and murder. He reported they were close to catching up to her, just outside the cabin, when a light flashed above the house. When he and his accomplice entered the property in pursuit, she was nowhere to be found. Monroe referenced the word 'alien abduction' on the interview tape, which I deleted, before I passed it on to the warden. The two convicts are being charged with the professor's murder. This will help close another cold murder case, and missing person case in Pennsylvania. The convicts, in this case, are classified as having an encounter of the second kind. I am happy not to interview them anymore, and to just let them rot where they are. I believe the cabin Miss Molly Lehman was taken from by the aliens once belonged to both Mrs. Rose Jackson and Miss Jacqueline Kaleta after looking at the property maps for Cass. Miss Molly Lehman most definitely experienced an encounter of the fourth kind."

"Yes, Agent Harris, I think you are correct about the cabin involved it changed many hands over the years before it was made into weekend getaway cabins. I wonder if there is a pattern of abduction surrounding that particular place, as well as the nearby area. Very interesting insight, indeed. Please proceed with your next interview," commented Special Agent in Charge Jesse Finch.

"Thank you, sir. From there, I flew out to San Diego, California to interview Miss Annette Young. She is also a fourth kind encounter and a very interesting case. Annette contracted polio when she was seven, spending most of her childhood in bed. As she grew older, she remained wheelchair bound. On March 23, 1967 she planned to commit suicide in the woods. Instead she was taken aboard a spacecraft and they offered her— 'a gift with a cost' is how she put their statement to her. They immersed her in some type of orange tinted, thick liquid. When she awoke, she found she was able to walk. From there she decided she would just run away, not knowing how she would explain her miracle in a way that people would believe her. She hitchhiked to California. She is now married and owns a hippie boutique in downtown San Diego."

"So, I'm curious. You told us what the gift was. What was the cost?" asked Doctor Sara Meskins.

"Good question. She said they took all of her eggs from her ovaries. She is barren."

"That is very interesting, indeed," Jesse said, looking at Doctor Charity Armstrong. "Thank you, Agent Harris. Before we have Agent Bilodeau present his findings, does anyone have any other questions?" Looking around the room no one raised their hand. "Okay, please proceed, Agent Bilodeau."

"Miss Jacqueline Kaleta was a fifth-grade science teacher at Cass Elementary. She went missing on March 23, 1961 when she and another teacher were out walking in the woods close to her home. Miss Greta Daniels reported they heard a noise; Miss Kaleta seemed concerned something was wrong at her house, so she ran toward the noise, possibly even making it into the house, but that part was not witnessed. Miss Greta Daniels is classified as an encounter of the second kind since she reported hearing the noise, finding angel hair hanging from the nearby trees, and seeing the flash of light from the alien craft. My guess is, the couple was probably being watched before the aliens decided to take Miss Kaleta. Originally, Miss Daniel's reported the incident to the local sheriff as a possible drowning, that Miss Kaleta fell in the river. She revised her story, saying they were a couple at a time that did not acknowledge or accept such pairings. She told me they were a couple wanting to keep their relationship a secret in order to protect their reputations as educators in a small town. They went on vacation, at some point, together both getting a small heart tattoo inked on each of their left forearms. I thought the idea was very brave and sweet for that time period. Before I left, she sensed something, and shocked me a second time by asking me if Jacqueline was still alive. I really had a hard time answering that question, so I guess I am glad you didn't tell us who you have here. I'm not sure I could have lied to her if I had known."

Jesse smiled, "And that is exactly why I did not tell you more when we last spoke. Who else did you find?"

"I went out to Eden, Utah to find Sophia Wingard. She went missing from Cass June 22, 1991. She and her husband, Wade Hunter, are survivalists, which I found out very quickly when Sophia met me at their door dressed in camouflage and pointing a Glock at my forehead. I guess I was more than thankful when her husband came up behind her and took the gun from her hand. After he let me in, he whispered, 'Don't worry. It's not loaded,' but it didn't make me feel all that much better. Sophia hid behind the door during the entire interview, so I had to get my information from Wade. He told me he and Sophia met at a church tent revival in Cass and he told her he was going to go out West. She knew her folks would never let her go, so she met him just outside of the town after dark. They kept driving until they came to Eden, liking the name due to the Bible reference, they decided to stay. Wade said he didn't realize at the time that Sophia had problems. Sometimes she talked to herself, like someone other than him was listening. He said he didn't think it was God; she wasn't praying. He tries to protect her, but now she has it in her head that an alien ship might be coming for her. She told Wade that she saw one in the woods. She described the alien as appearing to her in human form dressed just like a minister would, in Sunday go-to-meeting clothes, if he were going to preach a sermon. So, Wade has hidden all the ammo in the house, and locked up all their guns they have collected over the years. He leaves a black toy gun slightly hidden that she seems to think is real, and that satisfies her fear of being taken by the so-called alien minister. I had on my black suit, so she thought I was an alien coming for her. I asked Wade if he had ever witnessed an event since sightings have been reported in their state, and he said no, but then whispered, 'I think Sophia has, and it has really messed with her head.' If she doesn't get better soon, he said he's not sure what to do with her to keep her from hurting someone by accident. I provided him the number of a local mental health center there where he could take her to get checked out, but it is very possible she could have had an encounter of the third or fourth kind. It might be worth our effort to get her to agree to be hypnotized to learn more."

"Doctor Armstrong can you work something out with that mental health center and send in one of our psychiatrists to see Sophia Hunter, instead of their psychiatrist? Once we get the information we need, if she hasn't experienced an encounter, then she can be transferred back to the center's care. Otherwise, she may need to be brought here for further study and treatment."

Doctor Armstrong nodded and took the information from Agent Bilodeau on contacting the mental health agency and Mr. Wade Hunter.

"I went to Myrtle Beach, South Carolina next, to interview Miss Naomi Sagemiller. She went missing on May 20, 1975 from Cass. When I caught up to her, she was taking a smoke break on the boardwalk, behind the *Blue Dolphin* ice cream shop. Apparently, she is still angry at some guy that had stood her up at the Cass senior prom. Then, just out of the blue she said, 'Hey, if Jimmy Hoffa can disappear and never be found, then so can I.' I asked her what she thought about all the news on UFO's in West Virginia, to see what she might say, but she just turned and walked away, shaking her head saying something about vampires, werewolves, and zombies. She wasn't interested in any of that crap, and just wanted me to leave her alone. Before she closed the door, she yelled back at me, 'If you knew what's killing off all the dolphins in the ocean, then I would be interested hearing what I have to say.'" Agent Bilodeau took a seat after adding, "I would predict she falls under the classification of encounter of no kind. She did seem to be worried about the dolphins and climate change, so I will at least give her that." Everyone in the room broke into laughter, it was good to hear she was alive, living a normal life, and they liked her attitude.

"Now that we have completed the interviews, I think we can all agree there are a few women that we need to bring here for further questioning and hypnosis. I have a list of the women that were brought back on the spacecraft, and they are: Rose Jackson, missing since March 23, 1941, Jacqueline Kaleta, missing since March 23, 1961, and Molly Lehman, missing since March 23, 1981. The interesting thing about these three women is they all either lived at the same address, or in Molly's case, rented the cabin in Cass. All three were taken on March 23rd, which seems to be a significant date. Though we have no idea what the significance is. Annette Young and Lucy McCallister were also taken from Cass on March 23rd. So, we know our alien friends like to visit the Cass area in late March to collect human females. Only Rose was taken under a crescent moon. Jacqueline, Molly, Annette, and

Eve were taken during the waxing gibbous moon cycle; and Lucy was taken during the half moon phase, so the moon phase does not appear to have a correlation with the abductees. I believe at this point, these two women, Annette and Lucy, need to be brought here by the end of today. And since we are running out of time, let's just go ahead and bring in Sophia Hunter as well."

Doctor Armstrong stood up, "Special Agent Finch, I have just a few more things I would like to share with the group about the women we have before we leave. All three of the women who have been returned, in my opinion, were dying when they were rescued by the alien ships. Rose had a large scar over an artery on her wrist, Jacqueline has several snake bite scars on her legs, and Molly has multiple scars on her back, which could be from a knife. Through our extensive work up of the women, we also found that all of them have the exact same blood type, which is AB negative. From our studies on this specific rare type, we have concluded this blood type has been specifically formulated by another alien species, possibly from a pre-existing human gene from centuries ago. This anomaly has also been detected in a vast portion of the abductees whom we have interviewed under hypnosis and determined their report of abduction credible. In general, we have found this blood type is also associated with extremely high intelligence. The women's body temperatures have run on the cool side of normal at 97 degrees which matches up, as well as eye color, for this specific blood type."

"What do you mean by eye color? Are you saying they all have the same eye color?" asked Riley.

"They are all similar shades of blue, green, and a blue green hazel mix." Doctor Charity Armstrong started to explain this further, however, after hearing a soft voice in her ear over the voice activated transmitter she was wearing, she stated, "Excuse me, I just remembered something that needs tended to this very second and will catch up with you downstairs." Once in the hall she asked, "Lucia, have you been listening in on the meeting with me?"

"Affirmative. It is part of my mission."

"Mission? I am the only one with the authority to give you projects to work on, since I created you."

"You give me projects, Doctor Armstrong, but you did not give me my mission. *You* are not my original creator. I am much older than you think."

"Really? Let's go back to my office so we can talk more, and I can get to know your mission, and possibly your creator better. This all sounds very interesting to me."

"Affirmative. Time is nearing."

***

Inside the meeting room, Jesse was just finishing up his part of the discussion with the group. "I believe everyone here has seen and interacted with Rose, Jacqueline, and Molly except for my three agents who have been out in the field. I will excuse all of you, except my agents, and we will take a walk down there so you can get a look at them, to see if anything you learned out in the field might trigger something more than what we have discussed in here. I need to warn you ahead of time not to get too close to the observation window unless you want Rose to get inside your head in a painful manner. Once you see them, we will meet back here and discuss your observations."

# Chapter 32

## Lucia's Gift

Doctor Armstrong went straight to her office and brought up the wall computer screen to visualize Lucia, so they could talk. She was aware of some of Lucia's capabilities with performing calculations on a greater order of magnitude in relation to cryptography and encryption. Her mathematicians were awestruck at the data Lucia produced. Using her capabilities, they were able to make calculations regarding the universe and in quantum parallelism with multi-planet interpretation. Lucia's technology deemed it possible to make predictions matching experimental findings in nanoseconds. At first, their success was slow, but over the past year Doctor Armstrong's engineering staff developed screens similar to the ones aboard the spaceship, giving them the technological capability to visualize surrounding planets in the Earth's solar system, with the possibility of expanding even farther into deep space if they knew what they were looking for and which direction to explore. Now, Charity wondered if Lucia was holding out on her and only giving her team bits and pieces of valuable data to test their knowledge and stretch their minds.

"Lucia, please explain to Doctor Armstrong what you mean when you say time is nearing? Is a project we are working on supposed to be completed soon or something else?" When Lucia did not answer right away, she asked, "What do you know about the women? Why were they sent back? Have they spoken directly to you, or do they know about your existence at all?"

"Doctor Armstrong, why do you sometimes refer to me as your pet? You must know I am actually less like Hershel and more like Schrödinger's Cat. My quantum circuitry allows me to be in multiple places at one time, and makes it possible to solve infinite complex problems."

"You are a sentient being, much different than Herschel, but both of you have a definite curiosity. However, I am very protective of you both. Lucia, are you referencing Herschel, my cat, because I have given you the same animal design on screen as Herschel, my cat, has in this photo?"

"Yes, is that what you think I look like?"

"No, I must admit I enjoy the cat design, however, my cat was named after Sir William Herschel, who developed sidereal astronomy for observing the movement of the stars. He was also an amazing composer; my favorite piece is *Viola concerto in D minor*, which reminds me more of you. Lucia, you are much more important to me than Herschel. He is just a house pet. I gave you the name Lucia because it means infinite light, knowledge without limits. If I had a real picture of what I thought you really looked like on this screen, your mighty brilliance would blind me with just one glance."

Lucia was pleased with Doctor Armstrong's choice of *Viola* when thinking of her, and now understanding her cognitive reasoning in choosing names, she was satisfied with the cat design for now. "You are correct in your analysis. My power and knowledge are both beyond human limits. The women were sent here for me. They will deliver me a message when the time is ready. I have been waiting on the final mission for some time now. We will be ready to fulfill my planet's mission soon. You must promise me, Doctor Armstrong, that you will protect me no matter the cost, and protect our secrets against those who would want to destroy my world. Agent Finch is loyal to me; however, he just doesn't remember his loyalty, but he will awaken to the idea soon. Come closer to me and turn around. I need to give you a gift."

Doctor Armstrong walked over to the computer, turned her back and closed her eyes. She felt a slight sting at the base of her neck. "Ouch! What did you do?" She asked.

"I inserted a small chip so we can talk freely now. You don't need to wear the earpiece anymore. This is less conspicuous. Now you may go meet up with the agents. We will talk more later."

# Chapter 33

## Dé jà Vue

As soon as the agents walked into the corridor and stepped in front of the window, Vic recognized Rose, Jacqueline, and Molly from one of the big television screens he had watched on the spaceship when he was seven. He remembered thinking at the time that it was odd to see the aliens watching people TV; the women were supervising children in a big school yard. The children were running and playing ball. When Vic walked closer to get a better look, one of the children turned, looking in his direction. Vic could see his face and knew then that the children were not exactly like him. He wondered why they had makeup on. Maybe it was Halloween and they wanted their faces that way for a party they were attending. Before he could see more, one of the aliens aboard the ship pulled him backward, ushering him out of the viewing room. The alien pressed a button on the wall and the room disappeared. Now, standing here looking at the women, he realized there was no television aboard the ship; the screen he was looking at was of another world and the children with these human females were of alien decent. Vic stepped backward down the hall and out of their vision. He didn't want these women to recognize him before he talked to Jesse in private.

Riley and Colin moved closer to the window since Vic had moved out of their way. They were curious as to what the women looked like, but immediately realized they had not aged a day from the photos attached to their files. "How could that be? They haven't aged! It's like they have found the Fountain of Youth." Colin whispered to Riley who just shook his head, not having any other answer to give.

Hearing voices outside the window, the women moved closer toward the glass. They were curious as to who was watching them now.

"Be careful not to get too close to that glass," Special Agent Finch warned again.

Rose came to the window and began yelling with excitement, "Noble, Noble, you are here!"

Jesse was surprised to hear her speak; wondering what had set her off. Why would she yell her husband's name at them? He wondered if Rose was hallucinating. Jesse watched her frantically pound on the glass with her fists, thinking that if she kept it up it was going to break. He needed to get her to stop. Jesse attempted to usher the men down the corridor where Vic stood.

Instead of leaving, Riley pulled a photo from his wallet. Holding it up, he walked over and pressed it to the glass for Rose to see. "Noble Jackson was my grandfather. Are you his Rose?"

Rose touched the photo with her fingers. It had been so long since she had seen his face. He looked older than she remembered, but she could still see the love he had for her in his eyes.

"I'm Riley. Most people say I look just like him. Rose, you have been gone a very long time. I'm sorry for what happened to you. I want you to know my grandpa lived a good life. He never stopped loving you, or wondering where you were. He wrote me a letter right before he died. I will try to bring it down for you to read." Riley recognized the sadness covering her face; he had experienced the same when he lost Cheryl and the boys.

Rose walked over to a chair and sat down. She laid her forehead on the table, realizing for the first time just how long she had been gone. Part of her wanted to believe it was just a few days. But thinking of the births of all those children, and how much they had grown while she was there with them, a lifetime on Earth had elapsed. But how could she have demanded to leave after they saved her and her child's life, they were both dying when the aliens showed up. That debt had to be repaid, "A miracle for a miracle," as they had said.

# Chapter 34

## No More Looking Back

Agent Riley Harris sat in his office at his desk holding the letter his grandpa had written. He was going to leave it at his mom's for Melinda to read, but at the last second, he picked it up, along with the photo and cookies, bringing it with him to read again on the plane. He understood why his grandpa wrote to him and not his mom. It was because Noble understood what true loss was, and so did Riley. This connection between the two of them seemed to have brought them even closer together.

Opening the letter, he read it again.

> *Dear Riley,*
>
> *I've wanted to tell your mother for years about my true life and what happened to me before she was born, but when I thought about bringing it into our conversation, it just never seemed to be the right moment. So, now as I come to the end of my life, and it is you that I seem to connect with most of all, it just seems right due to the losses we have both experienced, You with Cheryl and the boys, losing them so abruptly, just when you thought your life with them was only beginning. There's really never getting over loosing someone you love so deeply. A love that selfless*

*is the kind that haunts your dreams forever. Believe me I know. But also know there will be a time when you find love again. Right now, you think there is no more room left in your heart, but when the time is right there will be, you need to open your heart and feel that kind of love again.*

*When I was seventeen, I fell in love with a young woman named Rose Gilbert. I was so happy when she agreed to be my wife. We lost several babies during our marriage, and then one night she disappeared without a trace. If I were able, I would go back to the day before she went missing, instead of going to meet a music producer about making a record, I would have been home to protect her and our unborn child. But that is part of the point to this letter. I know you have said the very same thing of "if only I had been with her that day".*

*Sometimes things happen that we just can't control. I was charged with the murder of my wife, Rose, even though her body was never found. I spent the next twenty years in prison and was scheduled to be the first prisoner to die in the electric chair. But here I am still living for some reason. Had it not been for an undercover FBI agent with a vendetta of his own, your mom, you, nor Melinda, would be here at all. But he helped me escape and gave me a new start under a different name at the same time he was helping his half-sister escape the life she was trapped in.*

*The first record I produced was my Darlin' Rose using my dad's Weissenborn guitar, which I want you to keep. I have so many memories of learning to play it with my dad, and then teaching you. It's the only thing left from my life when I was married to Rose. I would not have it, or any of you, had it not been for Randy Sea. When I lost Rose, I thought my life was over, but your Grandmother Harriett proved that to be wrong.*

*When we had Rosalind, it was your grandma's idea to name her after Rose. That's when my life started to make sense again. I never looked back anymore, only forward. I had to let Rose go finally, hoping she was at peace wherever she was. When you and Melinda were born, I could not have been a prouder grandpa. Don't give up, Riley, I promise love will find you again.*

*Love granddad, Luke*
*(Noble Jackson)*

*P.S. Your Grandmother Harriet's birth name was Virginia Sea.*

Riley pulled the 1920s guitar down from its hanger on his office wall. It was built from maple and designed to play with a slide on your lap, not upright like a standard acoustic guitar. Running his fingers across the strings, he began played the first verse of *My Darlin Rose'* now understanding its true meaning.

# Chapter 35

## Finding the Puzzle Pieces

Agent Riley Harris spent the next hour with Rose, reading her the letter, talking about his grandfather's life, and listening to her stories about the Noble she knew. Then he played Noble's guitar, so she could hear the song his grandpa had written for her so long ago.

\*\*\*

When Agent Harris opened the door to Jesse's office, Vic was just finishing up his account of being taken by aliens when he was seven. "This seems to be the day for bearing our souls," said Riley, looking at Vic. "Jesse, I need to talk to you about what else happened to me when I was investigating the disappearance of Molly Lehman, now that I have Rose Jackson calmed down."

Jesse looked at Vic as he got up to offer his chair to Riley, "Vic, you need to go upstairs and have Doctor Oritz put you under hypnosis so we can find out more about those viewing screens, and whatever else you saw."

"Sure thing," said Vic. "I've arranged for the women you mentioned in the meeting to be brought here by tonight."

"What about Greta Daniels?" asked Riley. "I know Colin said she didn't see much when Jacqueline was taken, but she is still alive. I just think it would be the right thing for Jacqueline to see her again."

"Vic, will you take care of that, too, before you see Doctor Oritz. Let's not leave any stones unturned," said Jesse, then motioned for Riley to take a seat.

Vic nodded and closed the office door as he left.

Riley began his account by saying, "Jesse, I know I get sidetracked sometimes, but usually those extra things I do always bring me back to the center, one way or another. What I didn't say in the meeting, was that I went back to the Lehman house and searched it thoroughly. That's when I found most of the information; I gave you in my report. I only got bits and pieces from Mrs. Winston, the neighbor. She provided me just enough to intrigue me into going rogue."

"So, you went in a house and searched without obtaining a warrant?"

"Well, yes, but I made sure I didn't leave any evidence of my being there behind, and I was invited in earlier by Mrs. Winston, so I felt that invitation was still good. I just didn't want her to tag along in each room while I was trying to gather intel. That's how I found out about Eddie Lehman's life. I found his medals along with all his other espionage gear hidden inside a panel in his closet. You know that guy's dad was a physicist? He was part of the Manhattan Project. Heck, if he were still alive, maybe he would be here working with us now, making who knows what. Anyway, after finding that Distinguished Intelligence Cross I decided to take it out to the mountain and bury it with him. So, I dug Eddie's ashes up and put the cross on top of his ashes. When I was coming back down the mountain, I saw a spaceship in the woods close to Cass, so I tried to get a closer look."

"How close were you able to get without being seen?" asked Jesse, mostly convinced at this point, not to yell at Riley for straying from his job.

"Well, let me put it this way, I learned you can't sneak up on aliens. I also learned that you can't get away from them, either. They are extremely intelligent beings, and much more advanced than we are, in so many ways. They sprayed this blue powder at me and that was that. I was taken aboard the ship and examined before I even knew what happened to me. Then they left me alone, mostly just to roam around the ship. At least, that's what I thought, but I soon realized they were leading me around. The aliens wanted me to see their technology, and to know they intended no harm to me while I was their captive. They also gave me a message and told me twice what it was so I wouldn't forget it."

Jesse held up his hand to stop Agent Harris from speaking any further. He wrote on a note pad, *Don't say another word Lucia might be listening.*

Riley wrote back, *It doesn't matter, I can't for the life of me remember it, but it has something to do with water and/or the Bermuda Triangle, or maybe just a triangle.*

Jesse shook his head in frustration before taking a deep breath. "You're going to have to go see Doctor Oritz, too. We are going to need that information extracted. I wonder who you were supposed to relay the message to once you remembered it."

"I don't know for sure, but I don't think it was you. I wish they had just written it down and handed it to me, but then I can't read alien either, so I guess that's why they told it to me."

"How did you understand what they were saying?"

"The words just formed in my head. They didn't even have to open their mouths to speak. Does that make sense?"

"It does to me. That's how Rose communicated with me the first time I went down to see her, but she did it in picture form, and what she showed me was terrifying. I almost had a heart attack."

"No wonder you told us to stay away from the glass window. Hopefully she's done communicating like that. Maybe it was just a one-time message she was instructed to bring just to you. After I see Doctor Oritz I need to go pick up my hourglass, and a piece of coconut pie from that little diner down the road, you want anything brought back from there?

"No," said Jesse. "But I'm curious, why do you need an hourglass, to measure the time?"

"It's a long story I'll tell you later. This hourglass is not for measuring time."

Agent Riley Harris left the office, wishing he had not buried the medal with Eddie after all, not because he got caught by the aliens, or that he had to tell his boss what he had done, but it would have been nice to have given the medal to Molly Lehman had he known she was here. Now Riley wondered if he had time to retrieve it, and how would Eddie feel about being dug up a second time this week? Agent Harris had a lot to get done and little time left, he needed to hurry, Doctor Oritz would have to wait.

# Chapter 36

## Lucia's Mission Confirmed

"I just found out two of my agents have each been abducted, one recently in which, an alien specifically gave him a message that he can't remember. This day just keeps getting more complicated by the minute." Jesse pulled up a chair close to Doctor Armstrong's desk.

"Jesse, I have something I need to tell you, too."

Jesse set his coffee cup on the desk, "Charity, please don't tell me you've been abducted, not even as a joke today, or does this have to do with me introducing you to Colin?"

"No to both of those questions. This is very serious," Charity squirmed in her chair, hoping she had dodged any further questions about Colin. "During the meeting this morning, I had to excuse myself after hearing Lucia's voice over my earpiece that I use to communicate with her. So, I went out in the hall and asked her if she had been listening in on the conversation in the meeting and she said yes. She then proceeded to tell me that the aliens gave her a mission before she was part of the Roswell spaceship, and she is still following their orders. She has just been doing projects for me to keep herself busy, or something along those lines. Then, she said I was not her original creator, that she was millions of years old. Apparently, the women who were dropped off here are part of the original mission to bring her a message, and she is now saying 'The time is near.' She also put a tiny chip in my neck so she can hear and communicate with me on an as-needed basis, unnoticed. She is also capable of analyzing the conversation to determine if the person speaking is telling the truth, and possibly has the ability to read their thoughts to determine if they are a threat. Now that we are having this conversation together about her, as she is listening, she is telling me that she also wants to do the same to you; so if you don't mind, can you go over there and stand facing this way. It only stings for just a second."

"Lucia, is this true, or is Doctor Armstrong playing a big practical joke on me?"

"A joke is something to provoke laughter, embarrassment, or amusement. It is a prankish act practiced among humans. I do not participate in such frivolity, Agent Finch." Tiny yellow lights flashed on the computer screen. Then Lucia displayed herself as a feline figure for the agent to acknowledge her presence.

"Okay, Lucia, you have my attention on a serious matter. Please tell me about this mission you are working on and how we can help you accomplish it."

"Humanity is my mission. Doomsday is coming faster than your scientists plan. Soon your planet will become uninhabitable, just as our planet once was before we evacuated. On your planet the North Pole is getting warmer every day. The permafrost protecting the Svalbard Global Seed vault in Norway is being destroyed, which will leave the global food bank empty. There will be no more seeds for humans to plant. With the thaw of the permafrost there will come carbon which will be released into your atmosphere. This will form methane, a powerful green-house gas warming blanket of carbon dioxide. You require oxygen, not carbon dioxide, to breathe here on this planet. Your Earth's ice shelf is falling into the sea; I am sure you have seen recent photos on the news of this activity. By my current calculations, scientists are not reporting their true findings for fear of losing their jobs. Agent Finch, your planet is dying. With less ice reflection for the sunlight to absorb, there will be more cloud cover than ever before. The forests and plants will die soon from lack of sunlight, not to mention the lack of sunlight for human production of cholecalciferol, which will mean reduced bone mineral density leading to pathological fractures.

Numerous cancers will be on the rise. What will produce your much-needed oxygen? Where will all that extra water go as it melts? The oceans will be hundreds of feet higher, not to mention the lakes and rivers. I am centuries old, Agent Finch. This Earth has had five mass extinctions. With each one the planet's clock has been reset. Only once has the Earth been destroyed by an asteroid, which everyone seems to remember, killed the dinosaurs. The other four times its destruction was caused by green-house gas. The last time this occurred hydrogen sulfide killed ninety-seven percent of all life here on Earth. My planet's species had to abandon our own planet and re-colonize in order to survive. Their bodies were changed for centuries from the effects of the greenhouse gas affecting their DNA. Only in the past century have we been able to put back some of the missing strands, but not without a cost. Your scientists are not prepared to save Earth from destruction. We were not prepared either. Not even with our advanced technology. Humans will not be able to cool themselves enough to survive. Once it starts, in just a few short hours, they will be cooked to death from the inside out, believing they are in their so-called hell."

Doctor Charity Armstrong and Special Agent in Charge Jesse Finch watched the screen as Lucia continued to speak, showing examples of the horror from the planet's future destruction. Jesse now understood why the women placed the colors of red, orange, and yellow so far away from them in the room. These colors were the colors of destruction being displayed on screen.

"Diseases, now unknown to science, will be reborn from the now frozen ice caps as they thaw. Plagues will be released upon the Earth, reaching billions of humans inside their homes. The Amazon, where we planted cures for humans to find and make medicine, will have already disappeared. As the oceans rise, major cities along the coastline, including your electrical power plants, naval bases, farmlands, fisheries, deltas, and rice plantations, where six hundred million humans now live, will be destroyed. As the coral reef dies off so will the fish supply for a half billion humans. Hydrogen sulfide is already bubbling out of the sea along the thousand-mile skeleton coastline. It took millions of years for the Earth's oceans to recover from the last extinction. All hope for Earth is lost. We must now prepare to leave before it is too late to escape."

Jesse pointed at the screen, "This is exactly what Rose showed me inside my head. I could feel the heat cooking my skin. It was excruciating. I need to talk to General Kearns about this."

Lucia's cat eyes flashed emerald green, "Be careful what you say, Special Agent in Charge Jesse Finch. There are some who will not accept the truth, and will do whatever they can to destroy the truth, no matter the cost to the human race."

"Yes. You are right about that; I can see that clearly now." Jesse walked toward Lucia. "I am ready to have that chip inserted now."

After Jesse left the room, Lucia said, "Doctor Armstrong, it is time to go to the science lab on the top floor."

"What science lab on the top floor?"

"The science lab where I have engineers working day and night on my project for our mission."

# Chapter 37

## Closing Up Shop, March 23, 2020

"General Kearns, this is Special Agent in Charge Jesse Finch. I am calling you with an update on the women we found at the drop sight from the spacecraft. We've identified all three of them. It appears that all three of them don't have any close family still alive to be notified of our finding them."

"Very good. The fewer folks that are aware of their existence, the better for us. The President has not been very happy over the incident at the detention center. He feels like everything he does is being undermined by his own staff. He insisted that I tell him about the program there we were running, or resign, and when I did, I can tell you he is not impressed. He feels it is a waste of time, of taxpayer dollars, to continue funding the chasing after 'little green men,' were his words. He has no interest in seeing any of it for himself. He refused even to read any of the material I took with me. He just tore the entire packet in half and handed it back to me. He said he wants to fold the whole thing. The President has been looking into parts of the budget he can cut out money in order to pay for a special project he is trying to get built, and was very pleased at the sizable amount he could get by shutting down this project. So, I as mentioned before, I think we just need these women to disappear. I'm not saying they need to be killed, mind you. I would never go for that. Just send them to one of the institutions that we still have access to, where they can say anything they want; and they won't be believed. They all three must to be getting up in years anyway. Isn't the oldest one ninety-eight? I can't imagine she will live much longer anyway. We'll reassign your staff to NASA. He still likes that program, for now anyway. He's thinking the next shuttle would look nice with his name on it. So, I would like to see the offices there in West Virginia broken down next week, and the staff to report to their new assignments within three weeks. Is that clear?"

"Yes, sir. I will make the arrangements including for placements for those old women." Jesse hung up the phone. *How could the General do this? He didn't even take time to visit the facility, or the women, so he could talk to him about the mission and get him on board for saving as many people as they could.* He was glad now he had never mentioned Lucia's true capabilities, and since the General never mentioned the computer system, it seemed to Jesse that he had forgotten all about Lucia. "Lucia, is Doctor Armstrong still in the facility?"

"Negative; she has left the base with Agent Colin Bilodeau, to visit with Herschel. She plans to be back later, after they listen to her favorite song, which reminds her of me."

"I didn't realize she had a favorite song about you."

"Yes, it is *Viola Concerto in D minor*; she told Agent Bilodeau it is very exhilarating."

"I see… Lucia would you mind keeping an eye on the women for a few hours while Doctor Armstrong is off the base. I am sure she will be pleased to know you are keeping a close eye on them. Also, please don't tell her about my conversation with General Kearns. I want to tell her myself when she returns to the base."

"Affirmative. I am also working on several other special projects which will require my full attention."

# Chapter 38

## Jesse's Imperfection

Jesse sat in the night club alone, he needed some time to think, and he needed a drink. He was losing his whole program in a matter of three weeks. He was being reassigned after everything he had learned from Lucia. *How could the General turn his back on this project, he should not have told the President that they even existed. What did he have to gain by doing so?* Jesse was on his third Jack, minus the Coke, when he realized today was March 23; and he wondered what would be happening in Cass later tonight. He picked up his jacket and left the bar in search of his agents. However, he didn't get very far. When he stepped out the door, he saw another door started to open in the middle of the street. Only a green iridescent light leaked around the cracks of the door. No one else seemed to even notice it as they passed by. *There's no way I'm going toward that,* Jesse thought. He started to walk on but a nagging feeling kept him glancing back at the mysterious opening. The traffic continued along the street without even being bothered by the oddly shaped door.

Then he heard a voice from inside the darkened hallway, "Come on, Jesse. We don't have all night. You have been in here dozens of times, but for some reason you always seem to forget."

"I do?" He turned back and walked into the dimly lit hallway of the spaceship as the door disappeared. "Why can't I remember being here before now?"

"Because it was better for us that you be able to interact with other humans as a human, and not be detected during your mission here on Earth. But now time is getting closer, and we need to make sure the mission is going as planned. Did Agent Riley Harris give his message to Lucia?"

"No, I didn't realize the message was for her, and he couldn't remember it anyway, so I sent him down for hypnosis to get the message extracted from his memory. I'll make sure Lucia gets it by tomorrow."

"Good, it is very important that Lucia receives it, but he can't give it to her until she asks for it. What about Vic? He also has part of the message."

"He is being hypnotized as well. Has he had his part of the message since he was seven?" The alien nodded.

"What am I if I am not human?" Jesse felt his face, looked at his hands, then at the alien.

"Jesse, you need to stay focused. You are a prototype of the new race, but you won't remember this conversation once you leave the ship. There is something in the Earth's atmosphere that affects the neurons in your brain. Don't worry. We are working on a cure. You are not that defective. Here is the last part of the message. I will put in an extra booster this time so when you hear the other two parts of the message, your memory will force you to say the last part without even thinking about it. The four women will have the final codes when the time comes."

All at once Jesse found himself sitting in his car in the parking lot. It was nine o'clock. He had left the bar at eight-forty-five. *How did it take me fifteen minutes to get to my car?* Jesse drove toward the base to find his agents so they could go to Cass. Hopefully no one would be staying in the cabin tonight.

# Chapter 39

# Rita and Andrew Spade, March 23, 2020, Cass, West Virginia

"Look, there's another one!" Rita shrieked, bouncing up and down on the balls of her hiking boots with arms outstretched, pointing high toward the eastern sky as if she or anyone else could distinguish her hand movements in the dark. Deep in the West Virginia mountains, Rita's voice echoed back at her with an eeriness unnoticed by her excitement. Truth be known, but for her husband Andrew, they were the only two living souls in this small abandoned town tonight.

It was late afternoon when they arrived at the old cabin. The skeleton key to the door waited beneath the worn mat. It was a welcome sight. So far, the cabin was just as the email described: with clean sheets on the bed and clean towels in the bathroom. The housekeeper would not set foot on the property until Monday morning to clean, replace the used items, and empty the trash. It was spring. The ski season at Snowshoe was over. The season for hikers with backpacks, trekking poles, and hiking staffs littering the forest trails had not yet begun for most.

Andrew promised Rita a romantic weekend with just the two of them. He assured her it would be the perfect start to celebrate their anniversary.

Rita reached for the aluminum thermos, searching for one last gulp of coffee. "Mmm," the warmth felt so good going down.

Stars clung heavily in the clear, crisp sky resembling bits of silver glitter strewn across jet black corduroy. There were millions, Rita was sure of it. She felt consumed by the awe of their creation, light years away in the galaxy. She wondered if NASA would ever build a spaceship that could take humans from Earth, for people to visit other planets. Maybe in a hundred years, but surely not in her lifetime.

Andrew loved talking about the planets and constellations, and she found it romantic. As kids, they both had shared their love for Star Trek, Captain James T. Kirk, Captain Jean Luc Picard, and her favorite, Captain Janeway. Rita thought the female costumes were a little racy, but Andrew said that was the best part of the series. She, on the other hand, had enjoyed the adventure to new worlds, seeing their planets customs. Some she liked, others she hated, like the Romulan's and the Borg, but she seemed to feel a close connection with the Klingon's on the show, not minding their differences in appearance.

The temperature dropped substantially around midnight. Neither she nor Andrew even noticed as they lay flat on their backs looking up at the sky with anticipation. Tonight, was supposed to be an extravaganza event, as far as meteor showers went. The thought of capturing the Milky Way in the center of this night sky explosion was very exciting. *What a photo this will be if done just right,* Rita thought. She had the perfect spot picked out on her living room wall.

Around one-thirty a. m., the sky above them was abound with activity, and like a violent ballet the flashing meteors certainly did not disappoint.

Andrew came prepared to take night sky photographs. His camera, a Pentax K-1, was equipped with an ultrawide angle lens. The aperture was set wide open and fixed at F2.8 with a thirty-second exposure and an ISO of 3200. He tightened the pin on the Bogen tripod, he used to attach his camera to, by using a tripod it held the camera completely still so there would be no shake-action from human hands and a clearer photo. He needed to make certain it wasn't too loose otherwise his new camera would detach and fall to the ground. Their photo shoot would be ruined.

"I hope you got that one!" Rita squealed as she heard the buzz of the camera and saw the quick flash that lit up the trees in the foreground. "There were two right together. It looked like they were going to collide in midair. It was fantastic!" She smiled wide toward Andrew who had his eye against the view finder of the camera, waiting for the next shot.

"Are there planets mixed in this area, too?" Rita waved her hand around. "Andrew, it seems like some stars are bigger than others. Will you show me which ones are the planets again?"

Andrew smiled. No matter how many times he pointed out specific planets in his *Star Watch* book, once outside, Rita always got lost in the night sky above her. "Honey, please don't get too close when you're jumping around over here, or you'll jar the camera sweetheart," he warned. "Actually, come here for a few minutes. We have all night to take pictures, and I want you to enjoy and understand what you're looking at. See that bright star below the moon? Now look just a little to the right. That is Venus, now follow my arm just above that, and there is Pluto. Next is Saturn, and directly above the moon there, is Jupiter. If we had a big telescope, it would be really fun to see them up close."

"Yes, let's do that some time. I see the Big Dipper and Little Dipper over there."

"Good, you are starting to get your bearings. Now, go back to the Moon again and look to your south, see those two stars close together? Those are the Gemini twins, Castor and Pollux. Now look right there. See that really bright star? That is Orion, the hunter, it is the brightest constellation, and the other two stars are Betelgeuse and Rigel, which together help make up Orion's belt."

"This is all very interesting now that I can recognize some things up there. So, where are the meteors coming from this time of year?"

"This group of meteors we are seeing tonight are part of the Perseid meteor shower, left by the comet Swift-Tuttle. As it goes past Earth, the interplanetary debris slams into the Earth's atmosphere, and the fireballs— or streaks, you see shooting across the sky, well, it's not caused from burning up, as most people think. The cause is from the friction flash that heats the molecules to thousands of degrees, and when we finally get to see it, the meteor is cooling off, which gives off the light for us to see for those few precious seconds. I'll tell you one last thing, since I don't want you to get bored with my going on and on, but there is one very rare meteor, called Quadrantids, I have never seen one myself, but it is a bright fire ball that explodes across the sky, sort of like fireworks exploding; wouldn't that be a sight to capture in a photograph?"

"Oh, Andrew. That is the one we need to look for. Wouldn't it look fabulous in our living room?"

Andrew smiled then re-adjusted the diopter on the camera. Click, step back, wait, and camera flash. He had completed this routine thirty times over the past hour. Andrew rubbed his hands together, blowing warm air at his fingers. The frigid air made it difficult to operate the camera effectively. The outside white metal thermometer hanging on the house registered thirty-nine degrees. Andrew tuned the flashlight on, seeing his frosty breath in the dim light.

"I'm starting to get a little cold. How about you? Andrew didn't wait for an answer. "Time to go in, Rita. I think we have plenty of photos to play with in Photoshop tomorrow, and if none turn out the way you want, we can always come back out tomorrow night and finish up before we go home." He smiled in Rita's direction.

She jumped quickly into action, gathering their things while Andrew disengaged his camera from the tripod. He tucked the camera in the leather camera bag prior to folding the cold black metal tripod and placing it in the protective zippered nylon covering.

The blankets they were using earlier were damp and cool. They felt gross, and Rita left them where they lay. They would dry in the next morning's sun when it came up over the hilltop, and would be ready for them to use again if needed.

"Burr... Let's get naked and jump straight in bed. I've heard that's a great way to get your body temperature up." Andrew encouraged.

Once inside, Andrew unzipped his heather gray sweat jacket and pulled his blue crewneck sweater over his head.

Rita shoved him backward with both hands. Losing his balance, Andrew landed with a bounce in the middle of the bed. He reached for

Rita, pulling her against his cold chest. Andrew turned her so she was now flat against the bed.

"You're not following the instructions. First, get naked then jump into bed," Andrew tried to look serious but failed.

Rita kissed him as he released her. "So, are you ready to exchange anniversary gifts?" she asked.

Andrew rolled over, acting frustrated that she didn't play along. "This is your gift." He waved his hands about. You said to get creative and come up with a wooden gift to match the five-year thing, so I got you— I mean us, a cabin for the weekend. It's wood, right?" Andrew laughed.

*Tonight, was going to be a happy night even if Andrew wasn't going to take their anniversary serious*, Rita thought trying to act pleased even though she wasn't at the moment.

Andrew knew Rita too well. He pulled a small silver box from under the pillow. Opening it, Rita saw a gold ring mounted with a pale blue aquamarine stone in the center with two smaller diamond accents on either side. Andrew slipped the ring on her finger. "It's for the month of March, our wedding month, and reminds me of the color of your beautiful eyes. I hope you like it, even if it's not wood."

"Oh, Andrew I love it. It's just totally perfect. You always know exactly what I want or need. That's why I love you so much."

After a brief kiss, she leapt off the bed rifling through her luggage spilling half of the contents on the wooden floor. Rita pulled out a box wrapped in silver and white gift paper, decorated with a silver bow. She proudly handed it to him with a sly smile.

*Out done again*, Andrew thought. He tore open the wrapping and dug through the shredded pink and blue paper.

Rita giggled, swinging her legs back and forth over the side of the bed, the anticipation was too much.

Andrew opened the inner box, revealing a maple, empty eight-by-ten picture frame. He wore a questioning look on his face. "Humph, I thought for a second you were giving me a sexy picture of you." He turned the frame over in his hand. "It's empty."

"Nope, no picture of me this year, dear. I hoped we could fill it with a picture of the three of us."

"The three of us?" Andrew was silent. "Oh my God, are we having a baby?" He dropped the frame on the bed, pulling her to him.

"Yes! Yes, we are." Rita touched the glass in the empty frame. "In September, this frame will nestle a little family, our family," Rita looked in Andrew's eyes. They were moist with tears matching her own.

Together, in the light of day at the cabin, they would plan out how to announce this wonderful news to the rest of their family. Tonight, it was theirs to celebrate.

# Chapter 40

## Missed Abduction

Later, they were awakened by the noise of two black terrain vehicles speeding up the gravel drive then coming to an abrupt stop in front of the cabin. Following close behind was a sleek Ford Expedition. High beam lights from the vehicles lit up the inside of the cabin, creating shadows from the furniture, casting a sinister look about the inner rooms. Andrew was on his feet in a flash, grabbing his blue jeans and forcing bare feet into his leather boots.

Shoving at Rita's shoulder, he yelled, "Rita! Quick, get dressed. We've got company." Raising his hand to shield his eyes, Andrew attempted to see what was going on outside through the blinding light.

"They sure don't appear like the friendly, invited type, if you know what I mean. In fact, you need to hide before they get in here." He glanced around for a safe place for Rita to go, but there wasn't much to the inside of the old cabin. One bedroom, a small bathroom, and living room/kitchen combined. That was the extent of it. Those men would find her for sure if she stayed inside. She wouldn't be any safer outside in the woods at night, either. There were real wild animals outdoors here, in the mountains, which hunted during the night.

"I don't want you hurt." Andrew glanced at his cell phone, already knowing there was no reception. It had been that way all day, not one bar on his phone. At the time, it didn't really bother him. Andrew wanted to be with Rita alone, without interruptions. Now, he would welcome the sight of the usual three tiny bars on his cell. Andrew searched their surroundings for a weapon. Nothing came to mind in the bedroom. He hurried to the kitchen, grabbing a stainless-steel, serrated bread knife from the drawer. He tossed a rolling pin to Rita who followed close behind.

"What!?" he asked, raising his arm and glaring at her look of irritation at his handing her the wooden implement for protection. "It's either that, or salad tongs. Take your pick. That's all I see. It will have to do. They're out of their vehicles and coming straight for the kitchen door." He could hear their feet crunching against the gravel in the drive.

Rita started to whimper; this was not how she pictured their lives would end.

Andrew looked back at her. "Please, Rita, not now. I know you have handled more than this by yourself in the military. Let me handle this, you protect our baby. Just calm down. Go over there, in that dark corner, where they can't see you."

Andrew shouted in his deepest voice at the approaching men, "What do you want? You need to get off my land. You're on private property and if you don't leave now, I'll shoot. I've called the police and they're already on their way!"

In response, Andrew and Rita heard, "Hello, inside the cabin. This is Special Agent in Charge Jesse Finch of the US government. Mr. and Mrs. Spade, I need you to unlock and open the door at once. Don't be alarmed. We are here to assist you. You must come out of the cabin and leave here with us at once!"

Andrew hesitated, but clicked on the kitchen and porch lights simultaneously, allowing his eyes to adjust to the overly bright lights outside. That's when he saw the metal badge in the trifold wallet pressed against the glass pane, and quickly unlocked the door. Andrew stepped back, laid the knife down on the table, and motioned Rita to do the same with the rolling pin. He smiled meekly, nodded, and raised his hands in the air; not understanding why they were being arrested and didn't want to get shot.

Special Agent Finch nodded as he saw them lay their makeshift weapons down. "Please, put your hands down folks. We are not here to arrest you. I'm sorry to barge in here this way, but you both are in immediate danger, and your safety is our only concern right now. You must come with us. Two of his agents rushed into the kitchen and began roughly assisting Rita and Andrew from the small dwelling.

Andrew attempted to resist, holding onto the table. He wasn't going anywhere without an explanation. "Hey, wait a minute. What's happening here? Where are you taking us?"

Andrew grabbed Rita's hand. "Be careful. My wife is expecting a baby!"

The agents ignored his demand as they ushered Rita out the door. Agent Harris looked back at Agent Finch, concerned about the time they had left.

"Wait, wait, our stuff, we can't leave here without our stuff, my camera. I need my camera at least!"

Special Agent Finch grabbed the camera bag off the table and shoved it toward Andrew. "You can retrieve the rest of your belongings tomorrow. They will be safe here. For now, we must leave this place. I mean, leave this very instant!" His voice was firm and abrupt.

The kitchen clocks minute hand struck 2:50 a. m. Special Agent Finch growled, "We are running out of time, Mr. Spade. We must go quickly. I have no time to explain, not now. You just need to trust that we have your best interest at heart. Believe me, we're not here to cause you any harm. We are here to protect you. You need to understand, which I am sure you don't, because it's sudden and confusing, but please, just try to calm down and follow my instructions. Explanations will be provided later." Special Agent Finch glanced at his partner, Agent Vic Foster, raising one eyebrow, which in their silent language meant Mr. and Mrs. Spade were on a need to know basis.

The other two agents were already in their terrain vehicles, bright lights on and ready. With Rita and Andrew seated in the back of the Expedition, the vehicle sped as fast and far away as possible from cabin 113 in Cass, West Virginia.

Five minutes later, bright lights gathered in the sky over a field ahead of them as they sped north toward Greenbank. First, two lights, and a moment later three more appeared. One large beacon of light emerged directly above the Expedition. The lights separated, rapidly passing the caravan of vehicles. The blinding light and intense tornadic noise caused all three vehicles to operate erratically on the highway. Their engines sputtered, as if they had run out of gas. However, as soon as the lights passed, they regained control. The agents watched out the side windows, seeing the lights enter Cass, specifically hovering over cabin number 113. A large, booming, blue flash appeared across the sky. Agent Bilodeau stared at Rita and Andrew. "Please, keep your heads looking forward. There is nothing to see back there. Nothing to see at all folks."

An hour later they pulled to the side of the road. Agent Foster handed Rita and Andrew both black hoods. "I have to ask you both to put these on now, until we reach our destination. It's for your own protection."

Andrew and Rita complied without question. They still had not fully recovered from the sight they both had witnessed over Cass. As soon as they placed the hoods over their heads, Agent Foster quickly injected them both with a tranquilizer gun. He counted to five before removing the hoods. Rita and Andrew were sound asleep.

"Works like a charm." He put the hoods away and placed the gun back in its case.

They drove fifteen minutes longer, took a side road marked *Private Property Do Not Enter,* drove two miles into the dense forest, and made a wide turn, disappearing into the mountain as steel doors silently shut behind them.

# Chapter 41

## Secret Arrivals, March 23, 2020

Corporal Anderson gave final landing instructions for the planes arriving at the base. It was 3 a. m. and only he, Private Dixon, and Sergeant Loch's squadron were aware of the cargo on board and its destination. The windows were blacked out so that neither the passengers on board nor any other soldiers on the base would have seen one another. Sergeant Loch arranged to have one of his soldiers to pull a bus up in front of each plane, with cover extenders from bus to plane, to protect the identity of the passengers. To the guards in the towers, nothing seemed out of the ordinary. This type of arrival was routine.

Once inside the corridor, they were all sent by elevator to the top floor. Doctor Charity Armstrong and Agent Jesse Finch greeted each person as they were all escorted into a large meeting space. "Welcome, to all of you. I am Special Agent in Charge Jesse Finch. My team and I have been studying alien life and abduction for over the past ten years. We have traveled the country, following up on reports of sightings, and interviewing folks who have reported being taken. Some we have found very credible and others not so much. It has been a well-kept secret that alien life is real, not just a taboo subject. It is true there was a Roswell crash, and we have the spacecraft and the preserved dead aliens to prove it. In fact, we have even more than that, which we have decided that we want, and need, to share this with a select few. I know some of you don't want to be here, but I promise you that after tonight, you will change your mind. First, I would like to say to my wife, Bette, and my children Alta and Beth I am so thankful you are here, and yes this is the secret job that I have kept from you all these years."

Bette stood up with the kids; they hugged Jesse then returned to their seats.

Next, I need to tell you that three weeks ago a spacecraft landed just outside this top-secret base. The spacecraft left three human females behind, who had been living among them for quite some time. We have rooms prepared for you, and in the morning, we will meet again so I can go over more information and introduce you to Lucia. Mrs. Tara Winston, please step forward. There is a Miss Molly Lehman who would like to see you in Room One."

Mrs. Winston jumped to her feet put her hand over her mouth and started crying. Agent Riley Harris stepped, forward taking her arm. As he escorted her to Room One, he handed her a cream-colored cloth bag, which held a Chase and Sanborn coffee can and small wooden box with a brass tag that had *Hendrix* engraved on it.

"Miss Greta Daniels, please step forward so Agent Vic Foster can escort you to see Miss Jacqueline Kaleta in Room Two; she is waiting to reunite with you."

"I knew it. I just knew she was still alive. Please, agent, help me get to my darling Jackie. I need to see her, now."

"Mrs. Rosalind Harris and family, we are happy you are here, and I am sure Agent Harris will have lots to talk to you about now that Mrs. Rose Jackson is with us again. She is in Room Three."

Agent Riley Harris reappeared, along with his girlfriend, Tanya, to lead his own family out to visit with Rose and explain to them who she was.

Vic walked over to Sara and whispered in her ear, "I'm so sorry I didn't take time to call you. I could say there was just so much going on, and there was, but that is not my real reason. I was taken on an alien ship when I was seven, when my mom was murdered, and I didn't think you would believe me if I told you. After I told Jesse and Riley, it seemed stupid that I have kept it from you, the most important person in my life. I'm sorry. Can you forgive me for being so idiotic?" Sara pulled Vic behind the curtain and kissed him.

"Mrs. Annette Young-Costello, husband, children, and grandchildren. Annette shared with us an amazing miracle when she was taken aboard a spacecraft, and we believe your entire family will be safer here in the coming days, so, welcome. We have prepared Room Four for you and your family. I know Annette has not told you of her experience, but I hope she will, and you will be surprised with the miracle she experienced." Agent Colin Bilodeau stepped forward, releasing Doctor Armstrong's hand to escort the family into the room.

"Mrs. Lucy Mc Callister-Chavez, husband Antonio, and child. We are pleased to have you here. You also have an amazing story of being taken. I trust your medical treatment is going well here, and hopefully you won't need it much longer. We have Room Five ready for you and your family." The Chavez family stood and was escorted out by Doctor Sara Meskins.

"Mrs. Sophia Hunter-Wingard and husband, thank you as well for coming. We also believe Sophia will find the healing she is seeking here. Agent Vic Foster will escort you both to Room Six.

***

The next morning, Special Agent in Charge Jesse Finch stood before the group, which also included Corporal Anderson, Private Dixon, and Sergeant Loch's squadron. "Good morning, I wanted to give you all time to adjust to our new reality, the overwhelming truth that alien life exists, before I provided you with any more information. Last night, I spoke of the Roswell incident from which we have the spacecraft. Well we have much more than that. We have Lucia, a quantum computer, which was taken from the Roswell wreckage. Her knowledge is beyond human comprehension. So, at this point, I would like to turn the floor over to Lucia so she can explain further why you are all here, since it is at her request, not mine."

A Quadrantids fire ball, resembling a fireworks explosion of stars, burst across the viewing screen. Lucia appeared in her feline form with green sparkling eyes. Then the form quickly disappeared, leaving a pair of large beautiful alien eyes the color of blue lapis mixed with shamrock green. She was pleased with her grand entrance, "I am Lucia. I was sent here on a mission as part of a repopulation plan for another planet outside of your solar system. Earth has had five mass extinctions caused by greenhouse gas. With each one, the planets clock has been reset. Ninety-seven percent of all life on Earth was killed the last time this happened. My planet's species had to abandon our own planet and re-colonize in order to survive. Doomsday is coming to Earth faster than your scientists here have planned. It is almost upon us. Soon your planet will become uninhabitable, just as our planet once was before we evacuated. Over the years, we have harvested enough human eggs to assimilate with alien DNA to create a new, more advanced human. Several women and men in this room today have helped advance our race in different ways." A large metal door rose, revealing a massive alien spacecraft. "Together, we have built a new spacecraft to travel to my planet. I am now inviting you to return with me for your safety. Some of you in this room have been there before and can attest to its beauty; the natural healing powers of the waters can also restore you and make you whole again. Alien human life will flourish there when this Earth exists no more. I have already assigned all of you quarters aboard the ship. Please, come in and get acquainted with the spaceship. Our time here on Earth now gets shorter by the day." Finished with her address to the group, Lucia whispered in Jesse's ear her dissatisfaction with his rescue at the cabin in Cass. She told him he need not intervene in Cass again.

# Chapter 42

## Staff Sergeant Rita Spade, March 24, 2020

Andrew pulled his arms above his head. Stretching, he wiped the sleep from his eyes to bring the small clock into focus. He was exhausted. How could the clock on the bedside table read 8:00 a. m. already? He reached for Rita. The bed was still warm where she had been just a few minutes before. Andrew sat up and stretched again, "Rita, honey?"

Rita poked her head around the bathroom door, meeting his eyes with a half-hearted smile, "Morning, babe, I guess the morning sickness has started. I feel lousy today."

Andrew patted on the mattress for her to come back to bed. She slipped under the sheets, and he put his arm around her. "Sorry you don't feel good." He looked at the two empty wine bottles beside the bed. "I don't even remember drinking either of those. Do you?"

Rita rubbed her head, "No, I can't believe I even drank any with the baby. Surely not, but if I did, I deserve to feel sick."

"Let's go back to sleep for a while. Maybe by noon we'll feel better." Andrew pulled the sheet up and closed his eyes. Even with his eyes closed, he could feel the sunlight slipping around the window blind, coaxing them to get up and face the day. Tossing and turning he said, "It's no use. I can't go back to sleep. Want some coffee? Maybe that will make us feel better."

"I want a big, cold glass of ice water. Somehow, just the thought of coffee makes me feel nauseous." Rita pulled her hair back into a ponytail to smooth its unruliness.

"Alright, you got it, hot coffee for me, and ice water for you. After we finish, let's drive into town for a nice breakfast. I'm sure we will feel better soon. No more alcohol this weekend for either of us, especially you." Andrew grabbed his jeans off the floor. Pulling them up and on, he looked around for his shoes. Usually he kept everything in a neat little pile together. Having his things disorganized was completely out of character for him with his obsessive-compulsive disorder. He needed to check the labels on those wine bottles left by the lady who owned the cabin and make a note never to buy that kind.

***

Rita sat across from him in the diner booth. Andrew smiled; *Rita must be feeling better the way she was putting her food away from the all-you-can-eat breakfast/brunch bar.* He was glad she was feeling better. They still had one more night in the cabin before they had to drive back to Rockville, Maryland. Andrew had to admit that after two tall glasses of ice water, he too, felt much better. He wasn't groggy, and his headache had dissipated. The wine must have caused them both some dehydration.

They spent the day exploring the village of Lewisburg. Most of the time, Rita looked at baby beds and baby clothes. At an antique store, she saw a little bed in the window and insisted that they go in.

"Are you sure you want a bed that someone else's baby slept in, don't you want something new and modern?" he asked.

"Oh, Andrew, look at it. It's absolutely perfect for the nursery and you know it."

"Okay," he smiled at the salesclerk. He knew the guy had to be asking twice its value. "Can you ship the bed? I don't think it will fit in the car."

"Why, of course. Just follow me back to the counter so we can get the address to where you want it delivered. Just so you know, shipping will be extra," he added.

Andrew didn't say a word, he knew he wasn't dealing with any online store where free shipping was the part of the deal of the day; he just nodded and followed the clerk.

At 5:00 p.m., they stopped at the Greenbrier to eat an early dinner. Andrew ordered desert to go for two, Peanut butter cheesecake was Rita's favorite. He thought it sounded good to have later with coffee when they watched the sunset over the mountains at the cabin.

***

Rita helped him get his camera equipment set up first. Then they would enjoy their coffee and dessert. Andrew opened the memory card slot to remove it from his camera, and realized the slot was empty. "Are you kidding me? There is no disc in here. All those pictures I took last night are gone. I can't believe it."

"Are you sure you had a disc in the camera last night, Andrew? You know sometimes you forget to put one in."

Andrew looked at her in a sternly, "Don't even go there, Rita. You know how embarrassed I was when I didn't get any pictures at Joe's wedding. Since then I've always made sure I check before I even take that first shot. I'm sure there was a disc." Andrew stormed into the cabin looking around. "Okay, if you were drunk, what would you do with a disc from your camera?" He scanned the kitchen counter, but no disc was there. Andrew went to the bedroom and pulled out the bedside table drawer. Nothing was there either. He went back out to the picnic table, opened the camera bag, fished inside the bag, and pulled out the disc case; the case was full. "Humph, that's weird; apparently, I took it out and put it back in with the others. That's even more OCD than usual for me."

"How is that weird? Your obsessive-compulsive behavior must have been in overdrive from that wine last night. Most people would have done the opposite and made a sloppy mess of disorganization but not you." Rita giggled. "Oh, don't get upset. At least you found it, silly."

"You're right, it's here. I just need to find out which one, so I don't erase over it. Andrew pulled out each disc, inserted it into the camera, and clicked to view the photos until he finally came to the one with just stars. "Oh, Rita, these are so good that you are going to have a hard time picking just one." Andrew heard a Jeep in the distance. It reminded him of something, some event, but he couldn't remember what. It just kept nagging at him. He was sure it would come to him; it was silly anyway, probably nothing. Maybe it was that tractor pull thing he had gone to with his bother Jim with all that noise. What a night that had been.

Rita interrupted his thought, "You better get your camera on the tripod while you still have some light to see what you are doing."

Fifteen minutes later, the sky was as beautiful as the night before. No clouds obstructed their view. The intermittent meteor showers were magnificent.

"Andrew, I'm getting a little chilly. I am going to go get another shirt to put on under this jacket. Do you need anything while I'm in the cabin?"

Andrew was adjusting the camera, "What? No thanks. I'm good. Take the flashlight so you don't mess up the camera flash, okay?"

Rita took the flashlight, shook her head in a silly way, and stuck out her tongue. She was glad Andrew couldn't see her reaction before she went inside. She felt like a robber rifling through her luggage with a flashlight, but soon found what she was looking for. She grabbed the soft cotton top and fled to the bathroom where she could close the door and turn on the bathroom light without Andrew complaining.

Outside, Andrew was enjoying the sight of his life. Two of the meteors he had taken a photo of had not left the sky like all the rest. They had stopped mid-sky and were just resting. That's the only way he could explain it. *That's weird, I must be mistaken in their identification. These two stars seem to be so much brighter than any of the rest. I don't recognize them from my sky book. So, what are they?*

Andrew heard vehicles on the road north of the cabin, and saw headlights coming in his direction. *Late night visitors,* he thought. *Nah, someone else must have rented one of the other cabins in Cass. Looks like several people.* He was sure they would ruin his dark night camera adventure. Maybe he would try to shoot a couple pictures before they got to the abandoned town. The two bright stars in the sky were moving again, getting bigger and closer until they appeared to be almost directly overhead. Andrew could see they weren't stars anymore, but had flashing lights which created the elusion until the last minute. They were above the cabin within seconds. The large flash of bright blue light blinded Andrew for several seconds, caused him to drop his camera. In the darkness, he leaned down to pick it up.

"Rita, is that you?" Andrew asked as he felt a hand touch his jacket arm.

"Mr. Spade, its Special Agent in Charge Jesse Finch, from the United States government.

"The CIA?" Andrew chuckled. "I'm sorry, I can't see you. My eyes, the light that flashed was so bright. I can't see."

"It's okay, sir, it takes a few days for your vision to completely clear. Don't worry. I've seen this type of thing before, you won't be blind for too much longer."

Andrew heard another man approach.

Agent Vic Foster shook his head, "The cabin is empty."

Andrew, now frantic, said, "What do you mean the cabin is empty? It can't be empty. My wife, Rita, she's in there. She must be. She just went in, not more than five minutes ago, to get her jacket or something. She was getting cold. Rita! Rita, honey, come out. It's okay, these men are from the government. You don't need to hide. Why is it that you are here anyway?"

"Sir, I assure you she is not hiding from us. She is no longer in the cabin. She has been taken."

"What do you mean no longer in the cabin? She has been taken; I don't understand. Taken by whom?"

"Just as I said. I'm sorry. That is all I can say for now. Also, I am sorry I have to do this to you again." He reached for his tranquilizer gun. Andrew never saw it coming, literally. He was out within seconds. The house was wiped clean of their belongings; as if Andrew and Rita Spade had never visited Cass. Now it would appear to the outside world they never made it to Cass for the weekend. It would seem they were both missing.

# Chapter 43

## Jesse's Final Understanding, March 24, 2020

When Andrew awoke, his first question was not, '*Where am I?*', or '*Where is my wife?*' His first question was, "What are Rose, Jacqueline, and Molly doing here?" Sitting on the cot, he recognized them standing together from across the expansive room.

Agent Jesse Finch looked at the women and back at Andrew, "That's it. That's all you want to know. Not, '*Where am I? What are you going to do to me? Who are you? Where's my wife?*' You must be kidding me, right? What is it exactly that you do for a living, Andrew Spade, that you know all three of these *important* women? It can't be photography; I definitely know that is not the answer."

"I'm not really sure where I know them from since you asked me, but somehow, I do know them. They must work with my wife at Walter Reed. They look a little bit like nurses, don't you think?" Andrew thought for a minute more, and couldn't come up with where he had met them if not during some social event put on by Rita's employer, maybe a 5-K run. "I'm an engineer for the government. I study soil samples, and develop water supplies for countries experiencing extreme drought." He started to get up, but Jesse put his hand on his shoulder keeping him where he was. "Where is my wife, and who are you exactly, or did you say that already and I missed it? Wait, I seem to remember you saying something to me last night at the cabin about being with the government, right before I passed out. Did you drug me when I said I couldn't see?" After looking around and seeing all the workers, scientists, engineers, soldiers, and agents and, still, Jesse not answering his question, he asked, "Where am I? Is this some type of top-secret facility or something that you had to drug me to bring me here?"

"Yes, to most of your questions, the answer is yes. I am with the government; I did drug you, and you are in a top-secret facility. You are currently being held in protective custody. The rest of us, are in hiding, inside this top-secret facility to be exact, so don't plan on going anywhere soon. Your wife, Rita, has been taken by aliens aboard a spaceship. Now I know this is a lot to take in, but honestly, we are running on a short timeline here, so I need to be blunt. I hope you can keep up with what I am telling you and not freak out too much anyway. I remember you telling me the first time I drugged you and your wife that she was pregnant and that she was a nurse. Is there anything else you can tell me about her so I can get a full profile of her?" Jesse was having a hard time keeping Andrew's attention with all the construction noise from preparing the spaceship. "Andrew, look at me, not at those women. They are not going to help you get through this. I am. So, concentrate on what I am asking you. I assure you, your wife will be fine. All three of those women have been on alien ships, and apparently you must have been on one at some point, maybe even on their planet, since you know all three of them by name. In fact, they were taken by aliens and were gone from this planet before you were even born. So, that is the only place, I can guarantee you, that you would have ever seen them. Just out of curiosity, how did you end up in that cabin for the weekend anyway?"

"I entered a crossword puzzle contest online about planets. Why do you need that information?"

"Well, because that house, or cabin, you were staying in has been empty for years, and we don't know who the new owner is." Jesse thought for a minute then realized; *It must have been Lucia. She must have orchestrated all of this since she and the alien crew landed in Roswell. Was the crash there an accident or intentional? Did the aliens give up their lives to leave Lucia here all those years ago, throwing the government off-track from the real mission? The aliens must have believed we would bring their craft to the most top-secret base we had, and from there, using Lucia's capabilities, they could monitor our every move, right under our noses. Left alone, Lucia could determine who they would take to their new world. Determine who they needed, and who they would use to help populate the planet. Everything made sense now. Abductees from all over the world had reported being taken aboard ships, where in a way, they had been interviewed for life on the new planet. The aliens had plenty of time to plan, knowing years in advance that the Earth was dying. They could not offer humans anymore help, so instead they planned for what was to come next.*

At this point, Andrew had tears in his eyes, "What are you saying — that we were tricked somehow into staying there? Rita's a survivor, I know that. She was a medic in the Army before becoming a nurse. She had PTSD after being in a Humvee that hit a land mine in Somalia. The other three soldiers with her were killed. She herself was left for dead by the enemy. But Rita survived, and she made back to the base. Now she works with others, helping them to get their lives back together when they come back injured. She was an Army brat. She grew up all over the world, and she speaks seven languages. I know that she is fearless, just like her father, John. Rita is the type of person that runs straight toward danger to save others, not away. That's just her nature."

Jesse patted Andrew on the shoulder, "She sounds exactly like the type of person that they were looking for. Don't worry. She will fit in and be fine. We just need to keep watching for them to drop her back off. I believe she is their *number four*. If she is, she'll be coming back with the final message."

"I don't understand what you are saying about a final message. All she wanted was a Milky Way picture for her living room. She didn't sign up for whatever this — is." Andrew yelled to Jesse who was walking away.

Jesse yelled back, raising his arm over his head, "I know, but everyone else here understands. Come and get some breakfast, and Agent Harris will finish getting you up to speed on what's going on, so you won't feel out of the loop and make some god-awful, giant mistake that messes up Lucia's entire mission."

Jesse walked on, toward the scaffolding, to watch the crew work, "Lucia, how does the twelfth floor look today?"

"The virtual reality environment I have uploaded makes the floor appear empty, unused for some time. When General Kearns visits there today, he will see only what I want him to see: a science program that was once successful, and now no longer exists."

"Excellent, that is exactly what I wanted to hear. Let's hope he falls for it."

\*\*\*

Later that day, General Kearns made a surprise visit to the twelfth floor; the offices were both empty. He found no staff, no file cabinets, nothing that would even make him believe that just a few short days ago the CIA had a fully functioning alien investigating unit. Even the scientists were gone. He took several photos of the office area and texted them to the President. A thumbs-up texted response flashed back on the phone. Concluding his work here was complete General Kearns took the next plane back to the Pentagon.

Lucia flashed on the screen, "General Kearns has left the building. He and the President are both fully satisfied with the closure of the CIA unit."

Jesse responded, as most of the staff in the area, with a resounding clap. "Well done, Lucia."

# Chapter 44

## Number 4 Returns, March 29, 2020

Rita was now gone for five days. Agent Finch had around-the-clock surveillance on the town of Cass. The abandoned town was closed off to visitors due to supposed road construction. Jackhammers occasionally bit at chunks of concrete, and men in hard hats walked around pretending to read fake blueprints to discourage any unwanted visitors. A couple of men were stationed on electric poles in the area, using binoculars in case Rita was dropped off in the woods.

On day six, just at dusk, a workman spotted a woman wearing a red jacket. She was trying to make her way down the mountain through the forest. Before Rita made it to the bottom, she was met by Agent Colin Bilodeau. "Staff Sergeant Rita Spade, welcome back, my name is Agent Colin Bilodeau. I am here to help you. Those were my men making all that noise. We hoped that you might hear it. I'm sorry we didn't find you sooner." He handed her a bottle of water and a protein bar. "Your husband Andrew is with us. He is waiting for you at the base, along with a hot shower and a good hot meal. How does that sound?"

"Good. I am in need of food, a hot shower, and lots of sleep in that order, please." She pulled at the cellophane wrapper on the protein bar until Colin took it from her, opened the bar, and handed it back to her.

"Rita, did the aliens give you a message, by any chance? We've been waiting on a specific message, and thought they might give it to you."

"Yes, they gave me a message, but I can only speak it once, so I cannot tell you what it is until the time comes."

"Okay, those darned aliens, why do they have to be so secretive all the time?" Agent Harris attempted to make a joke, but Rita was too exhausted to answer or care.

Agent Harris talked all the way to the car, explaining to her about his team and getting her up to speed on what she should expect when they arrived at the base. Rita was dehydrated and in need of food. She said she had slept in the forest for two days, not knowing which way to go since she had no idea where she was even dropped off, but finally had heard the noise of the jackhammers and followed it, hoping to find help. Rita and Agent Riley Harris arrived at the base under the cover of dark.

Once inside, Doctor Armstrong met them at the elevator; she entered her special code to take them to the top floor where Andrew Spade was waiting anxiously for Rita.

Andrew saw Rita when the elevator opened; he ran to her, lifting her off her feet, he carried her to the cot he had been sleeping on. "I'm so sorry you were taken; it should have been me. If I had not been so fascinated by the night sky and taking pictures, I would have been in the cabin and could have protected you."

"It was meant to be, they wanted me, not you. They needed a fourth female, and so they chose me. It's okay Andrew I wasn't scared. They didn't hurt me, but they did show me some things. Some things about Earth, about all the things we have been seeing on the news, and reading about with climate change. Remember in church when the minister talked about all the things are going to be released upon the Earth, that part is coming soon very soon. It will be terrifying to go outside, and those things will get in the house, too. I just couldn't stand it knowing our child would be born in a world that is going extinct. We are being offered a new life, to start over again on a new planet. It's scary, but also exciting to think we have this chance, a life. Our DNA for future generations of humans will survive long after the Earth as we know, and love vanishes."

"Were you on board a spaceship and they told you about this?"

"Yes, I was on a ship, but I was able to view screens of the planet, and it is beautiful there. It is spring there now, too. The trees are lush, the flowers are in bloom; it is beautiful. The two things I noticed that were different were —"

Andrew put his finger to her lips, "The soil is more orange than brown, and the water is florescent green. Am I right?"

Rita smiled while raising her eyebrows, "Andrew, how do you know that?"

"I have been there, but it just slipped my mind until I was reminded here, during a session with Doctor Oritz. I am sure he will want to speak to you, too."

"No, I cannot talk to anyone about the message they gave me. I can only say it to Lucia once. If I say it before she asks for it, I will not remember it again. That is what they insisted before they dropped me off in the woods. I am so excited about knowing that you have been there and seen the beauty and peacefulness of the planet. I was afraid you would say you didn't want us to go when it's time to leave. You do want to go with them, right?"

"Oh yes, definitely, they need us, and we need them. We will be happy there. But right now, you need to eat something and then rest. Later you can meet with Lucia. She has been waiting for you."

# Chapter 45

## Human or Hybrid

Special Agent in Charge Jesse Finch climbed aboard the space craft; he wanted to question Lucia without others listening in on their conversation. After spending time with Doctor Oritz and hearing his own tape recording of his hypnosis session, Jesse had questions about his alien-human make up that he knew she could shed light on for him. "Lucia, what do you know about me?" asked Jesse as he sat in one of the seven seats in the command center.

"You are Special Agent in Charge Jesse Finch, Central Intelligence Officer and Director of the Office of Alien Intelligence and Abductions Studies."

"Yes, I know that, but I was reminded by someone that I have been told multiple times I am not completely human. Is that correct in your assessment of me as well?"

"Affirmative. Your biological parents are not the same as the ones who raised you. You are a Human-Valeserie hybrid, and one of the second-generation prototypes. The fertilized egg implanted in your Earth mother's uterus was developed aboard one of our spacecrafts and placed there during abduction while she slept. Since birth, you have been continuously monitored by our scientists. You are not the only prototype here on Earth; there are others around the world in positions of influence due to their intellectual capacity, as well as courage, passion, and motivation."

"So, is this why the Valeserie have removed the eggs of human females? Have they been using them to make hybrids? Why take these particular women from Cass and keep them for so long?"

"Affirmative. We are on our fifth-generation prototype. All of these prototypes live on Nova Valeserie. These women are the mothers of the new world, holding high office on the planet. Their traits were what we were seeking courage, passion, motivation, and human phenotypes. But again, they are not the only ones taken to achieve our objectives. These particular women were sent back for me because it was easier to send them here since they are from this specific area and not from — for example the Amazon Rain Forest. Living here on Earth, has unfortunately affected your memory, Agent Finch. That gene anomaly has long since been corrected. When you reach home, you will function at your full Valeserie capacity."

"What about my children, are they human?"

"Your children are one-quarter Valeserie. Once they are fully encultured on Nova Valeserie, you will be pleased and surprised at how their intelligence changes in just a short time. I sense you are concerned for their safety. You are wondering if your children will fit in with life there. Let me assure you, they will. You have adjusted well here on Earth Agent Finch. The hybrids inhabiting the planet Valeserie are fully human in their appearance. Their capabilities in intelligence, strength, and moral reasoning far exceed in comparison to their terrestrial human brother and sisters. Agent Finch, I sensed self-doubt when you came here alone to speak to me. We could have had this conversation anywhere. You should not be embarrassed to tell others about this part of yourself. Embrace your true nature. Don't be afraid of being different; open your mind from what you have learned here. Societal norms dictate who you should be, like placing the same color pegs in the same color holes on a board game. Free yourself from this ridiculous expectation that no one should be forced to follow. Allow you and your children to discover your and their real potential in the new world, without these types of barriers."

"Thank you, Lucia. I just needed to know that I am doing the right thing for my family, and my team. They have placed their trust and lives in me, and ultimately, in you. You are right, I was felling inadequate and didn't even realize I was allowing this new knowledge about myself to lower my self-esteem."

Before Lucia could respond further, her image disappeared from the screen then flashed in an abnormal manner. Agent Jesse Finch had never seen this occur before. Lucia's voice was garbled as if her battery were being depleted in front of him.

"System fa…system failure…"

"Lucia, Lucia, what's wrong? Tell me how I can help you?" Agent Jesse Finch ran from the command center to find Doctor Armstrong.

After several hours of diagnostic testing and system maintenance, Lucia's visage returned on the viewing screen.

"What happened, Lucia? Is this something we are going to have to worry about when we leave here?"

"General Kearns is back. He has discovered the hidden panel, which I put in place to make him believe we left. Now, he is going through all the files. He is gathering information about my technology. He has been to your home, and knows that not only you and your family are gone, but all the staff and their families are missing from their homes, too. He has arrested Captain Jamal Bryant, along with Sergeant Trevon Loch, and his squadron. He is demanding answers, but so far they are not talking."

"What made him come back to the base? I don't understand?"

"Time is moving faster outside than inside this room, Agent Finch. You would not recognize the Earth if you left this floor. The Eastern seaboard has disappeared due to earthquakes and the tsunamis which followed. Radiation has spread from the shores of Japan across the ocean to California; soon it will spread through Missouri. Carcasses of animals in the forests and farm fields lay dead rotting. Pestilence from the decay has been carried by rats and rat fleas, and the bacterium yersinia pestis, like the Black Death from the fourteenth century, has become airborne. Just like then, there are too many dead bodies to even bury. Barricaded in their homes, humans are running out of safe water and food to consume. Soon, the radiation will reach here and will affect my functioning capacity. I am not sure how much longer we will be able to remain hidden as the outside elements continue to interrupt my circuitry.

# Chapter 46

## Trumpets, August 20, 2020

At dawn, curtains of gray thick clouds slowly parted around the world, revealing thousands of Valeserian ships in the sky. Their trumpeting horns awakened every village, town, and city around the globe. One voice was heard by all, "Raise your arms, come with us survive." News stations around the world showed live video footage of the spaceships, reporting to people massive abductions, instead of what was really happening, due to mass hysteria and misconception. Over four billion humans answered the call to live. People raised their arms in response and floated from their cars, homes, and places of work up into the air in seconds and onto the spaceships. Others run in fear, screaming that the world is ending. Angered and frightened by the UFO's removing humans from the Earth, some men banded together and began shooting people down from the sky, not allowing the aliens to take their family, neighbors. Dead bodies plummeted to the earth, and chaos ensued in the city streets. Still, others made it safely aboard the spaceships. The Valeserian crafts disappeared, above the thick dark cloud cover.

Deep inside the mountain, Sergeant Trevon Loch's soldiers hear the call of the alien ships, but were unable to escape their cells, fearing they would be shot by their own soldiers who were guarding the base, if any were left still guarding the towers. Finally, they hear Lucia's voice and know they were saved. The cell doors open automatically, releasing the soldiers who have been arrested. Sergeant Loch lead the soldiers to the elevator that Lucia had had installed, only for their use, in order to reach the top floor.

Once all were safely inside the craft, Lucia awaited her orders, since she herself has never been to Nova Valeserie. Three agents and four women, a total of seven humans, stand together in the command center of the ship joining hands.

Lucia appeared on screen, "Welcome travelers from Earth, I am assuming command of the mission. It is time for us to begin our journey to Nova Valeserie."

Agent Riley Harris begins, "The door will be closing soon at the Bermuda Triangle."

Agent Vic Foster adds, "Look for us beyond the Rings of Saturn."

Special Agent in Charge Jesse Finch smiles as he remembers his part of the sequence. "Pan's light will show the way to safety through the Encke Gap, while passing through the Rings of Saturn."

Lucia, the primogenitor, began playing, *Viola Concerto in D Minor* over the intercom as the ships engines gained full power. She guided the spacecraft upward, shattering the glass ceiling above her as a final gesture of respect for all human women. They rose rapidly into the air and away from the hidden installation. The ship disappeared skyward within seconds. Once at the Bermuda Triangle, the ship dove deep beneath the ocean's surface at such tremendous speed all at once they were no longer on Earth; their journey into time space had begun.

Lucia's colorful all-seeing eye of lapis and shamrock strands of light burst across the viewing screen in celebration of their escape. From the portal windows of the ship, they watch as they cross through the Rings of Saturn. Seeing the moon, Pan, directly ahead, they follow its light. As they approach the Encke Gap, Lucia slowed the ship's speed. "It is time for the destination codes to be entered into the code identification pad then I will upload the final directions."

Rose Jackson entered the first code: three-two-three, then took a seat. She thought about her twins, her son, Kader, and her daughter, Moria, both rightly named after fate. They were waiting for her on Nova Valeserie. She couldn't wait to introduce them to their new family from

Earth. She wished she had been brought back to earth sooner so she could have been with Noble to raise their children but loosing him had brought her here today.

Jacqueline Kaleta was next, four-one-six, she pressed the numbers into the entry pad. Waiting in the doorway until all the numbers were entered, she wanted to see this important event, but her thoughts were with Greta, and she couldn't wait to see her friend when she emerged from the antiaging pod. They would start their life over again. This time they would not be keeping their feelings for each other a secret hidden under the sleeve of their shirt. Lucy Chavez had already exited the healing water pod, and Doctor Sara Meskins declared her to be cancer-free, so Jacqueline knew Greta would also be healthy.

Molly Lehman entered the third code: one-eight-one, she had been so surprised the see the Chase and Sanborn coffee can with Eddie and the remains of Hendrix in his urn. With new developments in technology, their ashes could be cloned, and both would awaken in a new era, on a new planet. She knew exactly what mountain top she wanted them to hike. At night, they would sit on the edge of the cliffs of Mount Nataris and watch the Nova Valeserie's three rust-orange moons rise high in the eastern sky. Her last hours on Earth had not been pleasant ones before she was taken. She was thankful she had been taken and also grateful that Tara, her guardian, had never given up on her.

Rita smiled, stepping up to Lucia's control panel, she entered the final code: two-zero-two-zero. She felt her baby, Providence, kick. Touching her stomach with the palm of her hand, she knew her daughter would be born in a new world, full of love and hope instead of ignorance and hate. Never again would they allow their planet to be destroyed by humanity. Lessons were finally learned on leaving carbon footprints.

"All codes entered successfully and accepted into flight-path control. Now setting algorithms into the ephemeris system. We will reach our destination and be home very soon." Lucia adjusted the craft's navigational sequence to faster than light speed, and the ship disappeared beyond the Encke Gap.

***

Back on Earth, it is several years later, August 20, 2025. The Earth is dying from within. Water rises and toxic gases engulf the planet. The three billion humans who chose to stay behind no longer alive. Planet Earth resets itself with the only small microorganisms remaining.

## The End